DIRTY MONEY

DIRTY MONEY

Ashley & Jaquavis

ISBN-13: 978-1-60162-077-4

First Mass Market Printing October 2009
Printed in United States of America

10 9 8 7 6 5 4

This is a work of fiction. All characters, incidents, and dialogue in this book, with the exception of some well-known historical and public figures, are products of the author's imagination and are not to be construed as real. Any resemblance to actual events or locales, businesses, or real persons, living or dead, is entirely coincidental.

Submit Wholesale Orders to:
Kensington Publishing Corp.
C/O Penguin Group (USA) Inc.
Attention: Order Processing
405 Murray Hill Parkway
East Rutherford, NJ 07073-2316
Phone: 1-800-898-0910
Fax: 1-800-220-2665

www.urbanbooks.net

Urban Books
1199 Straight Path
West Babylon, NY 11704

ISBN-13: 978-1-60162-077-4
ISBN-10: 1-60162-077-2

First Mass Market Printing February 2008
Printed in United States of America

10   9   8   7   6   5

*This is a work of fiction. Any references or similarities to ac-
tual events, real people, living, or dead, or to real locals are in-
tended to give the novel a sense of reality. Any similarity in
other names, characters, places, and incidents is entirely coincidental.*

Submit Wholesale Orders to:
Kensington Publishing Corp.
C/O Penquin Group (USA) Inc.
Attention: Order Processing
405 Murray Hill Parkway
East Rutherford, NJ 07073-2316
Phone: 1-800-526-0275
Fax: 1-800-227-9604

First, I would like to thank God for giving me strength and for blessing me with talents that will help me achieve my life's goals. I would like to thank my best friend and co-author, Jaquavis, for understanding me and for inspiring me to do unbelievable things. You have always stood by my side and if I don't say it enough, "thank you and I love you". I would like to thank my mother, Jackie Hill, for helping me to become a strong black woman. You have given up so many things in order for me to have what you didn't, I love and appreciate you for that. I only hope that when I have children, I can be half the mother to mine that you have been to me. I would like to thank my father, Yul Snell, for helping me to be strong. You instilled morals and wisdom into me that I will honor for the rest of my life. You have always been an inspiration to me, I know that you work hard to give me what I need, and a whole lot of what I want so I would like to say I love you. I promise to you that I will always look after my sisters and brothers. I would also like to thank Tammy Snell for opening my eyes to new things. You have pushed me to be great ever since I was five years old and you believed in me. I admired you as a child and now as a young woman I still hold that same amount of admiration and love for you that I always have. To Mario, Sydney, Lil Yul, and Yulanai, I love you all with all of my heart. Thank you for looking up to me and giving me motivation to pave the way for you. I want to thank Raven for believing in me, loving me, and for always being there. I know that I will always have someone to talk to because of you. I want to give thanks and love to all of my grandparents, Grandma and Papa, Grandma Annette Snell, and Grandma

Juanita Snell. I want to thank Aunt Kamela for putting me up on game and for being there at times when I needed her most. I would like to thank Shay, my girl, for loving me and being one of my favorite cousins. I hope that I can be a positive role model in your life. I will always be here when you need me. I would also like give thanks to Char (my closest friend), Rudy, Tamia, Shonda, Erin, Beev, Amber, Margo (my biggest fan), Courtney, Aunt Monya, India, Jasmine, Joy, Brent, Wayne, Kiara, Jada, Camrin, Uncle Reggie, Aunt Pearlette, Aunt Nichelle, my "Nannie", my god son Robyn, Mrs. Roshell, Ashley Cain, Mrs. Couch, Ms. Green, Mrs. Gulley, and Mrs. Murphy. All of you have contributed to me in so many different ways. Some are family, some are friends, and some have taught me many things but I thank and love you all.

♥Ashley

First I would like to thank God for blessing me with the talent to paint pictures with words. I would like to thank my environment for giving me the knowledge and the experiences to compose this book. I want to thank my co-author Ashley for collaborating with me to compose this urban tale. You gave me motivation to put what I lived, what we lived, into words. Thank you to my block, y'all give me the stories and circumstances to write about. Berkeley and Chevrolet is always my home, y'all know who y'all are. Thank you to Jackie Hill for bringing my gift to life. I want to give a big thanks to Kamela and Shay. When nobody fucked

Chapter One

Anari watched the clock, tapping her pencil against the desk and wishing the class would hurry up and end. She glanced over at her best friend Tanya, who slept with her head propped in her book, and laughed to herself. She tore a piece of paper from her notebook and threw it at Tanya.

"Tanya, wake yo' ass up," she whispered.

Tanya raised her head groggily and wiped the spit from her bottom lip. Just as she was about to throw the paper back at Anari, the school bell rang. The girls walked out of the classroom into the hall and out the front door.

On their way home, they ran into a group of girls who didn't like Anari too much. Anari stopped walking when she noticed them. This particular group of girls thought that she was conceited and were always writing stuff on the bathroom walls or spreading rumors that Anari slept around. In actuality, that was the last thing she did.

Anari was still a virgin, so the rumors bothered her to the point that she avoided the people who started spreading them. Tanya noticed Anari hesitate, so she spoke up loudly.

"Fuck them, Anari. They scary asses ain't gon' do nothing. All they do is run they damn mouths."

Anari walked past the girls, hoping that they wouldn't start anything with her. She picked up her pace while Tanya walked past the girls, mugging each one. Tanya made sure that she made eye contact with the main girl to let her know that she was not intimidated and that she would not let them intimidate her best friend.

When they finally passed the group of girls, Tanya looked at Anari. "I told you them hoes ain't want none," Tanya said.

Anari laughed it off, trying to pretend as if the girls didn't bother her, but on the inside, she was trying to stop her heart from beating so fast. They walked home, talking the whole way. They never walked home without one another. They felt safer walking home together. In their neighborhood, it was common for young girls to get hassled by dudes who did not understand the word "no."

As they looked at the rundown subsidized housing projects they called home, Anari said, "I am not living here. As soon as I turn eighteen, I'm out."

Tanya looked at Anari, knowing that her friend was tired of living in the hood. She knew how it felt to want more out of life. "I feel you, but until then, we just got to deal with it."

"Tanya, get your ass in this house and do your damn chores!" Tanya's mother yelled as she stuck half her body out the second-story apartment window.

Tanya rolled her eyes at the sound of her mother's voice. "Here I come!" she replied. She turned to Anari and shrugged her shoulders. "I have to go, but call me later. I want you to put my perm in for me."

Anari said, "Okay," and began to walk to her building. She was almost there when she heard sirens in the distance and saw a boy running through a hole in the fence. Anari nosily kept her eyes on the boy and saw him throw something in the bushes as he raced past it.

Anari paused for a minute and took a look around to see who he was running from. She didn't see anyone, so she walked over to the bush to see what the boy had thrown. Anari picked up a sandwich bag full of what looked like crumbled peanuts. She put the peanuts in her book bag and quickly walked into her building. When she entered her apartment, she saw her mother cuddled up with some strange man. "I'm back, Ma," she yelled and ran upstairs to her room.

Anari looked out her window and saw two policemen push the boy to the ground. She cracked her window so she could hear what was going on.

"Where is it?" yelled one of the officers.

The boy kept his face pressed against the ground. His voice was muffled. "Man, I don't know what you talking about. I ain't got nothin'."

The other officer checked the boy's pockets. "I think he might have thrown it somewhere."

"Check behind those bushes over there, and if it's not there then check in those garbage cans, too," his partner replied.

The officer thoroughly searched the bushes and the trash, but he didn't find anything. "Let him go. It's not here."

The boy got up from the ground with a cocky smile on his face. The officer roughly removed his handcuffs. "You got lucky this time, you little piece of shit."

Anari closed her window and pulled the sandwich bag from her book bag. She poured the peanuts onto her bed and counted out twenty of them.

So, this is the stuff that be making niggas rich.

Anari heard a knock at her bedroom door and scrambled to put the stuff back into the sandwich bag. She threw it under her pillow and yelled back, "Hold on, Momma. Here I come."

Anari's mom just yelled through the door, "I'm 'bout to go. I'll be back later, and when I come home, I want that damn kitchen clean. And when Maulie get home, tell him to clean up my room before he goes outside."

Anari opened her door. "Okay, Ma," she said.

After her mother left, Anari got right to her chores. She wanted to hurry up and finish so that she could figure out what she would do with the drugs she found.

Maybe I'll give them back to that boy. I think Tanya knows one of his friends.

Anari finished her chores and went into the kitchen to get something to eat. She opened the refrigerator and found some milk and some baking soda.

Damn, it ain't even nothing here to eat.

Her stomach growled, so she did what she always did when she was hungry. She drank water.

She took a glass back up to her room and called Tanya. After two rings, Tanya picked up.

"Hello?" Tanya answered loudly.

"What up? What you doing?" Anari asked.

"Nothing. I just finished my damn chores. My momma swear I'm her slave."

Anari laughed at Tanya and quickly changed the subject. "What's that boy's name that you talking to? You know the high yellow boy that you always be flirting with?"

"Oh, you talking 'bout Lance. What about him?"

"I need to talk to his friend. The one that he always be with. Do you know his number?"

Tanya put Anari on hold and came back with the number. "Anari, you still there?"

"Yeah, do you have it?"

Tanya continued, "His name is Maurice and his number is 686-5114. Since when you start liking him?"

Anari was in a rush to call the boy, so she told Tanya that she would call her back. She started to pick up the phone then hesitated. Would he be mad because she took his shit? What if he beat her ass or something? Maybe she would just keep it and not say anything.

The more she thought about it, though, Anari realized she couldn't keep the drugs in her room without her momma finding them, and she would rather take an ass whooping from Maurice than her mother any day. She picked up the phone and dialed the number.

"What up?"

"Hi, can I speak to Maurice?" asked Anari.

"This me. Who is this?" replied Maurice.

"Well, you really don't know me, but this is Anari. I saw what happened to you today and I just wanted to call you and let you know that I have your stuff. I took it out the bushes so the police wouldn't find it."

Maurice was silent for a while. He finally spoke up. "I'll pick it up later tonight. It's too hot outside right now. Is twelve o'clock okay?"

"Okay, but don't knock on my door or ring the buzzer," Anari replied. "I'll meet you out front."

Maurice hung up the phone and Anari went to get his stuff. She was looking at it when she heard the door slam downstairs. She went to her door and yelled, "Maulie, is that you?"

Jamal raced up the stairs with Tanya following behind him. "Yeah!" he said, running from Tanya as she playfully hit him on the back of the head.

"You it," he said as he hit Tanya back and ran into his room.

"That boy getting big. I ain't gon' be able to beat him up in a couple more years." Tanya laughed as she walked into Anari's room. "So anyway, what did you call Maurice for?" she asked as she plopped down on Anari's bed.

Anari walked over to her door, shut it, and locked it. She walked back to her bed and reached under her pillow. She held up the sandwich bag and showed Tanya what she had. "This is his stuff. He dropped it and I want to give it back to him."

Tanya took the bag from Anari. "It's like four hundred dollars worth of dope in here," she said. "You can buy you some fly shit with four hundred dollars."

Anari shrugged her shoulders and frowned her face up. "How in the hell you know it's four hundred worth?"

Tanya smiled and lay on her stomach. "I watched my friend Lance bag that shit up. He told me what goes for what and how shit is. You should try to sell that and make some money."

Anari ignored her friend's suggestion and changed the subject. They talked for about an hour before Anari's mother interrupted them.

"Hold on, T. I'll be right back."

Anari went downstairs to watch her mother inspect the kitchen. When her mother appeared to be satisfied, Anari walked past the strange man sitting in the living room and up the stairs. When she went back into her room, Tanya had the bag of stuff.

"Nari, I miscounted. It's only like three hundred dollars worth in here."

Anari took the bag from Tanya. "It don't matter how much is in there, because I'm giving it back to him."

Tanya rolled her eyes, knowing that Anari was a goodie-two-shoe. "I don't care what you do with it as long as you don't smoke that shit," she said. "I don't want no crack head for a best friend."

"Don't even play." Anari laughed at the thought.

Anari was nervous about meeting Maurice that night, so she tried to think of something else for the rest of her day. She put in Tanya's perm and tried to do some of her homework. Tanya went home around 10 o'clock and Anari got ready to pretend she was asleep. She walked down the hall and knocked on her mother's bedroom door. "Ma?"

Anari could smell the scent of weed coming from the other side of her mother's door and she knew that her mother's usual rituals were taking place. She opened the door.

"I'm going to sleep. Do you want me to do anything else before I go?"

"You ain't going to sleep until you finish them damn chores," Anari's mother replied.

Anari frowned in confusion. "You said that I was done with my chores. I thought I did a good job."

Her mother looked at her and scowled. "You didn't wash the clothes."

Anari was frustrated and just wanted to get her plan in motion. "But you didn't tell me to wash clothes."

Anari's mother walked over and hit her upside her head and raised her voice. "Get your trifling ass down there and wash them clothes! I shouldn't have to ask you. You're the oldest. I do my job by keeping a roof over your head. The least you could do is help out. You are an ungrateful little ass."

Anari wanted to spit in her mother's face, but she wasn't disrespectful. She hated when her mother acted like she was a good parent, but instead of saying this to her mother, she thought everything that she wished she could say.

I hate you! You don't keep nothing over my head! I could pay the fucking thirteen dollars a month. I'm walking around here in Tanya's clothes cuz you blow all the money on drugs. You can't even keep food in our refrigerator.

Anari walked out of the room with her heart filled with rage. She was so upset, she knew it was best that she just keep her mouth shut and do as she was told or she was bound to say something that could get her into trouble.

She went downstairs and started separating the

dirty clothes. All her mother's clothes smelled liked vomit, liquor, and weed. She frowned as the smell overwhelmed her. Anari threw the clothes into their separate piles, cursing her mother out in her head.

When she finished separating all the dirty laundry, she saw that she had four huge loads to wash, dry, and fold. She sighed heavily and shook her head as she put in the first load. She would be up all night trying to finish these clothes.

Anari was sitting on top of the dryer when she saw that it was 11:30, almost time to meet Maurice. She hopped off the dryer and ran up to her room. When she passed her mother's door, she didn't hear anything, so she assumed that her mother and her company were asleep. She went into her bedroom and put on a pair of blue jeans and a pink shirt.

Anari was anxious to give Maurice the drugs that she had found. She grabbed the sandwich bag and walked out of her room, trying to be as quiet as possible because she didn't want her mother to wake up and find out that she was sneaking out. She ran down the stairs, put in the third load of clothes, grabbed her house keys, and quietly walked out the front door.

As soon as she walked outside, she saw Maurice waiting for her in a raggedy black Ford Tempo. She walked over to his car and got in the front seat. As she sat down, she felt her heart speed up, and wondered why she was so nervous.

"Here's your stuff," she said, pulling the sandwich bag out of her pocket.

He took the bag from Anari and pulled out a wad of money. Anari turned her head, thinking that it would be rude for her to stare at his money. He placed five crisp twenty-dollar bills on her lap.

"I don't want your money," Anari said. "I was just helping out."

Maurice looked at Anari and licked his lips. "I want you to have it," he said. "I appreciate you being straight up with me. I saw you go into the bushes and get the dope. You could have just kept it, but you was real with me. You didn't try to pull nothing grimey. I like that."

Anari smiled as she took the money and put it into her purse.

"So, what you say your name is?" Maurice asked as he pulled away from Anari's building.

"Anari," she answered in her cutest voice.

She looked over at Maurice and was immediately attracted to him. He had a brown complexion with strong features. She noticed that he had a scar above his left eyebrow.

Even that looked good to her, she thought as she rubbed her hands together in her lap.

"So, you trying to chill with me tonight?"

Anari wanted to stay and chill with Maurice, but she knew that her mother would have a fit if she found out that she had sneaked out of the house.

Maurice peeped the look on her face. "I'll take you home, little mama. I don't want your moms to trip on you or nothing."

Anari was relieved that Maurice understood. She wasn't trying to get into any trouble, and she didn't want to come out and tell him that she had to go home.

"How old are you anyway?"

"Fourteen," she replied. "How old are you?"

"Eighteen," Maurice replied.

Anari didn't know that Maurice was so old, but she didn't really care. He seemed to be nice enough. Besides, he was only four years older then she was.

When Maurice pulled back up to Anari's apartment building, he said, "All right, youngin'."

Anari blushed as she got out of the car. She closed his door and walked toward her apartment building.

When she looked back and waved, he rolled down his window and yelled, "I'll pick you up for school tomorrow."

Anari laughed. "Okay."

She watched Maurice drive off. She couldn't wait to call Tanya and tell her about him. He was so fine. Anari hoped that he thought she was cute too. Her excitement died down when she realized that she had to sneak back into her house.

Anari slowly put her key in the door and opened it, praying that it wouldn't make any noise. The washing machine had stopped. Deciding she would finish the clothes in the morning, she started to ascend the steps, trying to stop them from squeaking. Every step seemed to squeak louder and louder as she walked up. After what seemed like forever, Anari crept past her mother's room and slowly opened her own bedroom door. As soon as she closed the door, she leaned up against it and sighed.

She took off her clothes and got underneath her covers. As soon as she closed her eyes, she felt something hit her in the face. "Ouch!"

Anari got out of bed and ran around her dark room. She turned on her light switch and saw her mother standing by her bed with a belt in her hand.

"You might as well get ready for this ass whooping. Your fast ass had the nerve to sneak out of my house."

Anari's mother came at her with full force, smacking her in the face repeatedly. Her smacks turned into punches as Anari curled up on the ground.

"I'm sorry!" Anari screamed, trying to get her mother to stop hitting her. She didn't fight back though. She had learned a long time ago that it was better to just take the hits.

Anari curled up even tighter and tried to protect herself from the forceful blows and unrelenting kicks that were aimed for her head and stomach.

"Momma, please!" she begged, hoping that the beating would stop.

Anari realized that her mother didn't plan on stopping until she was ready, so she lay there wincing as her mother hit her over and over again. She felt the pounding in her head and the swelling of her face with each kick that connected with her face. Anari tasted the salty blood as her lip busted, and she began to cry.

Finally her mother's male friend came in and pulled her mother off of her. "That's enough! Look at her. She can't even move."

Anari's mother stopped hitting her. She stood there breathing heavily. When she eventually caught her breath, she yelled, "Now take your fast ass down there and finish those damn clothes! And shut up before I give you something to cry about!" Anari was left in her room, lying on the floor in agony.

Jamal had heard the whole thing, and he lay in bed praying that his mother would stop. He loved his sister because she was the one who he came to when he wanted to play. Anari was the one who helped him with his homework, and she was the one who performed all the motherly duties that were not being done by their real mother. After he was certain that his mother was back in her room, he got out of bed and tip-toed into his sister's room.

"Are you okay, Nari?" Jamal asked as he knelt down beside her.

She tried to compose herself so that her little brother wouldn't see that their mother had beaten her again. "Yeah, I'm okay, Maulie. Go to bed so you won't be sleepy for school in the morning."

Anari tried to get up off the floor as if she wasn't hurt, but the pain was unbearable. She grimaced as she felt stabbing pains all over her body. Maulie helped her up then she walked her little brother to his room and tucked him in. Anari stayed there with him until he was sound asleep. Tears flowed down her face as she watched her brother sleep peacefully.

I hope I can get us out of here before it gets worse.

She kissed his forehead and walked into the bathroom. Anari looked into the mirror and saw that her lip was busted and she had a small cut underneath her eye.

I hate her stupid ass. I hope she dies. I hate being here. As soon as I get enough money, I'm out. I will never do my kids like she does me. The only thing that's keeping me here is Jamal. He needs me more than anything. If I ain't here then she will start beating on him, and the day that she touches him will be the day that I start fighting her back. I hate her. When I leave, I'm never looking back.

Anari ran some cold water into the sink and tried to stop some of the swelling by putting a cold towel onto her face. She didn't want to go to school tomorrow looking beat up. It wouldn't be the first time that someone asked her, "Damn, who beat your ass?" As she looked at her mangled face she began to cry again.

I hate her.

It had taken Anari all night to finish all the loads of clothes. By the time she finished, it was time for her to get ready for school. She got dressed and made sure that Jamal was up and ready to catch the bus. She took the money that Maurice had given her and sprinted out the door.

When she got outside, Maurice was waiting for her, just like he had promised. Anari got into his car and he took her to school. Before she got out of his car, he asked, "What happened to your face?"

An embarrassed Anari replied, "Nothing."

He kissed Anari softly on her lips and she got out of the car.

She didn't hear from Maurice a lot after that. Most of the time he was in the streets with Lance and his other friends. But Anari always looked forward to him surprising her in the mornings or waiting for her after school.

Anari didn't know how it happened, but she

started to see him more and more, and within a year she became known as Maurice's girlfriend. Even though Maurice and her had never actually talked about it, she saw herself that way, too. It seemed like people treated her differently now that she was Maurice's girl. The girls who used to hate on Anari now envied her and tried to befriend her.

Even though she had adopted new associates, she knew that her one true friend was Tanya. Anari and Tanya had formed a bond that couldn't be broken by anyone. Eventually, Anari stopped borrowing Tanya's clothes and they began to trade them instead.

Maurice kept Anari in fly clothes and always gave her money to eat and buy things with. After Maurice found out how Anari's mother treated her, he always made sure that he was around when she needed him. He even bought Jamal shoes and clothes whenever he went shopping for himself.

The day Anari came out of her house with a black eye was the day he demanded that Anari move out with him. Although Maurice was only nineteen, he handled the situation like a grown man. He talked to her mother and convinced her that it would be better for Anari to come and live with him. The five hundred dollars that he gave Anari's mother just gave her all the more reason to say "yes."

At the tender age of fifteen, Anari had her own apartment and a man who was willing to take care of her and make sure that her little brother was okay. Maurice made sure she went to school every day and he spoiled her. Anari literally got anything and everything that she wanted. Maurice hustled, and although he was small-time when Anari first met him, he was quickly rising to the top. With stability now in her life, her grades were improving in school and she was finally happy.

Maurice was barely at their apartment, so Tanya and Jamal came over all the time to spend the night. Anari started to notice things about Tanya. She would make comments about other chicks' asses and breasts. Anari used to laugh it off and paid it no mind. Tanya never came out to Anari with her preference, but Anari had her suspicions.

A few months after Anari left home, she received a phone call from Jamal. "Nari, something's wrong with Momma. She locked herself in the bathroom and hasn't been out in two days."

Anari's eyes bucked. "Why didn't you call me sooner?"

There was fear in Jamal's voice as he answered. "Because she always locks herself in there. But she's never stayed in there this long."

Anari dropped the phone to her side and took a deep breath. She instructed him to go over to Tanya's apartment until she got there. Anari called Tanya and let her know what was going on then called Maurice to come home. She was used to this, but this time she knew that something was terribly wrong. It was just this feeling that she had in her heart that something wasn't right. Anari knew that this time was different from the others.

Maurice finally picked her up, and as they drove over to her mother's apartment, her chest felt heavy. When Anari arrived, she found her mother dead in the bathroom. Her mother's death was caused from an overdose of heroin.

Anari was hurt by the death of her mother, but she didn't attend the funeral. She had a lot of animosity built up toward her mother, and she didn't want to disrespect her soul by showing up at her funeral full of hate. In a way, she felt responsible for her mother's death. Anari hated her mother, but now that she was gone, it didn't seem right to dwell on her shortcomings.

Anari was finding it hard to deal with the fact that she was motherless. Although she was not a good mother, she was the only mother Anari had. Now that she was gone, Anari felt that a part of her was missing.

An overdose on heroin? Maybe if I had been there I could have stopped her. I shouldn't have wished death on her. She didn't deserve that. Why did she have to do that to herself? Why couldn't she just be a good mother? My mother! Why couldn't she just be here for us? I don't know what I'm supposed to do. What's going to happen to Maulie?

Jamal was forced to stay with his father, a man that he barely knew. The only good thing about it was that his father lived closer to Anari.

Since Anari didn't know her father, she became Maurice's baby girl. She liked it that way, though. He was the only person that she needed. Anari loved Maurice with all her heart. She depended on him and knew that as long as he was there for her, she wouldn't be alone. He took care of her and made her feel special. He loved her, and she never expected things to change. But as the years passed, they did.

Chapter Two

"**B**aby, can I talk to you about something?" asked eighteen-year-old Anari.

"Nah, I ain't got time right now," Maurice replied. "Holla at me when I get back. I got to make this run."

Anari wanted to cry. She just did not understand how he could pay her so little attention. Lately, he didn't even come home at night and if he did, it was only to change clothes and leave right back out.

"What do you mean you got to make a run? What the fuck is that supposed to mean? Baby, I'm tired of this shit. You spend more time running the streets with Lance than you do at home with me. Every day it's something new. I cannot handle this. The police are all on my ass and shit, like I'm the one out here moving dope. I don't want to live like this, Maurice. When is it going to stop? I'm tired of looking over my damn shoulder every time I step foot outside the house. You got me mixed up in this bullshit. You always filling my head with all these promises. Show me, Maurice."

Maurice just glared at Anari. He didn't reply, and that made Anari continue.

"You grimey, Maurice. You are full of shit. You just as dirty as your damn money. You claim that I'm trying to stop your hustle, but there are other ways to make money."

Maurice walked toward the door, shaking his head as if she were insane, as if the idea of him giving up the drug trade was ridiculous. She didn't talk shit about his dirty money when she was busy spending it on Gucci and shit. And she sure as hell wasn't worried about the shit when he bought her a Mercedes.

"Look, Nari, I ain't got time for this shit. I don't never bring no dope into this house, so them muthafuckas can't do shit to your old high-priced ass. I love you, so you just got to roll with it for a minute. If you can't do that then maybe you need to get the fuck on. I'll make sure you straight, but you ain't gon' stop my hustle." Maurice threw up the edge of his hand like a hatchet.

Anari stared at Reesey with hateful eyes. "Fine. When you get home, I won't be here."

That was the last conversation she had with Maurice before he died. She didn't even get to tell him . . .

"Mommy." The little voice snapped her out of her daydream. She stared into the eyes of her only remnant of Maurice, his son. Maurice Ronnell Jones II was the spitting image of his father. He was brown-skinned, with dark brown eyes. She knew he would grow up to be sexy as hell, just like his daddy.

Anari began to cry. She hadn't even had the chance to tell Maurice that he was a daddy.

She had become pregnant in the middle of her first college semester. She was forced to drop out, and said that she would go back after she had the baby. But after Maurice died, she never got back around to it.

"What's wrong, Mommy?" her two-year-old son asked, using a baby's language that only she could understand. Her son watched the anguish and defeat conquer his mother's face.

"Nothing, baby boy. Mommy's just a little tired, that's all. It's time for your nap."

As Anari put her son in his room, the tears continued to fall from her eyes. She missed Maurice so much. He was her heart. He was always by her side when she needed him most, but she could no longer turn to him. He was gone. He had been for almost two years now, and she still hadn't gotten over losing him.

Her pregnancy had been a hard one. She felt lonely, and all she wanted was to have someone to share her newfound joy with. She stared around her home, the luxurious home that Reesey had worked so hard to buy her. She stared at her furniture that she had imported from Paris and her white Italian carpet, and knew that none of it was worth the life of her only love.

"Baby, I miss you so much. I need you," Anari said as she felt loneliness and sorrow invade the depths of her heart.

She was the girlfriend of a hustler, so she knew the risk of Reesey's fast life. His death was inevitable. There had been so much blood shed and he had taken so many lives that everything just caught up to him. In his lifetime, Maurice had killed so many people that eventually it had come back to him. And even though Anari knew these things, she still couldn't let go. He was her reason for breathing, and now that his breaths had stopped, she felt as though hers should too.

She went to the bathroom and felt her stomach start to turn. She stared into the mirror at her perfect honey brown complexion, her light brown eyes, and her beautiful long, thick hair. She held her flat, neatly packed stomach and admired her curvy, enticing shape. She remembered that these assets were what had drawn Maurice to her in the first place.

She was so overwhelmed by her sadness that all she wanted to do was sleep. That's all she ever did. Ever since Maurice died, her days had been filled with exhaustion. She lay down on the gold satin sheets on her king-sized bed and drifted off into a restless sleep.

"Oh my God! Reesey, baby, what happened to you?" shouted Anari as she watched Maurice stumble into the house with bloodied and torn clothes. She noticed the hole in the bottom of his shirt.

"Tanya!" she screamed. *"He's been shot. Call 911. Baby, who did this to you?"*

Maurice weakly replied, *"Mann."*

Anari's heart dropped. She knew that Mann was no joke. He was another hustler from the East Side of Jersey, and for reasons that were unknown to Anari, Mann had a serious beef with Maurice. It had been going on for *about two months now, and she had no clue what it was about.*

Tanya came running out of the bedroom to see what was going on. She was amazed at how much blood could come out of a human body. She was frozen still when Anari shouted, "Bitch, call 911!"

Tanya snapped out of it and rushed to the phone. "Someone has been shot," Tanya screamed as Maurice slipped in and out of consciousness.

"Calm down, ma'am. What is your emergency?" asked a voice on the other end of the line.

"Someone has been shot! It's so much blood."

The voice on the other end remained calm. "Okay, remain calm, miss. Can you take the person's pulse?"

A frightened Tanya looked at Anari. "She wants you to take his pulse."

Anari, not really knowing what she was doing, put her fingers on the pressure points behind Maurice's ear. "I can't find it," she replied. "Tanya, tell them I can't find it."

Both girls panicked and Tanya yelled into the phone, "She can't find it. Just please hurry. We are at 9851 Brookview Road. Hurry!"

Tanya hung up the phone and rushed over to aid Anari as she tried to nurse her man back to health. As Anari rocked back and forth with a bleeding Reesey in her arms, she prayed, "God, please let him be okay."

She knew that he would never make it if they waited for the ambulance.

"Tanya, go get the car. We're driving him to the emergency room!"

As Tanya ran to the car, Anari half-dragged, half-carried Maurice to the car. As they were pulling out, a black Jaguar blocked them in. Her heart stopped when she saw the tall, dark figure step out of the car.

"Bitch, get out of the car," Mann shouted as he approached her car from behind.

Anari was frozen in fear. She didn't know what to do. She tried to roll up her car window, but Mann reached into the car and grabbed her by her hair. Anari screamed in pain as she tried to break loose of Mann's hold. She opened her door, banging it against Mann's leg, causing him to release his hold on her. Without thinking, she reached under her seat and grabbed the .22 that Maurice bought her for times like this. Despite the fact that she had never used it, she brought it up and released four shots into his head and chest, like a pro. She felt his blood splash onto her face and heard Tanya scream as she realized what she had just done.

The police locked her up, and it took her ten days to convince them that she had acted in self-defense. When they let her out, Maurice was in the hospital getting better and he didn't have to worry about the nigga who shot him because Anari had already handled that for him. The only thing she had to worry about was Mann's clique. They were bound to try to retaliate. She knew that she had just started a war that would end with more than Mann's dead body.

Her alarm clock woke her out of her dream. She was soaking in sweat and trembling at the thought of the man she killed. The phone rang, and still dazed she answered with a soft "hello."

"Hey, girl. Is you ready?" Tanya asked.

Anari remembered that she was supposed to go a birthday party with her girlfriend. "Shit! Girl, give me thirty minutes. I fell asleep, and I'm a little shaky. My nightmares have been bothering me lately."

Tanya knew that this would happen again, because Anari hadn't been the same since she lost Maurice. "Nari, are you all right? If you want to, we can just chill tonight. You know, like we used to. I'll go pick up some Jamie Foxx comedy shows and we'll kick it and eat some Chunky Monkey ice cream."

Although this was tempting to Anari and she really didn't want to go out, she had already promised her friend that she would go. Anari hated to break her word so she replied, "No, I need to get out of the house anyway. I'll be there in forty-five minutes."

Anari hung up the phone and called her brother Jamal. The phone rang several times before a loud voice answered.

"What up? Who this?" said her eighteen-year-old brother.

Anari had told her brother time and time again to talk like he had some sense, but since she needed him to baby-sit, she looked past it this one time.

"Hey, Maulie. This is Nari. Will you watch your nephew tonight?"

He agreed to watch Maurice for the weekend. "You need to get out anyway. Go have fun. I'll keep him for two days, but you owe me!"

She hesitated when Maulie said that. She knew that he would make her pay him back double for keeping Maurice on a weekend. She agreed, hung up the phone and hopped into the shower.

As she washed her body, she fantasized about Maurice. It had been so long since she had felt someone inside of her. She rubbed her breasts, pretending that it was Maurice's hands. She felt herself getting wet. She touched herself, wishing that Maurice was with her. She felt herself getting hot. Her fingers were soaked in her juices, and she pictured Maurice putting her on her back and massaging her insides with his tongue.

She was brought back to reality by the ringing of the phone. She rinsed off and stepped out of the shower, but didn't even answer the phone. She knew it was Tanya calling to rush her. Her answering machine picked it up and Anari heard her friend's voice.

"Anari, hurry your ass up. And don't be taking all day. Just throw something on."

Anari shook her head and mumbled to herself. "Okay, okay, I'm coming."

She rushed into her room and started to rummage through her closet, trying to find something to wear. She liked to dress to impress and couldn't just "throw something on" as Tanya had suggested. It took her twenty minutes before she found the perfect outfit. She put on a black Gucci halter with a short black Gucci skirt and thigh-high boots. She looked into the mirror and added her platinum Gucci accessories. She knew she would be the best-looking girl at the party. "I always am," she said to herself as she grabbed the keys to her Honda Accord and headed out the front door.

Anari drove over to Longway Boulevard to pick up her friend. When she got there, Tanya stepped out of the house in a two-piece pink Prada hookup.

I have to admit my girl looks good. From the looks of her, no one would ever suspect that she's a lesbian. Well, bisexual, as she calls it. I don't give a damn, though. If you getting down with bitches, you are a lesbian in my book. I mean don't get me wrong. I'm not homophobic or anything. She ain't never tried to come at me with that left-hand shit, so I don't have a problem with it.

"Hey, T. Looking good, girl," Anari shouted as she got geeked up to go to the party.

"I know, I know," Tanya replied as she walked over to the passenger side and got into the car. As soon as she got in, she turned the radio up loud. Anari felt the vibration from her 15-inch subwoofers. Tanya put her hands in the air and screamed, "Let's go!"

When Anari entered the party, some of the ballers aimed straight for her. She wasn't feeling that, though. Men could be so juvenile. Anari hated it when niggas tried to holla. They needed to improve their game before they came at her.

Instead of entertaining the thought of talking to any of those losers, she headed straight to the dance floor. She danced with her girlfriend to the smooth sound of reggae. She moved her body like a snake as she got into the groove of the party. She talked with some of the people that were around her and she was laughing and having a good time.

"I'm going to get something to drink. Do you want something?" she asked Tanya.

Tanya shook her head and stayed on the dance floor as Anari made her way to the bar. She ordered a Long Island Iced Tea and chilled at the bar for a while. It was getting too crowded on the dance floor.

She was chilling when she noticed this fine-ass dude sitting at one of the tables by the door. She knew he was somebody important just by his presence. Bitches were surrounding him like he had the magic stick or something. The dudes weren't any better. They were sitting around him, agreeing to his every word and anticipating his every move. Anari wondered if he could even breathe.

When she grew tired of that scene, she searched the party for Tanya. When she finally spotted her, she was freaking some nigga in the corner while some woman with a slim waist and a big booty danced on Tanya from behind. Anari laughed and motioned for her friend to come over to the bar. Tanya saw Anari watching her and made her way over to her side.

"Are you having fun?" Tanya asked.

"Yeah, it's cool. I don't even have to ask you that question," Anari replied, still laughing.

Tanya looked back over to the guy and the girl she had been dancing with. "Look, girl. I might leave the party with them. We going over to the Waffle House to have breakfast, so when you ready to dip out, don't worry about me."

Anari shook her head, amused with her friend. Tanya sashayed her sexy self back into the crowd.

Anari's attention was on the person sitting by the door. He intrigued her. There was something about him that she liked. She watched him chill as the people around clung to him. He didn't seem conceited, though. It appeared that he was humble. He just smiled sexily and entertained the people around him. While she peeped game, a man sat next to her with the cheesiest grin she had ever seen.

"Hey, baby. You look like you could use a drink."

Anari looked at the dude as if he were crazy. She couldn't believe this broke-ass nigga had the nerve to come over there trying to run game. Now she was attracting losers! She decided to get out of there before he thought something was up.

As Anari rose out of her seat, the man grabbed her arm. "I'm just trying to have a conversation, you know. See what's up for tonight," he said in a drunken slur.

"Ain't shit up for tonight, at least not between me and you. Besides, a conversation involves two participants, and since you only have one, I guess you're out of luck," retorted Anari as she snatched her arm from his grasp, got up and went to the bathroom near the back of the club.

She walked into the bathroom and looked in the mirror to make sure that her makeup had not smeared. It had been so hot in the party. When she was satisfied with her appearance, she walked out of the bathroom.

When she came out, the dude from the bar was waiting for her in the hallway. She wasn't comfortable being in the secluded area of the club with a drunk man, so she knew that she better hurry up and get around a group of people. She tried to walk past him and go back to the bar, but didn't get very far before the man grabbed her tightly by the arm and began rubbing his hands over her body.

"You like that, don't you?" he asked as he palmed Anari's ass, squeezing so tightly that it hurt.

Anari tried to pull herself away from him, but her efforts were futile. This man was three times her size. "You're drunk. Stop!" she told the man firmly as she pushed against his chest.

The man held her even tighter and ran his tongue along her neck. He began to grind against her, pulling her ass closer to him. She felt his nasty dick start to harden, and she became afraid, knowing that a drunken man, a hard dick, and a helpless girl with a smart mouth were not a good combination.

When Maurice was alive, shit like this would never have happened. They knew not to mess with Maurice's woman. Since he got respect, she got respect, but he was no longer here to protect her.

"Let me go!" she shouted angrily. She could not believe that no one was seeing this. The music in the club was loud, and she was in the back of the club, so no one could hear her screams.

In a room full of people, this man was about to drag her off against her will. He put his greasy hands on her breasts and tore through her tiny halter. He began kissing on her body, and she felt his slimy tongue as he forced it into her mouth. She kicked and fought him, but her efforts were no use. This man was going to rape her in front of almost two thousand people.

"Help! Stop, please, no!"

She knew that she was helpless. There was an empty pit in her stomach, and she could taste the salt as the tears streamed down her face and into her mouth. He snatched her arm violently and pulled her toward the back exit. He pulled out a knife and hissed that if she did anything, he would kill her.

She stopped breathing as soon as the threat came out of his mouth. Her stomach twisted tightly in knots and she tried to think of something that she could do to get herself out of this situation. Her thoughts scrambled in her head, but none of them made any sense to her. She was in a panic, and when she finally realized that there was nothing she could do, she slowly began to walk where he wanted her to go. She could feel the sharp blade of the knife against her back and her demeanor quickly changed from angry to afraid. Not only was she afraid for herself, but she was afraid for her child. There was nothing left to do but beg.

"Please, I have a little boy at home. Don't do this to me. Just please leave me alone. I'll give you anything you want. I have money," she pleaded with him, but it didn't help.

The guy seemed to get even more pleasure because she was begging. Just as he was about to force her out the back door, the men's bathroom door opened and the dude that she had been staring at earlier came out.

Anari screamed to get his attention. He looked at Anari and her torn clothing and immediately pulled his gun.

"What the fuck?" He grabbed the perverted man by the neck and hemmed him up against the wall with one arm while holding the gun at his head in the other. The drunk took the knife and sliced it over the man's arm, trying to get him to release his hold.

The man was furious. He slammed the drunk's head against the wall hard. His hand was wrapped around the drunk's neck so tightly that Anari didn't think that he could breathe.

Anari sank to the floor and put her hands over her ears, wishing that she had stayed home that night. When the drunk lost consciousness, the other man stomped him until he was unrecognizable.

Anari could not tell if the guy was dead or not, but after what he had tried to do to her, she sure hoped so.

The man, who had basically saved her life, picked her up and carried her out the back door and to his car.

"You all right, ma'am?" he asked as he took off his shirt and covered Anari's battered body with it. Anari was still in shock, so she just shook her head and continued to cry. "Where you live? I'll take you home," he offered.

Anari was so defeated that she couldn't respond. She just told him her address and stared out the window.

She was still in tears when he pulled up to her house. He found her keys in her purse and carried her into the house. She jumped out of his arms and ran into the bathroom. Staring in the mirror, she saw red spots around her neck where the man had sucked on it. She was disgusted. Her body felt dirty, and all she wanted to do was get clean. She quickly turned on her shower and scrubbed her skin until it was raw. She just wanted to get the scent of the man off of her. She scrubbed her body so hard that the water hurt as it hit her. She wet her hair and screamed loudly as she tried to get as clean as she possibly could.

Anari stepped out of the shower and saw that she had made her skin red from washing it so hard. She brushed her teeth and gargled to get the taste of him out of her mouth. She pinned up her wet hair, grabbed the man's shirt off the floor, and walked out of the bathroom in a short silk robe that hugged her body tightly, accentuating every curve. When she walked into her living room, the man was still there. She realized that he had saved her.

"Thank you. If you hadn't come when you did, I don't know what would have happened."

She began to tear up, and even though she did not know this man, she hugged him. He held her so tight. It felt good to be in the arms of a man again.

"Here's your shirt," she said as she pulled away from him.

He took it from her and put it back over his head. He looked at her. "Don't worry about your car. I'll have one of my boys drive it over here later on tonight."

She looked down at his arm and saw that it was bleeding. "Come here. Let me clean that up for you."

He followed her into the bathroom where she ran some soapy water into the sink. She grabbed a towel from the linen closet and slowly cleaned around the wound. The man watched her as she gently took care of the cut on his arm.

Anari looked up and saw him watching her, and she smiled shyly. "It looks kind of deep," she commented, "but I don't think you need stitches."

She grabbed some peroxide out of the medicine cabinet and poured it over the cut. She then wrapped it in gauze. "See, good as new."

He looked at her and she smiled. "Thank you," he said.

Anari appreciated all his help, but she still didn't feel safe. "Will you stay here until I fall asleep?" she asked.

He looked at this beautiful woman and felt his manhood start to harden. She was everything he wanted, and he knew it when he saw her staring at him in the club. "Yeah, I'll stay with you," he replied.

She led him to her sofa and she lay down. He sat on the floor and watched her as she drifted into a peaceful sleep. When he thought that she was safe, he kissed her on her cheek and left.

When she woke up the next morning, her body was sore from her confrontation in the club the night before. She remembered that someone had rescued her. He brought her home and was a perfect gentleman. She looked around, hoping he was still there.

"Damn! I didn't even get his name," she said. For some reason, she remembered that she was comfortable with the stranger. It was the first night she did not dream about Maurice.

Chapter Three

"*T*his is Reginald Ellis, reporting for CNN news. One of the biggest drug lords to hit New Jersey was murdered today. Maurice Jones was found in the apartment of Tasha Gross. Both he and Ms. Gross have been decapitated. The body of their son, Jonathan Jones, was found face down, floating in the bathtub. The police believe that these murders were drug-related. The police have also described this as one of the most malicious murders they have ever witnessed.

"Jones has flooded the streets of New Jersey with crack cocaine and heroin for over five years, and is believed to be responsible for over thirty unsolved murders. We will keep you updated on the details as they come in."

Anari could not believe what she was hearing. It was all over the news. Maurice couldn't be dead. She picked up her cell phone and dialed his number. When she got no answer, the pain began to sink in. She stared at the television screen in disbelief. She knew that this had to be a mistake.

Anari called Maurice's mom, searching for more an-

swers, but when she heard the muffled cries of Mrs. Jones, she knew that it was all true. Maurice was dead. Not only had he been killed, but he had a completely different life outside the one he shared with her. He had another woman and a child, and she found out about it on the damn 6 o'clock news. She knew she was not the only one who had seen this newscast. Her business would be all over New Jersey by nightfall.

She knew one thing for sure, though. Whoever had taken the life of Maurice could have easily taken the life of her and her unborn child.

"Oh God, no! Why did this have to happen to me? Why was Maurice lying to me? Why was he doing this to me?"

She hated him and loved him at the same time. She didn't know how to react to this situation. All she knew was that her heart was broken for two different reasons, and both reasons hurt.

There were so many things that she needed to know, so many questions that would remain unanswered. The one person who she trusted had betrayed her. Not only had he betrayed her, but now he was also gone from her life. She would never get to speak to him, to confront him, to touch him again. The last words they said to each other had been hateful ones, and she could not believe that she would never get to say "I love you" or "I'm sorry" again.

A loud shrill noise snapped her out of her trance. She looked at the phone and breathed a sigh of relief. She was glad that the phone had startled her from her painful memories. She let her machine pick up the call as she made her way to her car.

She looked at the three cars that she owned. One was a tan SL600 Mercedes Benz, one was a black Honda Accord, and the other was a candy apple red Cadillac Escalade. She decided to take the Benz, and drove to Maulie's house to pick up her little man. As she turned onto Jamal's street she saw trash, graffiti, hoodies, and nickel and dime men everywhere. They flooded the streets like a plague.

Jamal lived in the middle of the hood. His neighborhood was where all the statistics took place, but to Jamal this was home. They had grown up in the ghetto, and unlike Anari, it was still the one place where he felt safe.

"Jamal needs to move his ass out of this neighborhood," Anari mumbled to herself as a crack head knocked on her window, asking for money. Anari started to reach into her purse but changed her mind when she thought about what the fiend would spend her money on. "I can't feed your habit, baby girl," Anari said as she sped up to avoid other lowlifes.

When she reached her brother's home, Anari blew her horn because she was afraid to leave her Benz unattended. Jamal came right out, with her child dangling from his back.

"Say hey, Mommy," said Jamal, trying to teach him to speak. Her son just waved at his mother and continued to hang off of Maulie's back.

Anari laughed. "Boy, get your bad ass in this car." Maurice followed his mother's instructions and with a sad face got into the car. "You gon' have him spoiled," Anari said as she watched Maurice begin to throw a fit because he was leaving his uncle.

"Shut up. That's my nephew," Jamal replied as he kissed his sister's cheek.

Anari looked at her brother. "Whatever, boy. We'll see you later. And thanks again."

Anari always made sure that she thanked her brother for spending time with Maurice. Since Big Maurice had died, Jamal really had been a great male figure in her son's life. He made it a habit to be around to help her raise Maurice, and she wanted him to know that she appreciated him.

As she drove away from Jamal's rundown neighborhood, her cell phone rang.

"Yo," she coolly answered. There was nothing but silence on the end of the line. "Hello?" she angrily repeated herself. She hated when people played on her phone. It was so childish. She didn't have the time to sweat it, though. She drove around with Maurice, chilling in the back all day.

Anari took Maurice to Northland Mall. Li'l Reesey loved to go to the mall because he liked to throw coins into the fountain. As they walked around the mall, she bought Maurice everything she saw that she thought looked right on him. As she maneuvered his stroller and carried her bags at the same time, her cell phone rang.

"What?" she answered in a frustrated voice.

"Dang, girl, what the hell is wrong with you?" asked her concerned friend.

"Sorry, Tanya. I'm in the mall with like thirty bags in my hand. And I'm trying to push yo' bad-ass godson around in his big-ass stroller. I'm out here looking like a bag lady," she said as she sang Erykah Badu's popular song.

Tanya laughed at her friend. She loved Anari's voice. Her girl could sing. She had called Anari to see what had happened to her, and to tell her what she had done after the party.

"Girl, you crazy. But let me tell you what I did after I left the party last night. Well, the dude that you saw me with ended up being a complete flake, so me and this girl named Shonda hooked up. You know the girl you saw me dancing with?" Tanya didn't even wait for Anari to respond before she continued. "Anyway, girl, we went back to her crib and was kicking it. She cool as hell, and we got drunk. I mean, we were so tore up. We did a few thangs, but I don't think I'm gon' call her again cuz after we was through she was all clingy and shit. You know? Like we were in a relationship or something. And you know I can't be tied down. But I had fun, though.

"So, what did you do after the party? What was the rest of your night like?" she asked.

Anari forgot that her friend did not know about the incident at the party, and frankly, she didn't want to talk about it. Every time she thought about it, she felt chills go down her spine.

"Nothing. I went home," Anari replied.

"Well, I went to Ticia's Beauty Salon earlier today, and you know them hoes always gossiping up in there. So anyway, they were talking about some nigga that was driving your car. And since you won't even let me drive your whip, I thought that I was entitled to know why you was letting someone else drive it, missy."

Anari laughed at her nosey, misinformed friend and told her the whole story. When she finished explaining the situation to her friend, she was nearly in tears.

"Anari, I am so sorry. I should have never left you there alone. If we went together, we should have left together. Just like my momma taught me." Tanya was sympathetic. "But who was this mystery man that saved you?" she asked.

"Girl, I don't even know. I didn't get his name. He was nice, though, and if it wasn't for him, who knows what would have happened? But listen, let me call you when I get to the crib, okay?"

Anari hung up her cell phone before her friend had the chance to grill her some more. She already knew what was on her friend's mind. Tanya was probably going to ask her if she fucked him. Anari shook her head, thinking about Tanya. That girl was crazy.

She looked at her baby boy, who had fallen asleep in his stroller. "I guess that means it's time for us to go home," she said to herself. She made her way to her car and drove home.

After she put the baby in his room, she went into the living room and flopped down on her couch. After spending all day pushing Maurice around, all she wanted to do was sleep. Unfortunately, she was not at liberty to sleep right now. She had to fix dinner.

She got up off the couch and walked into the kitchen, checking in her refrigerator to see what she would cook. She decided to make lasagna, salad, and breadsticks.

She turned on the oven and prepared the meal. It took her about an hour and a half to finish cooking, and by that time, Maurice had awakened. She sat Maurice in his high chair and they ate a delicious dinner together. In the middle of their meal, the phone rang.

"Hello?" she answered.

"Okay now. Finish telling me about this dude."

Anari laughed when she heard Tanya's voice. "What do you want to know? It wasn't a big deal or anything. He just brought me home," Anari said as she wiped some food from Maurice's mouth.

"Bitch, whatever. Was you feeling him and was he tight? Did you kiss him? Ooh, Anari, did y'all fuck?" Tanya asked, saying exactly what Anari expected her to say.

Anari had to burst out laughing. "Damn, Tanya. Okay, okay. Look, he was tight, and I was feeling him. But we didn't do anything. He just brought me to the crib and stayed until I fell asleep. It doesn't matter anyway because I didn't even get his name. I will probably never even see this man again."

Anari hung up with her friend and finished her dinner. After dinner, she sat up and played with Maurice. They played hide and seek, and tickle monster. She played with him until he was exhausted.

When he fell asleep, Anari looked at her beautiful baby boy. "I love you, sweetie," she said to her son as she lifted his tiny body and placed him in his room. She didn't know what she would do without him. He was her life, and the only reason that she was able to survive his father's death. He was her pride and joy. She kissed her son again then went into her own bedroom and went to sleep.

The next morning, big Maurice's mother called. "Hey, baby girl. How have you been?" asked Momma Jones.

Anari recognized her sweet voice. Just thinking of Maurice's family made her cry. "I'm fine, Momma Jones. How are you?" replied Anari between tears.

"Oh, don't you worry about me. I am fine. I was just wondering if my grandson could come with his granddaddy and me to Hawaii. We're going on a vacation, and I haven't seen my baby in a while." Mrs. Jones sounded eager.

Anari was reluctant to let her son go anywhere without her. It wasn't that she didn't trust Maurice's parents with her baby, it was just that he was the only thing that she had left, and she just didn't want to lose him too. She knew she would have to get out of that habit, though, and who better to start with than his grandparents?

"Okay, when are you leaving?" asked Anari.

"Friday morning. We'll pick him up. We'll be gone for two weeks," Mrs. Jones replied.

Two weeks was a long time. She was already beginning to miss her baby and he hadn't even left yet.

"Besides, this will give you time to have a little fun. You haven't been happy since my son passed. I know you loved him, but you've got to move on with your life. Your love for him will haunt you for the rest of your life if you don't let go. He knows that you loved him, and I know that he loved you. You are the only woman he has ever said that about. I know he had that other girl Tiffany and everything, but she didn't compare to his Anari."

Tiffany? Maurice's mother is getting old. The girl's name was Tasha.

Momma Jones interrupted Anari's thoughts. "You believe that, child. So, go have fun and don't worry about a thing. We'll take care of that baby."

It was true. Anari did need time to breathe, and she couldn't do that with Maurice bouncing off the walls all the time. She hadn't had any time to herself since he was born.

"All right, Mrs. Jones. I guess he can go. We'll see you in a couple days." she said as she placed her phone back on the receiver.

On Wednesday and Thursday, Anari bought Maurice new outfits and accessories for his two-week vacation. She didn't want his grandparents to have to buy him anything while he was there. When Friday arrived, his grandparents were there to pick him up at 12:00 sharp. She helped them pack his suitcase in the trunk and kissed her child goodbye.

"Have fun, baby boy, and be good for Mommy," she said.

When they drove away, she went straight to the gym to work on her figure. It had been so long since she had worked out. She just didn't seem to have the time anymore. As she walked into the gym, she smelled the sweat that dripped from the hundreds of bodies that were there that day. She made her way to the Tae-Bo class, but found out that it was full.

"Damn, now I got to run on them damn treadmills."

Anari hated running. She would much rather join an aerobics class, but since the one she wanted was full, she didn't have a choice. She found a machine that was open and reluctantly began her hour-long run. As she ran, Anari felt her thighs tightening and burning with every stride. This shit was strenuous. She needed to work out more often, she thought as she began to sweat.

The next Tae-Bo class was about to begin, so she made her way to the basement level where the class was held. Anari signed her name on the list and noticed that she needed a partner. She looked around for someone in the class who appeared to be by themselves. Anari spotted no one, so she decided to leave.

Just as she was walking up the steps, an attractive, light-skinned girl with short hair and a nice shape asked if Anari would be her partner. Anari said "cool" and joined the girl as they maneuvered to the front of the class. The instructor had everyone practicing boxing techniques.

This bitch can box, thought Anari as she blocked all of the hits her partner threw at her. This girl was aggressive.

If she didn't know any better, she would think this girl had beef or something. The girl threw left-right combinations that would knock a bitch out but Anari wasn't intimidated. The bell rang, indicating that it was time to switch. The girl tried to hand Anari the boxing gloves, but Anari didn't take them.

"Keep 'em. I don't use gloves."

Anari cockily wrapped her hands in tape and took a boxing stance. When the instructor yelled "fight," Anari gave the girl a combination that would kill a bitch on the streets. Anari may have looked fragile, but she knew how to hold her own. Tanya had taught her how to fight in grade school. She was never one of those fighting types, but if push came to shove, she would knock a ho out.

Anari fought mightily with her partner, who blocked her hits with just as much force. The bell rang for them to stop, and when they did, all the other people in the class were clapping and staring at them.

Anari stared at the girl to see if she wanted to continue this shit for real, but she lightened up when she saw the girl burst into laughter. When Anari realized that she was being childish, she began to laugh too.

"Hey, by the way, I'm Shawna," said the girl.

"I'm Anari. Nice workout," she replied.

They walked back upstairs and went to the

women's locker room. "Hey, you want to go hit the next class?" asked Shawna.

"Nah, girl, I can't. I got to find out what's up for tonight. My baby is vacationing with grandparents, and I'm trying to relax and have fun while they're away," Anari said.

They slipped on some sweats and exited the locker room, heading for the parking lot. Anari waved and headed for her car. When she got there, she noticed that her back tire had caught a flat.

"Damn, I just got these damn tires!" she said as she put her hands on her hips and shook her head. She saw Shawna pull up behind her.

"You need some help?" Shawna asked.

Anari nodded her head and gratefully replied, "Yeah. Do you know how to put on a spare tire?"

Shawna laughed. "Nah, but we can give it a shot."

Anari smiled and went into her trunk to get the spare. She pulled out the tire, but after that she was lost. Shawna got out of her car and stood clueless next to Anari. They just pulled every tool out of the trunk, hoping that they would at least use some of them to help fix the tire. They both looked at each other, waiting for the other one to do something. After thirty seconds of dumbfounded silence, they both burst into laughter.

Shawna went back to her car and searched through her gym bag. She came back with a cell phone and offered it to Anari. "You might as well just call a towing company and have them fix it. I can wait with you until it comes."

Anari took the phone and smiled graciously. She dialed information and they connected her to a towing company.

"New Jersey Tow, how can I help you?" said a man's voice.

"Hi. I have a flat tire and I need it fixed. I'm at the gym on Broadway Ave."

Anari made the arrangements, and they told her that someone would be out in forty-five minutes. She gave Shawna her phone back.

"Thanks for waiting out here with me. At least I don't have to look stupid alone."

Shawna laughed and waved her hand in dismissal. "Girl, it's nothing." She looked across the street at a restaurant and asked, "Hey, are you hungry?"

Anari nodded and Shawna continued. "We might as well have lunch while we wait."

The girls walked across the street to the small deli. Anari was happy that she didn't have to wait for the tow by herself.

"I haven't seen you around. Are you from Jersey?" Shawna asked as she bit into her turkey sandwich.

"Yeah, I've lived here my whole life. I just don't get out too much. I usually just chill in the house. Just me and my baby."

Shawna shook her head. "Well, you should come out with me tonight. You know that P. Diddy release party that's going down, right? I got an extra invitation if you into that type of scene. Everybody who's anybody is gonna be there. You should come through and check it out. We can ride together, if you want. I'm going to the mall to buy something to wear as soon as I leave here," Shawna offered in an eager voice.

Anari usually didn't chill with females like that, but she was not about to turn that offer down. Besides, Shawna seemed to be cool. She was nice enough to help Anari with her tire, and Anari needed to make some new friends anyway.

"You think you could get one more invite for my girl Tanya? She's cool, and if I go without her, she gon' flip. I'll pay you for the extra ticket if you follow me to the ATM," said Anari.

"Yeah, it's cool, but tell you what. Don't even worry about the money. We'll all roll out."

Anari noticed that Shawna had a Lexus, so she knew she wasn't a broke ho. They exchanged numbers so that they could get in contact with one another.

Shawna looked out the window. "Oh, your tow is here." They got up and walked back across the street.

A man got out and walked around her car to see which tire had the flat. "It's gonna be forty-five dollars," he said when he finished replacing the tire.

Anari handed him the money, turned to Shawna and thanked her again. They said their goodbyes and agreed to meet later. Shawna gave Anari the two tickets and they went their separate ways.

Just as Anari was pulling into her driveway, Tanya pulled in right behind her. "Hey, girl. I was just about to call you. You will never guess where we going tonight."

Tanya got all excited. "Hopefully, somewhere where I can find a good man." Tanya smirked and added, "Or woman."

Anari put her hand in Tanya's face. "Ugh, bitch, you could have saved that gay shit. Anyway, we are going to Diddy's release party tonight!"

Tanya frowned her face up at Anari. "Diddy? Diddy who? Broke-ass Diddy that got nabbed over there by the south end of Jersey? When he get out of prison and who giving him the release party? Shit, I threw a party when his ass went in."

Anari was cracking up. This bitch was crazy.

"Tanya, not that Diddy. I'm talking P. Diddy, Sean 'Puffy' Combs, *Making the Band*, marathon-running, million-dollar Diddy. Yo' ass is crazy. And anyway, what I look like fucking with Diddy old bum ass?"

Tanya screamed in excitement, "Oh my God! How we gon' get in there? We haven't been to any release parties since Maurice died. You think you still can get in?"

Anari explained to Tanya about Shawna and the party. Tanya had heard enough. "We need to go find something to wear. No, never mind. I need to get my hair done. I'll see you at nine."

Just as quickly as Tanya had come, she had gone. Anari couldn't blame her friend, though. She was geeked too. She couldn't wait until tonight. She was about to party hard. She hadn't had a good time in a long time, and once her son came back from his vacation she would have another long stretch before she saw a good time away from the house.

Anari made her way into the house. She looked at her clock, which read 4:00 P.M. "Good. I have some time to rest," she said to herself.

Anari ran a steamy hot bubble bath, lit some scented candles, and turned on her Tamia CD. She sang along, "Oh, can't nobody do me like you. I'm officially missing you."

Anari was in the zone. She spent over an hour in the tub. When she got out of the bath after she saw that she was starting to wrinkle, it was 6:00 P.M.

Anari looked in her closet to find something to wear. She pulled out her black Versace mini dress with the slit down the breast line, a silver chain belt, and rippled, hip-hugging waistline. She pulled out her silver shoes and platinum accessories. By the time she finished choosing her outfit, it was almost time to go.

She made sure she put her .22 in her purse, just in case something happened. She hated guns, but she didn't ever want to be empty-handed and unable to defend herself, like she had been when she was attacked.

Anari put on her clothes and admired herself in the mirror. She loved the way the dress hugged her body. She had a figure that most chicks would die for. She turned around in the mirror and made sure that she looked just as good from the back, knowing that was the first place someone would look. She pinned her hair up in an elegant swoop, that sexy, sort of careless, wild look. She put on her diamond earrings and applied her makeup.

Just as she finished putting on her gloss, Tanya rang her doorbell. Anari looked at the clock and went to let Tanya in.

"Hey, girl. I like that dress," she said as she headed back to her room to do her finishing touches. Tanya followed her and threw her hands in the air in frustration.

"You still ain't ready? How you gon' not be ready? It's eight-thirty."

Anari shrugged. "We ain't leaving until nine, so shut up." She gazed over at Tanya and gave her a look of approval. Tanya had on a gold Prada dress with gold Prada shoes that laced up her legs.

"I like your dress," Anari told her.

Anari still wasn't completely ready, but when Shawna pulled up, she grabbed her shoes off the bed and put them on as they raced out the door.

Shawna had on a tight red dress that flowed at the bottom when she walked. "Hey, girlie," she said to Anari.

Anari smiled and made the introductions. "Hey, this is Tanya. T, this is Shawna."

My girls look nice, but I look better.

They all got into Shawna's car and drove to the party. When they walked in, all eyes were on them. There was no doubt that Anari was the classiest woman there. As the girls entered, Shawna spoke to several celebrities.

"Hey, Tiff. How's it going, baby?" Ludacris shouted.

Anari and Tanya looked at each other. "Why he call you Tiff?" asked Anari.

Shawna shrugged. "I don't know. You know how they talk down south. It's probably some new slang or something."

Anari had to admit she was impressed. This girl obviously knew a lot of people.

The girls found themselves a table and absorbed the scene. It was hot inside the party. There were a lot of people there, and it seemed like everybody was on the dance floor. The waiter came over to the table with a bottle of champagne.

"We didn't order this," said Tanya.

"This is compliments of that gentleman over there at the bar," replied the waiter. The girls looked over to the bar and noticed this fine-ass brother.

"I know that is not Camron," said Tanya.

Anari laughed. She could see the dollar signs forming in Tanya's eyes.

"Get 'em, girl," Shawna said, mimicking Camron's popular song.

Tanya laughed. "Don't worry. You know I'm gon' get him." She stood up, fixed her dress, checked her makeup then walked over to the man at the bar. Anari laughed at her friend. Tanya could be so blunt sometimes.

"So, how old is your little boy?" asked Shawna.

Anari frowned in confusion. She remembered mentioning her child, but couldn't remember saying that she had a boy.

"How did you know I had a son? I don't think that I ever mentioned that my child was a boy."

Shawna paused for a minute and then looked at Anari. "Tanya told me."

Anari let it pass, but she still didn't believe Shawna. When had Tanya and Shawna had a chance to talk without her? She sat there and thought about it for a minute, but didn't want to ruin her night over something petty. It didn't matter right now anyway. All she was doing was trying to chill and have fun.

A man approached Shawna and asked if she wanted to dance. She nodded and smiled at Anari as she made her way to the dance floor. Anari was left sitting alone. She was a little bit uncomfortable because the last time she had been out, that man had assaulted her. She looked around, trying to be aware of her surroundings. Everything was cool and everybody seemed to be having fun, so she sat back, listening to hip-hop's finest, D.J. Kid Kapri, spin on the ones and twos.

"How you doing, ma?" asked a sexy voice behind her.

"Can I help you?" Anari asked. She turned around and noticed a familiar face.

"I just wanted to check on you, see how you been doing. Oh yeah, and let you know I took care of that nigga that came at you wrong the other night."

Anari's eyes softened and she motioned for the gentleman to sit down. She looked across the table at the gentle face that she recognized from the other night.

"Oh, I'm sorry. I didn't know who you were. I want to thank you for the other night," said Anari in a gentle voice.

"It's nothing. Don't worry about it. Someone as sexy as you don't deserve shit like that," replied the mystery man.

A blushing Anari smiled and brushed her hair out of her face.

"So why is it that I don't see you around?" he asked as he pulled his chair closer to hers.

"It's a long story. I don't go to many places. I'm more of a homebody, you know?" Anari replied cutely.

The mystery man studied Anari. He wanted to know more about her, but he didn't want to pry so he just asked, "Would you like a drink?"

Anari nodded and the mystery man rose and walked over to the bar. Anari's eyes followed and watched him as he ordered. He looked back at her and she pointed to the bathroom to let him know that she would be right back.

She stood up and went into the restroom. She didn't have to pee, but she wanted to fix her makeup and make sure that she was looking as fly as this mystery guy was.

Anari exited the restroom and the next thing she knew, she heard a loud blast in her ears. She knew that familiar sound all too well. Immediately, she dropped to the floor and crawled under the nearest table.

"Oh my God, Tanya!" She screamed for her friend, but no one heard her.

Frozen in fear, Anari was unable to move. *Move, Anari, go!* She tried to will herself, knowing that she had to get out of there. She finally got up enough courage to run, but when she did, she felt a burning sensation in her right shoulder, like something was branding her with hot coals. Anari dropped to the ground, trying to apply pressure to her shoulder. She glanced down and saw a small hole in her dress and a dark, wet spot spreading. When she saw the blood, she felt herself become dizzy.

Somebody help me! I've been shot. Oh, God!

Anari wanted to speak the words she was thinking, but she couldn't bring herself to open her mouth. Anari was so scared. Her vision became blurry as she felt someone lift her from the floor. The last thing she remembered hearing was someone shouting, "Move, move! I need to get her to the hospital!"

When Anari woke up, she was in a hospital room with a wrap around her right shoulder. Immediately, she thought of Mann's crew. Someone was after her; she just knew it. She had to get out of there fast.

Anari called for her nurse.

"Well, you finally decided to wake up," said an attractive woman who appeared to be in her late twenties. "You're going to be sore for quite a while, and you might have some trouble with that hand because the bullet hit some nerves, but other than that, you'll be just fine. You lost a lot of blood, though, so take it easy. If it wasn't for your friend, you might have died. He was very concerned about you."

Anari looked confused. "What?" She didn't know who the woman was talking about, but she didn't care. She was just grateful that whoever had brought her here had done it on time. Now she was in pain and she just wanted to go home. She would not feel safe at the hospital knowing that someone had deliberately tried to shoot her.

As the nurse began to walk out of the room, Anari asked, "Can you bring me my release forms?"

"Baby, it's too early for you to check out of the hospital. You need to rest. The doctor will probably send you home tomorrow." The nurse walked out of the room, leaving Anari to her thoughts.

If I stay here whoever tried to kill me might come back and finish the job. No, fuck that. I'm going home.

Anari worked herself into a panic and struggled to get out of bed. She managed to put on her clothes and walk out of the hospital. She called Tanya to pick her up, but couldn't reach her. Just as she was about to call Jamal, she recognized a voice behind her.

"I thought you were going to be in the hospital for a while."

Anari turned around to find her mystery man staring at her.

Oh my God. I must look crazy.

Anari gave him a smile. "No, they released me. Will you take me home?"

He led her to his car and drove her home. The ride was silent, but when he pulled into her driveway, Anari spoke first.

"Thank you. You must be getting tired of saving me. By the way, who are you? I don't even know your name. You don't even know my name. Why are you always here when I need you most?"

The mystery man looked at her with warm eyes and smiled. She liked his smile.

"First, I'm Von and I know your name, Miss Anari Simpson," he answered.

"Von? Umm, I guess you all right. But you didn't answer my second question, and how do you know my government name?"

Von flashed that magnificent smile again. "Well, I'm here for you cuz I like your style. I just think you need a man to keep you safe. Oh, and I have ways of finding things out about people I'm interested in."

Anari smiled. This nigga was something else. She hoped he didn't think he was getting any pussy just because he had a few nice lines.

"Oh, so you interested now?"

Von rubbed his chin and laughed.

Even his laugh was sexy, Anari thought, not daring to say it aloud.

"Oh, and I don't need a man to keep me safe, but a friend for entertainment would be nice."

He nodded his head. "A friend? I can work with that. But look, let me help you out for a couple days. I talked to your nurse and she said you would be okay if you took it easy."

So, this was the boyfriend that the nurse was talking about, thought Anari.

They went into her house where her new friend ran her a bubble bath and fixed her dinner.

"Yo, is that bath for two?" asked Von.

Anari laughed. "Sorry. No, it's not."

She locked her bathroom door and took a relaxing bath. Her shoulder hurt like hell, though, and every time she moved the wrong way, it was like being shot all over again.

Anari got out of the tub, put on a Donna Karan two-piece short and jacket hookup then joined Von in the living room. They chilled, talked, and laughed together all night. She put in a movie and they watched it together, laughing and relating to each other. Anari didn't know that she could have so much in common with someone besides Maurice. Other than the fact that she had been shot, it was a perfect night. She sat on the couch opposite him and they entertained one another until four in the morning. When it was time for him to go, Anari felt sad.

"I'll holla at you later, li'l mama."

Anari smiled. Von made her feel so special. "Bye, and thank you for everything. It was really sweet, and I appreciate it."

Von grabbed Anari's face, bent over and kissed her cheek then he was gone. Just as she was settling in her bed, the phone rang.

"Hello."

A panicky Shawna was on the line. "Are you okay? I heard about what happened to you. I looked for you outside of the party, and when I couldn't find you, I freaked."

"Calm down, girl. I'm cool. As a matter of fact, I'm more than cool," Anari said. "My friend Von waited at the hospital with me. Don't worry, though. The bullet went in and out. I'm fine—just a little tired and sore."

Shawna offered to come over later, and although she accepted, Anari just wanted to rest until then.

Ten minutes after she hung up with Shawna, Tanya called.

"Are you okay?"

Anari was extremely tired, but she talked anyway. "I'm fine, and guess what? I met my mystery man. He was at the party. His name is Von, and he saved me again. He picked me up from the hospital."

Anari was talking so fast that Tanya had a hard time hearing it all. But Tanya was happy for her girl. It had been so long since Anari had been happy about a man. Tanya hoped everything worked out for her.

"That's good, and Shawna is real cool. She looked out with us. She invited us to the release party. Maybe when you get better we can all chill again."

Anari and Tanya talked until Anari could barely focus. "Look, girl," Anari said, "I got to get off this phone and get some rest, but I'll holla at you later. Look, we'll do breakfast the day after tomorrow."

"Why not tomorrow?" asked Tanya.

"Because hopefully tomorrow I'll be chilling with Von." Anari chuckled as she hung up the phone.

Chapter Four

"**F**uck that. You ain't going nowhere," yelled Maurice. He grabbed Anari's arm and pushed her against the wall.

"Maurice, stop it. You're hurting me." Maurice was acting crazy. He always did when he had been drinking. Anari could smell the Hennessey on his breath.

"What the fuck? What, you gon' hit me now? Nigga, I just caught your stupid ass all hugged up with some bitch and you got the nerve to be raising your fist at me. Is that the reason why you ain't been coming home lately? That stank-ass ho? I mean what, is her pussy better than mine? You's a lyin'-ass nigga." Anari snatched her arm from Maurice's grasp.

"Okay, okay, listen, baby. The bitch don't mean shit. She just a friend."

Anari smacked the shit out of Maurice. "I wish I could smack the truth outta your lying ass. Fuck you!" Anari grabbed her bags and got into her car.

* * *

The doorbell rang a thousand times before it woke Anari out of her sleep. She put on her cotton robe and house shoes then rushed to the door, which she opened to a face full of flowers and balloons.

"Are you Ms. Anari Simpson?" asked the deliveryman.

"Yes, come in."

Anari was amazed at how many flowers and balloons she was receiving. There were five dozen roses and more than thirty balloons. There were white roses, red roses, black roses, purple roses. She took the card that was attached to one of the bouquets. It read: *Look outside.*

What type of message was that, she wondered. Anari went over to the window and looked down in front of her yard. Von was perched on his car's hood in front of her house. A big present sat on top of his hood too. He picked up his cell phone and dialed her number. She laughed as she picked up her phone.

"Come here," Von said and then hung up his phone.

Anari looked at herself in the mirror. She looked good for her to just have awakened. Her hair had that wild look to it so she said fuck it and rushed outside. She walked over to his car.

"What is all this?" she asked.

"Just a little something to cheer you up."

"I don't need all this. You didn't have to," she replied.

He pulled her close. "I got something for you." He gave the box to her. As soon as she lifted the top, she saw the most beautiful puppy she had ever seen in her life.

"Aww, hello, little guy."

She was so excited, she laughed out loud. Her son would love this. Hell, she loved this. She picked up the puppy and cuddled him against her breast.

"Now that we got you that friend you needed, what's up?"

Anari smiled and kissed Von on the cheek, then on the lips. It was a soft kiss, one that made tingles travel down her spine and juices flow in between her legs.

"We'll see," she replied.

She invited him in for breakfast but he said he had to go handle some business. She said, "Okay," but Von could tell that she was disappointed.

"I guess I'll see you later then," she said as she walked back into her house with her new puppy in her arms. She was halfway up her driveway when she saw Tanya pull up.

Tanya hopped out of the car and looked at Von as she passed him. "Are you okay?" she asked Anari as she walked up to her.

Anari nodded. "Yeah." She looked at Von and introduced Tanya. "Von, this is my best friend, Tanya."

Tanya nodded her head. "What up?" She waved then she and Anari began to walk into the house.

Anari stopped and turned around. "Thank you."

Von watched her walk into her house. He was intrigued by Anari. There was something about her that he liked. He was tired of fucking with them hoodies on the block, but he didn't want to settle for just any bitch. Most of these hoes were just on him because of his money.

He didn't know about Anari, though. He couldn't read her. What was she about? He would see, though, because even if she wasn't wifey material, she was definitely worth fucking.

Anari and Tanya went into her house and played with her new puppy. She fed him and cuddled him and couldn't wait until her son came home so that he could see him.

She thought about Von. He was so sweet, but things always started out that way. After a while, sweet could turn to sour. There was no telling what he was about.

Tanya got up to leave. "I know you told me that this was Von's day, so I'm about to go. I just came by to see how you were. I'll call you later." Tanya hugged Anari then left.

When she was gone, Anari called Shawna, who answered on the first ring.

"What's up, Anari? You feeling all right?"

Anari was feeling more than all right. "Yeah, girl, I'm cool. Look, tell me why Von slick ass just came over here with five dozen roses and a puppy," explained Anari.

Shawna laughed into the phone knowing that Anari was feeling thick right now. "Ohh, sounds like his nose is wide open. Five dozen roses don't run cheap. So, you're feeling him, huh?"

Anari was feeling him all right. She told Shawna how much she wanted things to go good between them.

"Look, I'm right around the corner. I'ma drop by, okay?" said Shawna.

Anari hung up the phone and took a quick shower. When she stepped out, her puppy was barking at the door. Anari smiled.

"Good boy," she told the puppy.

She answered the door in her towel. Shawna walked in. Anari went into her bedroom and put on some clothes. She put on some blue Guess capri jeans with a red Guess shirt and jean jacket. She flat-ironed her hair and put on her gold jewelry. She threw on her Air Force Ones.

"Hey, Shawna, come here," she yelled as she tied her shoes.

Shawna walked into Anari's bedroom with the puppy in her arms. "What are you going to name him?" asked Shawna.

Anari thought about it for a minute. "I think I'll name him Lucky. So, what do you want to do today?"

Shawna didn't care what they did, so she said, "It's whatever."

Anari, Shawna and Lucky got into Anari's red Cadillac Escalade. They drove into New York to go shopping.

Shawna was cool. Anari liked her style. She didn't seem fake like so many other hoes that tried to be down. She reminded Anari of herself, which is probably why they were getting so close. They spent the day talking and laughing. Anari was learning a lot about Shawna, and Shawna could really relate to Anari.

On the way back home, Anari's arm started bothering her, so she let Shawna drive. She put her puppy on her lap and drifted into a restless sleep.

Shawna woke Anari when they pulled into a gas station. "Anari, wake up. I have to get some gas. I'm gonna go, okay?"

Anari nodded and lay back down. Soon after, Shawna's cell phone started to ring. Anari looked inside the store and saw Shawna looking down one of the aisles, so she answered it.

"Hello," said Anari.

A raspy voice was on the other line. "I won't miss next time."

Anari stared at the phone. "Excuse me?" she said.

"Tiffany? Is this you? Never mind. Wrong number." The phone went dead.

Anari shrugged, figuring that someone had dialed the wrong number. She sat back in her seat and went back to sleep. By the time Shawna pumped the gas and got back in the car, Anari had forgotten to tell her about the call.

She slept until they got to her house. As Shawna pulled onto Anari's street, Anari began to wake up. She looked at the clock. It was 2:00 in the morning, and they had been gone since before lunchtime.

Shawna parked the truck and yawned as she stepped out.

"Girl, you might as well stay here tonight and go home in the morning. It's way too late for you to be driving. You can sleep in the guest room," Anari offered.

Shawna didn't feel like driving this late, so she accepted. They entered Anari's house. The scent of the roses overwhelmed them.

"I still can't believe he bought you that many roses!" Shawna said as she hung her jacket in the front closet.

Anari smiled at the thought of Von and replied, "I know! It was sweet. He didn't have to do that."

They stayed up until 6:00 A.M. just talking. It turned out they actually had a lot in common.

They shared common interests such as fashion and music.

"Hey, Anari, have you ever lost someone who you were close to?" asked Shawna.

Anari stared at Shawna, remembering everything she had gone through with Maurice. She could feel the tears welling up in her eyes.

"Yeah, actually I have. Someone I was very close to. Why do you ask?"

Shawna looked at Anari and she could see the pain behind her eyes. Shawna lowered her head. "I was just wondering. I've lost someone before and none of my other friends can feel where I'm coming from. They all say that I need to let go. I was just hoping that maybe you could understand."

Anari understood exactly where she was coming from. She put her hand on Shawna's shoulder.

"I do understand. About three years ago, I lost my boyfriend. He meant everything to me." She smiled at the thought of their relationship. "His name was Maurice. He was killed, and I don't usually like to talk about it. I'm just like you.

"Everybody keeps telling me to move on, but they don't know how hard it is. I know exactly what you're going through. I'm glad you brought it up. You can relate to me. Maurice was good to me. We were planning a life together, and in the blink of an eye, someone took him away."

Shawna had tears in her eyes and Anari could see that this woman knew how it felt to lose a loved one. That is when her defenses broke down and she told Shawna the story of how she had lost Maurice and how much she missed him.

Shawna listened to Anari's story. "It sounds all too familiar. When I lost my boyfriend, it was like my whole world ended. He promised me so many things. I wanted a child so badly, but when he died, it was like my body stopped working.

"One day I started having these cramps. They were horrible. It was like my insides were twisting in knots. There was so much blood, but I didn't think anything of it. I thought it was just that time of the month, you know? That was the biggest mistake I ever made in my life because when I finally went to the doctor, I found out that I had been pregnant for two months and that I had miscarried. I lost my baby right after I lost my baby's father."

Anari's heartbeat raced as she listened to Shawna's story. She could see what Shawna was saying in her head, and although Anari had lost Maurice, she knew that Shawna had lost a child. Anari didn't know what she would do if anything ever happened to her baby. She didn't even want to think about it.

"I'm so sorry. I couldn't imagine what I would do without my son," Anari said as she held Shawna's hand.

Shawna looked at Anari. "I would have never believed that you have been through so much like me. You seem to be doing so well for yourself. I mean you have your son and your house and Von. You're lucky that you were able to bounce back so quickly. It seems like it's taking me forever. The only person I really have left is my little sister."

Anari looked at Shawna like she was crazy. "No, Shawna, I have my son. That's all. This material shit don't mean nothing to me. I would gladly trade all this shit in just to have one more minute with Maurice. It is so hard to invest so much of yourself into someone else and then suddenly have that person ripped from your life. It's like losing a part of yourself.

"And Von, he got game, but that's all it is. I don't think that any man will ever be able to do what Maurice did for me or make me feel the way he did. Von might be a nice guy, but so far he holds no place in my life. I don't know if I can ever love someone that much again. I mean, I just met him. No, the only thing that I have to live for is my son, and truthfully, he's the only reason that I had to keep living after Maurice died."

Shawna and Anari stared at each other in silence, both understanding the other's pain.

"We need to lighten the mood. You want some Chunky Monkey ice cream?" Anari asked.

"Girl, you ain't got to ask me twice," replied Shawna. She made her way over to Anari's movie collection and pulled out some Jamie Foxx comedy shows. She put in one of the tapes and they sat and laughed together until they fell asleep.

The next morning, the constant ringing of the doorbell awoke Shawna. Anari was still knocked out, so Shawna answered the door to see a smiling Tanya.

"Oh hey, girl. Come on in," Shawna said.

Reluctantly, Tanya walked in. She looked around Anari's living room, seeing the carton of Chunky Monkey ice cream and Jamie Foxx movies covering the floor.

Anari walked out of the room, still dazed from her short sleep. She looked at the clock. It was 8 AM.

"Oh my goodness, I only got two hours of sleep," Anari said as she pulled her hair up in a ponytail.

She yawned then looked at Tanya, remembering their breakfast date.

"Aww, T, girl, I'm sorry. We got in late and—"

Shawna cut her off. "Yeah, we took the big body truck and went shopping in New York yesterday. I guess I kind of wore her out. You know, with the gunshot wound and everything, she was knocked out on the way back."

Tanya looked at Shawna and laughed. "Oh, you drove back. You know, it looks like y'all had fun eating all that ice cream. Jamie Foxx's ass is funny, ain't he?"

She began to walk to the door then stopped, turned around and said, "Look, Anari, we can reschedule. I'll holla." Anari watched her friend walk out the door.

Shawna stared at Anari and asked, "What got her panties in a bunch?"

Anari laughed at Shawna. "Girl, I don't know, but I'm too damn tired to be worried about it."

Anari knew that Tanya was upset. She had known her for too long not to know when something was bothering her, but she just figured that Tanya would get over it. On that note, Anari and Shawna went back to sleep.

Chapter Five

When Anari awoke, it was about 6:00 in the evening. Her living room was clean and Shawna was gone. She stared at all her flowers and thought about Von.

Her arm was sore as hell, so she decided that the rest of the day would be her personal time to relax. She thought about everything that had happened since her son went on vacation with his grandparents. It had only been two days, and she had been shot, made a new friend, and had been wooed by another baller. For her, that was real progress because since Maurice had died, she was like a social zombie or something. Other than the fact that she had been shot, this had been the best she had felt in a long time.

Her phone rang and when she answered it, she heard her son's happy voice.

"Hey, baby boy. Are you having a good time? Momma misses you." Anari's son shrieked happily when he heard his mother's voice.

A minute later, Momma Jones picked up the phone. "Hi, Anari. How are things going?"

Anari would never tell Momma Jones about the shooting, but she did tell her about her new friendship with Shawna.

"Well, that's good. You needed this little break. Your son misses you so much we had to call you. All he kept saying was 'Mama.' We're having a nice time, though. We love you, baby."

Anari missed her son, but she didn't want to stop his fun, so she just replied, "I love you guys too. Have fun, and don't spoil him too much."

With that, she hung up the phone. She was so relieved to hear her son's voice. She had never been away from him for more than one weekend, and even then he was always in the same city. Now he was miles away and she couldn't touch him if she wanted to.

I guess I'll just have to get used to it.

Her phone rang again, but she decided to let the machine answer. "Yo, you've reached Anari. I ain't in right now, but if you leave a message, I'll holla when I get home."

"Yo, sis. Where you at? I ain't heard from you in a couple days. I wanted to pick up my nephew, so call me when you get in. Love you."

Anari wanted to pick up the phone and tell her brother she had been shot, but she knew that he would get all crazy. He would start a war with any and everybody who had ever looked at her wrong, so she didn't. Instead, she called Tanya to see what her problem was.

She dialed the number and let it ring seven times. She hung up and dialed Tanya's cell, but still didn't get an answer. This was a surprise because Tanya always kept her cell on. In all the years Anari had known her, Tanya had always answered her calls. Something was definitely up with Tanya, but whatever. Anari was not about to kiss her ass.

She can keep that shady shit. I know she ain't acting funny over that Shawna shit. Damn, I mean, Shawna cool too.

A frustrated Anari thought about calling Von but decided against it. If he wanted to talk to her, he would call.

"Lucky!" she called to her lovable pet. The adorable puppy came running from the back of her house. He had one of her shoes in his mouth.

"No, Lucky. Damn, you always eating on shit that ain't food." She took her shoe from her puppy and played with him until he went to sleep. She loved her puppy.

Her cell rang and it was Shawna. "What up?" asked Anari.

"Hey, girl. Sorry I didn't tell you I was leaving. You was knocked out," replied Shawna.

Anari heard the sound of Shawna's Lexus. "Where you on your way to?"

"This hotel on Stanley," replied Shawna.

Anari laughed. "Big date, huh?"

Shawna replied, "Girl, nah. My house being exterminated and I can't be in there for two weeks."

Anari thought about this for a minute. Shawna might as well stay with her for these two weeks. She really didn't like it when her house was so empty anyway.

"Come over here and stay for the two weeks. It's better than a hotel and it's free."

Shawna resisted for a minute, not wanting to

be bothersome, but when Anari kept insisting, Shawna finally accepted the offer. She was over there in lightning speed. When Shawna got there, Anari let her in and went to sleep.

The next day, Anari woke up and smelled food cooking in her kitchen. She got out of bed and saw Shawna fixing pancakes.

"I hope you made enough for two, cuz I'm starving," she said as she made her way over to the kitchen sink.

Shawna laughed. "Help yourself." Anari grabbed a plate and dug into Shawna's stack of pancakes.

"What you got up for today?" Shawna asked Anari.

She shrugged. "I don't know. What you got planned?"

Shawna sat at the table with her food. "This one guy I used to know bought me these passes to Sunset Spa. I was thinking about going today. You feel like going?"

Anari remembered that Maurice had gotten her day passes at the spa for one of her birthdays. The thought made her smile, and she pushed her plate of pancakes away from her.

"Hell, yeah. I'm always down to pamper myself. What time you trying to go?"

Shawna shrugged. "Whenever you ready. I already took a shower, so all I got to do is get dressed."

Anari got up from the table. "Well, let me start getting ready. Oh yeah. I got to call Tanya, too." She walked over to her phone and dialed Tanya's number.

"Hi, you've reached Tanya . . ." Her machine picked up, so Anari left a message.

"Hey, T, this me. I was just calling you to see what was up. Call me back when you get this message. As a matter of fact, just come down to Sunset Spa if you get this message anytime soon. I'm going down there for the day. Love ya. Bye."

Anari got dressed as fast as possible, and an hour later, they were on their way.

They walked into Sunset Spa and were immediately greeted by a friendly woman.

"Hi, ladies. Do you have appointments?"

Shawna shook her head. "No, but I have these day passes that I received as a gift."

The receptionist smiled. "Oh, of course. Follow me." She directed them to a room and handed them white robes. "This is the changing area. After you're done, you can pretty much enjoy our facilities for the day. We have massage rooms, pedicure and manicure specialists, hair stylists, and many other health and beauty areas available."

The woman walked out of the room and Shawna and Anari found a place to change. "What you want to do first?" Anari asked.

Shawna replied, "I'm about to get my feet done."

Anari looked down at Shawna's feet. "Yeah, cuz yo dogs need some work."

They both laughed and made their way to the pedicure/manicure center. The girls went from station to station, enjoying the relaxing atmosphere of the spa. Just as they were getting ready to get facials, Anari's cell rang.

"Hello," she answered.

"Where are you? I'm pulling up at the spa right now."

Anari heard Tanya's voice and sat up. "Okay.

Ask the receptionist at the front desk to show you where you can get a facial. We'll wait for you."

Tanya hung up the phone, wondering who Anari was up in there with.

A while later, Tanya walked into the spa and asked the receptionist where she could find the facial area. She walked into the room and saw Anari and Shawna sitting together, laughing as if they were old time friends.

This bitch . . . Tanya thought as she took a seat in the chair next to Shawna.

"T, you got to go get a pedicure. Look at my feet," Anari said as she held up her feet for her friend to see. "Oh, and don't worry about having ugly feet, cuz they work miracles. You should have seen Shawna's feet before they hooked her up."

Tanya just laughed and sat back as someone started on her facial. The girls spent the entire day at the spa, enjoying each other's company. Anari noticed that Tanya had been quiet, but she just figured that she was chilling.

The next day, Anari went to the doctor to see if her arm was healing like it was supposed to. It had been bothering her, but she figured that it would be sore for a while, so she really didn't think anything of it.

As she sat in the waiting room, she wondered why Von hadn't called her in a couple days. *I hope he calls,* she thought. She thought they had clicked the other night, but Anari didn't know how he was yet, so she really didn't know what to expect.

Anari picked up her phone and called Tanya so

she could get her mind off of Von. "What you doing?" she asked when Tanya finally picked up.

"Nothing. Where you at?" Tanya asked.

Anari was about to reply, but her phone beeped. She looked at the caller ID. "Hold on, T. This is Shawna on the other line."

She clicked over to the other line. "Hey, girl," she said, "what's up?"

Shawna replied, "Oh, I didn't want nothing. I was just calling you to tell you that your boy just called the house."

Anari smiled from ear to ear. "What did he say?" she asked eagerly.

Shawna laughed. "Nothing. He just asked for you, and I said that you weren't here. He said that he would call back, though."

Anari's conversation was interrupted when a nurse came into the waiting area and announced, "Anari Simpson, the doctor will see you now."

Anari nodded her head. "Shawna," she said, "let me call you back." Anari hung up her phone and turned it off.

She walked to the back of the doctor's office, where she waited in one of the examining rooms. A few minutes later, a handsome, young, black doctor entered the room. He looked up from her chart.

"Hi, Ms. Simpson, I am Dr. Erin. I'm going to need you to take off your shirt, please."

Anari stared at the doctor. "Hi, umm, where is Dr. Merlin? He usually examines me." She was referring to the old white doctor she had been seeing for years.

Dr. Erin smiled. "He's on vacation right now."

Anari shook her head and began to take off her

shirt. She hated that she had a new doctor. She had to take off her shirt in order for him to see her shoulder, and it made her a little uncomfortable.

The doctor unwrapped her arm and cleaned her wound. He also took x-rays to make sure that everything was healing internally as well.

When he was finished examining her, she put her shirt on quickly. "So, how does it look?"

"It looks like everything is healing well. Just keep it clean to avoid infection." He gave her a new prescription of painkillers. "Take it easy. This prescription will relieve a lot of the pain. If the pain becomes unbearable, that might be a sign of infection. If that happens, come back and see me immediately."

Anari nodded. "Okay, thank you." He handed her the written prescription and she walked out of the room.

She left the doctor's office and headed home. When she got there, Shawna was sitting on the couch, watching TV.

"Hey, girl," Anari said as she walked into the living room.

"Hey, you look tired. Did you get bad news at the doctor today?"

Anari shook her head, appreciating Shawna's concern. "Nah, it ain't that. I'm just gon' chill out for the rest of the day, though."

Shawna laughed. "Whatever, girl. You know you just trying to stay home so that you won't miss Von's next call."

Anari laughed at how much Shawna was beginning to know her. "Whatever. I am not thinking about him. I'm about to have another movie night.

You down, or do you have plans of your own?" she asked her friend.

Shawna shrugged. "My love life has been nonexistent for a while now, so you know I'm down."

Anari popped in another Jamie Foxx comedy show and Shawna got the ice cream out of the fridge. They chilled and got to know each other even more. Anari was glad that she and Shawna had become good friends. Shawna was cool as hell.

The girls spent most of the night up watching TV and talking to one another. When Von didn't call her by 2 AM, she went to sleep.

She was halfway asleep when she heard her phone ring. She groaned and looked at the clock beside her bed, wondering who was calling so late.

She answered the phone in a whisper. "Hello?"

Tanya was on the line. "Why you keep me on hold for so long earlier?" she asked.

"You called me this late to ask me that?" Anari asked in an irritated tone.

"Yeah. Why didn't you just tell me to call you back?" Tanya asked.

Anari sighed deeply. "I forgot. Shawna called me and when I finished talking to her, the doctor called me into his office."

Tanya was livid that Anari had chosen to talk to Shawna over her, so she said, "Whatever. Well, I was gonna ask if you wanted to go out tonight, but when you didn't call back, I forgot about it."

"It's cool," Anari said. "Me and Shawna just chilled in the house tonight anyway. You know, sat back and watched comedy shows." Tanya immediately became jealous when Anari told her about the movie night with Shawna. This was the second time Anari had done movie night without her. That was supposed to be their thing. They had been doing movie night since they were kids. Anari had been acting funny ever since she met Shawna.

Bitch better not forget who her real friend is, Tanya thought.

"Shawna just be over your house all the time now. Do she ever go home?" she asked.

Anari laughed. "It ain't even like that, T," she replied. "She's staying here for a couple weeks cuz she getting some work done to her house."

Tanya sucked her teeth. "Well, call me when that bitch goes home."

Anari sat up in her bed. "What are you tripping for? She just staying for a couple weeks. Shawna is cool. You act like it's something wrong with being around new people. We always invite you out with us whenever we go somewhere."

Tanya laughed sarcastically. "Yeah, y'all invite me. That's just it. How you gon' make me the third wheel?"

Anari was growing irritated with Tanya. "Damn, Tanya. You act like I'm your bitch or something. We ain't fucking. I don't have to explain shit to you. I got a new friend. That's it. You acting real childish with this jealous shit. This is a friendship, not a relationship. We can have more than one friend."

Tanya was not trying to hear what Anari was saying. She didn't like Shawna, and she didn't think that she should have to point that out to Anari.

"Whatever, Anari. You acting real funny—"

Anari cut Tanya off. "Well, whatever. I don't got time for this. Bye, Tanya."

She hung up the phone, and just as she was about to turn off her ringer, it rang again.

This better not be Tanya.

"Hello," she said angrily.

"What's up, ma? Is this a bad time or something?"

She recognized Von's voice and relaxed as she said, "Nah, it's cool. I thought you were someone else."

"I got a little problem," he said.

"What's that?"

Von hesitated for a minute. "Well," he said, "I got these floor seat tickets to the Nets/Lakers game for tomorrow night, and I ain't got no date."

Anari sat straight up in her bed. "Are you trying to ask me to roll with you? Cuz, if you were, that line was so tired."

They both burst out into laughter. "So, you don't wanna go?" Von asked smoothly.

"How can I pass a Lakers game? I would love to go." Anari felt her cheeks warm with excitement.

Von told her to be ready the next day at 7:00 and said goodbye. Anari hung up the phone, went back to sleep, and had a sexy dream.

In her dream, Anari stood in the doorway, completely naked, with a white flower sticking out of her hair. Von lay on the bed with nothing on but a smile. His muscular physique and sensual silhouette made Anari's inner thighs become soaked from the thought of him inside of her. She slowly walked over to the bed and straddled Von's face, riding his tongue and tightly gripping the bars on the headboard. She moved her body in a circular motion while moaning his name. Von caressed her behind as she rode him, gripping her cheeks tightly. Anari felt herself about to climax . . .

Anari woke up sweating and wet from her erotic dream. She calmed herself down and went back to sleep.

Chapter Six

behind at she rolled ping, her cheeks tightly. Anari felt herself close to climax.

Anari woke up sweating and wet from her erotic dream. She calmed herself down and went back to sleep.

Chapter Six

A t 6:30 the next evening, Shawna helped Anari get dressed for her date with Von. Anari wore a Burberry two-piece with purse and boots to match. She applied gold accessories and was ready to go.

"Have fun," Shawna said as Anari walked out the door, "and don't do anything I wouldn't do."

Anari looked back and laughed. "From the stories you've told me, that means there isn't too much I can't do."

Von picked Anari up in a stretch Navigator. Anari had to admit that she was nervous. She hadn't been out with another man before. Maurice was her first, so she didn't really know how to act around anyone else. Twenty minutes later, they pulled up at the airport.

"Von, where are we going? I thought we was going to the Nets/Lakers game."

Von smiled his magnificent smile. "We are. Oh, did I forget to mention that it's in L.A.?"

Anari was so geeked. "Oh my God, say you swear." She was so ecstatic that she almost pissed her pants. "But I didn't bring any clothes," Anari said.

"Then I guess we we'll just have to go shopping in Beverly Hills."

Anari wished she could call Tanya and tell her to stay at the house for the weekend, but Tanya was still acting childish. Instead, Anari decided to call Shawna to make sure she set the alarm on the house when she went out.

"Hey, have fun. And don't worry about the house. I'll take care of it," Shawna said when Anari called her.

Anari laughed. "You better, and hey, don't forget to set the alarm when you leave. The code is 1128."

They flew in a private jet Von had rented for the evening. He had everything set up perfectly. When they arrived in L.A., they were escorted to the Staples Center in another stretch Navigator. They entered the building and went straight to their floor seats.

Von looked at Anari. She looked damn good. She definitely had a nigga waiting, but he still didn't know about her.

During warm-ups, Kobe Bryant came over to Von as if they were old friends. "What up, Von? We missed you, man. You ain't been to the West Coast in a minute."

Von laughed. "Man, you know business be keeping me busy. Everybody can't make millions like you."

Kobe shook his head. "Yeah, I know, but look. Come to this party after the game. I'll leave your name at the door."

Anari couldn't believe what she was seeing. There was Von, having a conversation with Kobe Bryant—a fucking Barney-and-Friends-I-love-you-you-love-me conversation with Kobe! *Maybe Von was about something,* Anari thought, suddenly feeling special sitting next to him.

"Nah, that's all right. Me and my friend here got some plans," Von said.

Kobe smiled at Von then said, "All right, man. I guess I'll have to catch you later." Kobe ran back onto the court. Anari stared at Von in amazement.

"I hope you don't think you getting some booty just cuz you one of Kobe's groupies."

Von laughed. He was having fun with Anari. This was something he hadn't done in a long time. Anari was also having a good time at the game, and even though she wasn't a big fan of the Lakers or the Nets, she still found it hard to stay in her seat. Every time Jersey scored, she forgot about the soreness in her arm.

She noticed that Von was staring at her, so she leaned over and kissed him. Without talking about the kiss, they watched the rest of the game.

After the game, they went straight to a five-star hotel. They went up to their room, and as soon as she walked in, her breath was taken away. The room was bigger than her house. There were rose petals everywhere, candles all over the room, and chocolate-covered strawberries on the stand next to the bed.

She walked into the room with Von right behind her. He grabbed her and kissed on her neck as his hands slid down her body. She kissed him passionately. It had been so long since she had been with a man, and the romantic setting in the room didn't make it any easier for her to resist him.

He laid her down gently on the rose covered bed and kissed her all over. He softly kissed her breast and licked her from head to toe. She moaned as he tickled her insides with his tongue. She moaned his name continuously, wanting him to put his manhood inside of her. She stroked his hard dick. He was enough for her—way more than enough. Von lifted her legs and slowly penetrated her, making her gasp in delight.

He made love to her slowly, paying attention to the details. He kissed her body and touched her in places that made her tingle. She felt her legs start to shake as her toes curled and her back arched. She tightly gripped the sheets and felt Von pick up speed. All at once her body exploded and she felt an orgasm that she had not felt in over two long years.

"Von!" Anari climbed on top of Von and lay on his hard body. It felt so good to be in his arms. He looked at her and kissed her on the forehead then picked her up from the bed and carried her into the bathroom. He placed her in the huge bathtub, climbed in and sat across from her. He washed her and she washed him.

"Why didn't you . . ." She began to ask him why he hadn't pleased himself.

"Shh." He put his fingers over her lips. "Tonight was all about you."

She wanted him to be inside of her again. She needed to feel him rub against her clitoris. She made her way over to him and straddled him like she was a cowgirl. "Tonight is all about us," she said as she

rode him until he was satisfied. He carried her to
the bed and went to sleep with her in his arms.

Shawna was enjoying her weekend alone in
Anari's house. As soon as Anari left, Shawna kicked
back, turned on some music and enjoyed the peace
and quiet of the still house.

I love being here by myself. Anari has a plush crib, she
thought as she admired her friend's home.

She went into Anari's bedroom and turned on
the light. She had just met Anari and was curious
as to how Anari really was. She walked over to the
dresser and looked at the photos on top, picking
up a picture of Anari standing in front of a guy
with his arms wrapped tightly around her.

She immediately knew it was Maurice, remembering that Anari told her about him the night they
sat up talking. She picked up the picture and looked
at it closer. Anari looked happy in the photo.

Shawna traced the outline of Maurice's face,
and a tear slid down her cheek. He had died so
young, and she knew that his death had shattered
Anari's life.

Shawna knew exactly how Anari felt, remembering the day that her own man had been killed. She
put the picture back on the dresser and opened some
of Anari's drawers. She pulled out a couple shirts.

"I know you have some cute stuff in your closet,"
she said out loud as she walked over to Anari's
closet. She opened it up and had to take a step back
when she saw the vast amount of clothing that her
friend owned. "Oh, I am definitely gon' be borrowing some of these," she said as she began to pull
outfits of the closet.

Shawna tried on some of Anari's clothing and loved every minute of it. Anari dressed as if she were going somewhere important every day. It didn't matter if she was only going to the grocery store. She was always dressed to impress.

When Shawna had finished with the clothes she moved to the shoes. She reached for a shoebox and opened it to find a journal. She grabbed it, walked over to Anari's bed, and began to read.

I am so blessed to have him in my life. Maurice spoils me. It seems like we just met yesterday. I can't wait until the day that I become his wife. He is everything that I want, and he takes care of me and loves me. I have never felt this way before. The only complaint I have is that he is constantly in the street. I hate that I have to share him like that. I wish he would stop hustling, but I know that he won't, especially if I ask him. But it's good. As long as we're together, I'll be happy. Anari Jones. That sounds right.

Shawna closed the journal. She felt awkward reading someone else's thoughts, and she didn't want to be rude by continuing to read. She put the journal back where she had found it. She made sure that the room was as it was before she had entered, then went down to little Maurice's room.

She peered in and saw that his room was neat, decorated in blue and red. She saw a picture of him hanging on the wall. He was so cute. As she admired the room, she thought about how desperately she wanted a child of her own.

She couldn't wait until she had a son, knowing that it was probably the best feeling in the world to

Chapter Seven

Anari's weekend with Von was amazing. After their great night at the hotel, they went shopping and he bought her all types of fly shit. They talked to each other about everything—well, almost. He never really explained to Anari what it was that he did, but Shawna had already put Anari up on game. Von was a baller. He was a hustler who made his money from the streets. He had made a name for himself in Jersey, and the way Shawna described it, Von was the man.

Anari didn't know if she wanted to be the girlfriend of another drug dealer, but Von was the first person to make her feel alive again since Maurice. Besides, he hadn't actually made it clear what she was to him. She might just be another chick to him.

Anari had been so confused lately. She liked spending time with Von, but she knew how men like him could get. Anari just didn't want to fall too hard for a man who wasn't interested in her like that.

When Anari arrived back home, everything was as she had left it. Shawna was excited to hear that Anari had a good time.

"Tell me everything," she said as Anari unpacked her clothes.

Anari shrugged. "There's nothing to tell. We went to a game, that's all."

Shawna shook her head playfully. "Whatever, bitch. You ain't have that little switch in your ass when you left, so I know Von put it there. Now, what happened?"

Anari laughed and threw a pillow at Shawna. "Well, maybe a little something did happen, but it's no big deal. I mean, you see how he just shows up here and there. I don't know where this is going to lead to."

Shawna shook her head. "Yeah, but I see how he be buying you shit, too. A nigga ain't gon' spend his chips on a woman that he isn't interested in, Nari."

Anari thought about what Shawna was saying. Maybe he was feeling her. She didn't know. He might be buying every other chick the same shit.

"Money ain't everything, especially the kind of money he making," she told Shawna as she remembered how money made Maurice change.

"Don't be trying to change the subject. Tell me. I want to hear all the details," Shawna said as she sat on Anari's bed.

Anari smiled, remembering the amazing weekend. "Okay, okay. Well, let's see. We went to the game. Umm, we went shopping."

Shawna frowned her face. "I know all that. How was he? That's what I want to know."

Anari laughed. "I am not talking about this anymore. Get out." She playfully pushed Shawna. Anari wasn't thinking about Von. She was excited to see her son. Anari was determined to make sure that Maurice would have a nice homecoming.

"Did Mr. and Mrs. Jones call about my child?" Anari asked. "I know he must be driving them crazy by now."

"Yeah, Mrs. Jones called and said that the baby would be home tomorrow afternoon," said Shawna.

Anari was so excited to see her little man. She couldn't wait for Maurice to meet Von. She couldn't wait for Maurice to see the puppy.

"Oh, did Tanya call while I was away?" Anari asked, remembering that Tanya was upset with her.

"Nope, everybody else that called didn't leave names, but Tanya hasn't called at all. What's up with her?" asked a curious Shawna.

"I don't know," replied Anari. "T been acting stanky for almost two weeks now. The last time I talked to her was three days ago, and we usually don't go a whole twenty-four hours without talking to each other. I don't know what her problem is. I wish she would call me, though. I got to tell her so much shit."

She really missed her friend. Ever since she had met Tanya, they hadn't spent more than a couple days apart. It seemed like ever since Tanya had noticed that Shawna was getting cool with Anari, she didn't want to have too much to do with her best friend.

Anari didn't have time to think about it, though.

She sped through her day just so that her son could come home faster.

The next morning, Von gave Anari an unexpected call. "What up? I miss you."

Anari was definitely feeling Von. "I miss you too," she said, knowing that he could hear her smile through the phone. "But you know I can't chill with you today. My son is coming home. I haven't seen him for two weeks. I'll call you later on tonight, though."

Von was disappointed. "How about I just stop by to give you one kiss?"

Anari smiled. "Okay, but after that you have to go."

Von stopped by all right, but he got more than one kiss. He fucked Anari so good she was asking him to stay. They took a shower together, and before he left, she said, "Please don't hurt me, Von."

Von just looked at her. He saw her baby face and her perfect body and thought, *Why would I?* He walked over to Anari, grabbed her face and kissed her.

"I plan on being with you for a long time. I see you having my children. You're the only woman that I have ever thought about making my wife, and I haven't even known you for that long. Don't worry about little shit. I just got to make this money so that I can give you all the shit that you deserve. You mines, okay? Can't none of them other bitches do shit for me."

Anari melted with every word that came from his mouth. She kissed him then he left. He wanted to give her time to finish preparing her house for her son.

Von admired how much Anari cared for her son. That was the type of bitch he wanted to care for the shorty he planned on having in the future.

Everything seemed to be going perfectly. Shawna's house was done, so she would be leaving the next morning, and Anari's son was on his way home. At around 1:30 PM, her doorbell rang. Lucky zoomed to the door, barking and jumping around.

"Good, boy," Anari said in a joking way. She knew that her dog wasn't big enough to scare anyone away. She followed the dog to the door and opened it to greet her son. Momma Jones had a million bags in her hands. "These are all his souvenirs," she said.

Anari grabbed the bags from her hands and thanked Momma Jones for spending time with Maurice. She grabbed him out of her arms and covered him with a thousand kisses. He laughed as she tickled his stomach. Lucky came bouncing into the picture and Maurice went crazy.

He pointed and pranced up and down. "Doggy!"

Anari knew that he would love Lucky. A puppy was the perfect present.

Anari looked at Mr. and Mrs. Jones with a warm smile. "Thank you both. I really appreciate it."

They hugged her and she followed them to her door. "You call us more often now. We love you and we want to hear from you," Mrs. Jones said.

Anari promised that she would keep in contact more often. She closed the door and went back into the living room, where her son was running from his new dog.

"Whoa, now," she said as she picked him up.

Lucky jumped at her feet, trying to get to Maurice. Anari laughed as her son shook his head.

"You scared, baby boy?" she said as she picked Lucky up in her other arm. "See. He won't hurt you," she told her son.

Maurice reached over to pet the dog. Anari put them down and laughed. Lucky started barking and he took off again like a rocket.

Anari and Maurice spent the whole day together. They went to the park, where she let him run and play with Lucky as long as he wanted. While he bounced and played with his new pet, she decided to call Tanya. After the sixth ring, her girlfriend picked up.

"Hello," she answered with an irritated voice.

"Hey, T, what's up? Where the hell you been? I've got some shit to tell you."

Tanya didn't even reply. She just sucked her teeth. "I'm busy. I'll holla." With that rude and attitude-filled statement, Tanya hung up before Anari could even get out a word.

No, this bitch did not just hang up the fucking phone on me. Fuck it. I am not about to kiss her ass. We have been cool for too long for her to be acting funny now. Simple bitches. Damn. I mean, she act like we fucking or something.

Anari looked over at Maurice. He was yawning, and she knew it was time for them to head home. The trio headed back to their house.

When they arrived, she gave both of them a bath and put her son in his bedroom. Lucky jumped in the bed right next to him, and although she hated for Lucky to be on her furniture, Maurice looked too happy to resist.

"I love you, Maurice Ronell Jones," she said as she kissed him goodnight, then took a quick shower and set her house alarm. Once she felt safe, she went to bed.

"Maurice, where are we going? You know I hate surprises," Anari said, wondering why they were driving for so long.

Maurice just laughed at her. "Don't worry about it. Just ride."

Two hours later, they pulled up to the most luxurious hotel she had ever seen. Maurice opened her door and escorted her into a magnificent ballroom. The lights were low, and a live band was playing soft jazz music. Candles crowded the table, and she smelled the aroma of shrimp and lobster.

"What is all this?" she asked with a sexy smile on her face.

"This is our engagement party."

The lights turned on, and she saw all of their friends and family sitting at round tables in the room.

Maurice bent down on one knee. "Will you marry me?"

Anari was ecstatic. She practically screamed the word "yes" into his ears. "Yes, baby, yes!"

The sound of Lucky whimpering woke her out of her dream. She sat up in her bed and took her sleeping mask off of her face.

"I'ma kill this damn dog if he into some shit. It's too damn late for me to be getting up to check on him," Anari said as she sleepily stumbled out of bed. She put on her housecoat and walked into the living room to see what had happened. She turned on the light and saw that everything appeared to be okay.

She decided to check her son's bedroom. "Maurice?" she said as she peeked into his bedroom. When she saw that her son wasn't in his bed, she turned on the light.

"Sweetie, this isn't funny. It's way past your bedtime. We have a big day tomorrow. Maurice, come here this minute."

After looking in his closet, she walked back into the living room and checked her son's usual hiding spots.

Where the hell is he?

"Lucky!" Anari shouted, trying to get the puppy to reveal their hiding spot. Growing impatient she sternly said, "Maurice Ronnell Jones, you are going to get a spanking!"

This wasn't like him. Usually when she said that, his butt knew she wasn't playing.

Growing panicked, Anari rushed back into her son's bedroom and pulled back the covers. Anari's heart felt like it stopped beating, and she let out a scream when she discovered her son's blood-covered sheets.

"Maurice, baby, where are you?" Anari called as she knelt down on the floor. She pulled up the covers to look under his bed. Lucky was lying with his head in his paws. She pulled the puppy out from underneath the bed to find that a knife had been stabbed into Lucky's side.

Her breaths became short, and she felt as if there were no oxygen in the room. She gasped for air and stumbled back against the wall, trying to gain support.

"Maurice! Baby, where are you?"

Anari ran into her living room and rushed to the phone. She picked up her receiver and heard no dial tone. Anari rushed to the door and started to turn off the alarm so that she could go outside, but froze in fear when she realized that it was already off. She was sure she had set it when she went to bed.

She ran outside and tried to see if she could figure out who had taken her son. There were no cars on the street, and it appeared to be deserted. She jumped into her car to go get help. When she sat down, she saw a crisp white envelope taped to her steering wheel. She looked at the envelope, and with fear in her heart, she opened it.

Anari,
I want $250,000 delivered to 1265 Hemlock Street.
You got three days to get the money or your son dies.
Don't try no funny shit cuz if I think anything is
up, he's dead. If you call the police you might as
well had killed him yourself. Have my money ready
by Friday at 12:00.

Killa

Anari's heart dropped into her stomach. Unable to control herself, she threw up all over her lawn. Her stomach felt hollow, and she felt the pain start behind her eyes as her head began to bang.

Two hundred and fifty thousand dollars. Where was she supposed to get that much money from? This could not be happening. *God, please don't let them hurt my son.*

Anari didn't know what to do. She rushed into the house and called Tanya, praying she would pick up. She gripped the phone so tightly that her fingers hurt. Anari let the phone ring a million times before she hung up and called Shawna.

"Shawna, please help me," Anari pleaded.

"Nari, girl, what's wrong? It's four in the morning," replied a half-asleep Shawna.

"They took Maurice. Somebody came into my house and took my son. They left a note. They want money, but Shawna, I don't have that kind of money. What am I supposed to do?" Anari was frantic. She was losing her mind.

"Anari, don't move. I'll be there in twenty minutes."

Anari paced her house, thinking of ways to come up with that much money. She had about $40,000 left in her savings from when Maurice was hustling, but how was she supposed to come up with the rest of the money?

By the time Shawna arrived at the house, it was almost 6:00 AM. She ran into the house. Anari's face was ashy from her dried-up tears, and she was pacing back and forth across her living room.

Shawna ran over and hugged her in a reassuring way. Anari was hysterical. Her eyes were bloodshot from crying and she was shaking like a crack head that needed a hit.

Anari had gathered up all of her possessions. "I have to sell everything. I need to come up with this money." She threw on a gray sweat suit and some Air Force Ones then called her brother.

"Hello," answered Jamal.

"Maulie, help me! They took Maurice," Anari yelled into the phone.

Jamal was confused and didn't really understand his panicked sister, but he could tell that she was in trouble. Without hesitation, he raced over to her house.

"Anari, calm down. You got the forty thousand that Maurice left you. We'll come up with the rest. Come on. We gon' do this. You know I got something for whoever fucking with you. We gon' get your son back." Her brother tried to calm her down, but there was nothing that anybody could say that would make her feel better.

"Someone took my son out of my house. They came through my door, walked past my bedroom and kidnapped my baby." She wished it was all a bad dream.

Jamal left to see if he could go make some money, but Anari knew that he wouldn't. Jamal was only a small-time hustler who didn't make more that $500 a month out of the streets. Anari knew that he could never come up with $250,000.

Anari threw all of her clothes off her balcony down onto the front lawn. She kept all of her Guess, Tommy, and Roc-a-Wear shit, but all the high-end designer clothes, like Gucci and Prada, would definitely get her some money. She kept a couple of things, but everything else was about to get boomed for some quick cash.

She went into her garage and looked at her three cars, thinking she could get at least $100,000 for the Cadillac and the Benz. She decided to keep her Honda, knowing she would need a car. She pulled her cars in front of her yard and put "for sale" signs on them.

Shawna helped her set up tables to put her clothes on, and helped her pull out her furniture into the front yard. Anari made a sign that read: *Everything Must Go.*

Within hours, her home was flooded with all types of people interested in buying her belongings. Anari tried her best to bargain with everybody. She needed to sell everything for the highest possible price. She only ended up getting $30,000 for both of her cars because they were used. She sold most of her clothes, which earned her another $4,500—less than half of what she paid for them.

Her furniture went for $25,000. Maurice had bought her the imported furniture for over $100,000. But Anari couldn't complain. She just needed all the money she could get. Even with all of her possessions gone, she still did not have enough money.

God, please protect my baby.

Shawna approached Anari and handed her a stack of money. "Look, all I have to spare is five thousand. I wish I could do more, but I still have bills to pay myself. I hope this helps. Sweetie, I have to go. I'll call you though, okay? You be easy."

Shawna drove off and the customers moved the things they had bought off her lawn. Anari dropped onto the grass, put her head in her hands and cried. She felt so defeated. Even after selling all her shit, she had only raised half of the money. Two hundred fifty thousand dollars was a cruel ransom to demand. They had to know she didn't have that much money.

Why is this happening to me? He's all that I have left.

She walked back into her home and sat down on her bare floor. She looked around her empty home and cried. Lucky was dead, Maurice was dead, and it appeared that her son would be next. She couldn't go to the police. She couldn't tell Von.

What am I going to do?

Jamal called her later that night to reassure her that he would come up with the money. She knew that he would try to help, but she needed nearly $90,000. That was a lot of money to raise in less than two days.

She stood in the middle of her bare living room, knowing that she would have to sell the house. It was the only way she could come up with enough money.

Anari grabbed the phone book and called a real estate agent. After discussing terms and conditions with the agent Anari found out that her house was worth $250,000. That was more than enough.

The real estate agent said that she knew a couple who would probably be interested in buying it right away. The next morning, the agent called and told her that if she was willing to lower the price, the couple would give her cash right away. Anari sold her home for $140,000.

Anari had her car packed with all her remaining possessions. She packed hers and her son's clothes and shoes into her trunk. The suitcase of money was in the passenger seat. The only thing she had left was her Honda and her cell phone.

She checked her messages as she pulled away from what had once been her home. Von had called her several times. She had been so busy that she had forgotten about him. She knew that Von was a baller. He could easily come up with the remaining $6,000 she needed for her son's ransom, but she didn't know if she could ask him for it. She would pay him back as soon as she got on her feet again, but she still didn't know if she would go to Von.

That night, Anari slept in her car. She couldn't afford to pay for a hotel, and she couldn't get in contact with Tanya, Shawna, or her brother. She tossed and turned the whole night thinking about how she would get the rest of the money.

I have to ask Von. It's my only option, and I will easily swallow my pride to save my son's life.

The next day, Anari picked up the phone and called Von. "Can you meet me somewhere?" she asked.

Von could tell something was wrong just by the way, she sounded. He had been calling her for a couple days and she hadn't answered any of his calls then out of the blue she called him.

"Yeah, I'll meet you at the mall in twenty minutes."

Anari hung up the phone and felt a sense of relief. It seemed like Von really cared about her. He would give her the money.

When she arrived at the mall, Von knew that something bad had happened. He rushed over to her and held her as she broke down. He held her close and somehow she felt safe in his arms, as if he could protect her from anything. He put his fingers under her chin and forced her to look at him. He saw the tears fall from her face as she stared into his eyes.

Even though she knew he would give it to her, she could not do it. Anari could not bring herself to ask Von for the money.

Her world felt hopeless as she debated whether to ask Von for the money. She gently kissed him on the cheek. He watched her as she walked away in defeat. He didn't know exactly what was up, but he did know that she needed him and he would be there for her. When she was ready to ask, he would be there.

He jogged over to her car and grabbed her hand just as she was getting ready to open her door. He kissed her as if he would never see her again. As much pain as she was going through, she needed that kiss.

Anari looked into his eyes. "I have to go." She got into her car and drove away, leaving him there with no explanation as to why she was so hurt.

Anari pulled out her cell and as she was about to dial her brother's number, she dropped the phone. She felt weak and didn't know what to do. Her stomach was in knots and her hands were sweaty. Her body felt as if it was giving up on her, and she knew that she needed her strength to get through this. She had to think. How could she come up with the rest of the money?

Anari was afraid, more afraid than she had ever been in her life. She was confused and knew that she could not do this alone. She was thinking a million thoughts all at the same time and she began to feel flustered. Anari inhaled deeply to try and calm herself down, but it didn't help. She felt as if she were going to choke, so she turned off her car after pulling over on the side of the road.

What am I going to do? They're hurting my baby.

Anari could not take the pressure anymore. She needed help. She felt her mind go blank as she passed out in her seat. Anari fainted and her body slumped over onto her horn.

When Anari opened her eyes, she didn't know where she was. She remembered meeting Von at the mall and remembered driving away. Just as she was getting ready to become frightened, Von walked into the room.

"You all right, ma?" Von asked.

Anari shook her head. "No."

"I followed you from the mall. It seemed like you needed someone. When I saw you faint, I brought you home with me."

"Von, what day is it? Please tell me it's not Friday."

Von sat down at the end of the bed. "It's still Thursday. I found you about an hour ago. Calm down. What's going on with you?"

It was then that Anari broke down and told Von the whole story. Her eyes filled with tears as she told him how Maurice had been taken and how she had sold everything she owned to get the money she needed to pay the kidnappers.

Von was enraged. "Why didn't you say something earlier? I could have been handled this." Von made one phone call, and thirty minutes later, a man arrived with a paper bag full of money. Von and the man left the room to discuss something. Anari nosily got out of bed and listened at the door.

"Yo, man. Some crazy shit just happened. When I went to the bank to get the money, this stupid-ass kid tried to rob the muthafucka. He didn't even have a chance. The guards loaded that little nigga up like he was Scarface or something."

Anari immediately rushed to her purse to grab her phone. She called Jamal and received no answer. At that moment, she knew that the stick-up kid the man was talking about was her brother. She turned on the TV and saw her brother's face all over the news.

"Jamal Simpson was killed today while attempting to rob the Second National Bank."

Anari screamed. She could not believe this. This shit could not be happening to her. He was only trying to help her.

Von heard Anari's scream and rushed into the room. He watched her as she touched her brother's face on the television screen and fell to the floor. He went by her side and picked her up.

"It was my brother. He was only trying to help me. He's never stolen anything a day in his life. He was trying to help me! Me! My baby brother is dead." Anari felt her head spin and she fell back onto the bed. It was overwhelming. There was just too much going on at the same time. Anari felt her body shutting down. She was tired, her mind was numb, and no matter how hard she tried, the tingling sensation behind her eyes would not go away.

"You need to sleep," Von told her as he covered her body with a blanket.

Anari shook her head. "I need my son."

It was the last thing she said before she collapsed into a restless sleep.

Chapter Eight

Anari awoke the next morning to an empty room. Her body felt tired, and she knew it was because of the tossing and turning she had done the night before. She was still in pain from Maulie's death, but today she had to get her son back. She got out of bed and went into the living room, where Von and five other men were seated.

Anari heard Von say, "When she gets her son, nobody leaves alive. I want everybody in that muthafucka dead."

Anari called Von over to her and he escorted her back to the room. "I'm scared, Von."

Von pulled her close. "I got you. I promise."

Anari got dressed. She put on a black two-piece Adidas hook-up and strapped a .25 Beretta that Von had given her, to her leg. She wrapped her .22 up in a bun in her hair. The gun was so small that no one would ever suspect she had it on her. When it was time to go, Anari quietly followed Von to the car.

"Are you okay?" he asked, knowing that she was thinking about the potential outcome of all this.

Anari looked at Von and nodded.

She wasn't really okay, but it didn't make a difference. She knew she had to do this.

As Von drove toward Hemlock Street, the only thing she could think about was getting her son back. Her heart raced as they got closer and closer to their destination. Von parked a couple houses down from the drop-off spot and grabbed Anari's hand to let her know that everything was all right.

She walked toward the house and her heart beat faster and faster with every step. Standing in front of the building where the kidnappers had taken her son, she carried a large suitcase filled with the money they had asked for.

Her cell phone rang, and she was instructed to walk into the building. When she entered, she had butterflies in her stomach, but she knew she had to be strong for her son. The voice in her cell phone instructed her to take the stairs to the top floor. Anari walked up the dark staircase, afraid that if she made a wrong move, they would kill her son. When she reached the top of the building, she was instructed to leave the money there.

"Where's my son?"

The voice on the cell phone became enraged. "Bitch, don't get stupid. Leave the money on the roof and you'll get your snot-nosed son."

Anari didn't know what to do. Von had told her not to give them the money until they gave her back her son.

"Fuck that. I'll leave half on the roof, and you'll get the rest when I get my son." Anari opened up suitcase and set half of the money on the roof. She ran down the steps with the rest of the money and stopped when she reached the basement door. Anari opened the basement door and saw nothing but darkness.

Maurice, baby, I'm coming.

Her son was terrified of the dark. How could they keep a child locked in a basement like this? Anari rushed down the steps to find her son sitting in a chair with duct tape on his face. She ran over to him and untied his arms. Anari took the money and her son and ran up the stairs and out the front door.

As soon as she stepped out of the front door, she heard gunshots. She heard her son scream in pain, and she dropped to her knees.

"No, God, no! Not after all this. Please don't die in my arms." Anari ran as fast as she could, holding the money and her child. She looked around and saw Von run into the building. She heard gunshots go off inside, and she prayed that Von was okay.

She stared into the eyes of her dying son. "Momma loves you."

Anari screamed for someone to help her. Von ran out of the building with the rest of the money in his hand. She noticed that Von was bleeding and just as he was running toward the car, he was shot in the back of the head. Von hit the pavement hard and when he died, her baby took his last breath and died too.

Anari was snapped out of her daydream by the ringing of her phone. She had imagined so many different scenarios, and all of them ended in death. She was so afraid as she stood in front of the house on Hemlock Street. Anari could hear her heart beating in her ears and breathed heavily to try to calm herself. She was shaking from fear and anticipation, knowing that her fate was inside the building in front of her.

Anari answered her phone and heard Von's voice.

"I'm right here. If you have any trouble, shoot three times into the air and I'ma be in there."

Anari said okay and reluctantly walked into the building. It had been deserted for some time and it smelled of urine and liquor. She walked around the house, waiting to see someone. Instead, she saw a tape recorder in the corner of the front room. She walked over to it and pressed play.

"Leave the money in the upstairs room. Then go to the basement. Your son will be down there."

Anari rushed upstairs and dumped the money onto the bed. She ran back down stairs and into the basement where she struggled to see through the darkness that consumed the room. There were no windows, so she was forced to use her hands and stay against the wall so that she could find her way around the room. Anari was filled with fear and anticipation as she tried to find her son.

"Reesey, its Mommy. Where are you?" she asked, trying not to sound frightened. The room smelled like gasoline, and there was a horrible smell that contaminated the air.

"Baby!" she screamed.

Anari's stomach tossed and turned as she struggled to find Maurice. She let go of the wall to search the middle of the room, and as soon as she took a step, she tripped over something lying on the floor. Anari fell hard into something wet and sticky. As she attempted to get up, her hand brushed past the object she had fallen over. The stench of gasoline became unbearable as she touched the object on the floor.

Anari tried her hardest to adjust her eyes to the darkness of the room. She saw the puddle that she had landed in first. Anari felt the wetness seep through her clothes as she figured out that it was the blood of her son she had fallen into. Her eyes adjusted more, and she saw the outline of her son's tiny body a few feet away from her. Her heart pounded in her ear as she scrambled over to Maurice's body.

"No, no, baby, no!" she screamed as she grabbed her son up into her arms and rocked him. "No!" Anari's body felt numb as she realized what the horrific scent lingering in the basement had been. The basement reeked of gasoline and a stench that was so disgusting it made Anari gag. There were rats everywhere, and the smell was attracting them toward her.

She felt as if she would suffocate. It was all too much for her to take. It was then that she knew that this wasn't about the money. This had to be personal. Anari wanted to run, but the thought of her son had her frozen in disbelief and grief. A rat brushed past her and she shrieked in horror.

She laid her son down, pulled the gun off of her leg and shot it into the air. Von raced into the building after hearing Anari's distress call. He ran down the basement steps, and the smell made him hesitate as he struggled to find Anari through the darkness. He grabbed Anari and carried her out of the house, moving so quickly that he didn't even notice the child's body.

He placed her in the car and asked, "Where's the money?"

Anari just looked at him with tears in her eyes.

"Fuck," Von said as he ran back into the house to get the money. He ran up the stairs and into the room where Anari had taken the suitcase full of money. He looked everywhere for the money, but the suitcase was gone. He searched the house to make sure that it wasn't there, then ran back to his car and drove off.

Anari was hysterical, and Von didn't know what to do to comfort her. "What happened?" he asked, trying to figure out what went wrong.

Anari just cried as she weakly replied, "His face . . . it was burnt. I couldn't even recognize him."

Von knew what he had to do. They couldn't go back to the house to get her son's body. He couldn't risk being there when the cops showed up. He dialed 911 and reported a dead body at the address they had just left. Anari would be able to report the kidnapping later to claim her son's body from the morgue.

They arrived back at Von's house, and all he could do was hold her. She cried continuously, and Von knew she would be unable to make the funeral arrangements. He looked through her cell phone and called Shawna, but couldn't reach her. The operator said that the line had been disconnected, so he called Tanya.

He explained to Tanya what had happened, and she immediately came over to be with Anari. There was nothing Tanya could say. She had lost her godson, but Anari had lost her son. The two pains did not compare.

While Anari was in trouble, Tanya had been acting petty. Now she was sorry. She never thought that no shit like this was going down. Tanya held her friend close.

It was hard for Tanya to make the funeral arrangements, but she knew it would be even harder for Anari to make them. She arranged for Jamal and Li'l Maurice to have their funerals together, and Von covered all the expenses.

A week later, the funeral was held. It was a closed casket ceremony. Anari didn't want anyone to see her son in such a violent way. When Anari saw her son's casket sitting next to her brother's, she simply couldn't carry the pain anymore. She broke down.

This is all my fault. I'm sorry, Maurice. I'm sorry, Maulie.

Anari reached for Von, who stayed by her side through all this. He held her up as they walked past the coffin and took their seats. Anari went through the funeral in a blur. She didn't hear any of the speakers. All she thought about was the last happy time she spent with her son at the park.

I'm sorry, Maurice. I'm sorry that Mommy couldn't protect you. Mommy will always love you. I'm so sorry, baby boy. I'm sorry.

Anari had not spoken to anyone since the death of her son. She didn't even talk to Von. She just cried, and he just held her. He couldn't really expect her to let go easily, so he just tried to be there for her.

Anari sank into a deep depression. She didn't eat; she didn't talk. All she did was sleep. She didn't care about anything anymore. She had lost Maurice, her son, and her brother. There was no one left. Why was this happening to her? What had she done to deserve this? Anari wondered as she examined her life.

Von walked into the room and brought Anari some food. "I'm not hungry," Anari said in a cold way.

Von was fed up. "Anari, you have to eat. It's been six months, baby. I know it hurts and you miss your son, but you can't let the grief consume your life like it has. You have to keep living, if not for you, do it for me, and if not for me, do it for your brother and your son. You're killing yourself. It wasn't your fault. There was nothing you could do."

Anari knew Von was right, but it was so hard for her to let go. She needed time to heal, but she knew she would never heal if she did not start living again. "It's just so hard. But I'll try."

Tanya called her the next morning. "How have you been?" she asked her friend, knowing that this ordeal had not been easy for her. She too felt the pain of Li'l Reesey's death.

Anari paused for a minute and answered, "It gets harder every day. Von keeps telling me that I have to move on, but I can't. I miss him too much. How am I supposed to forget my baby?"

Tanya could hear the pain in Anari's voice. "Do you need anything? Can I stop by?" she asked, trying to be supportive.

Anari replied, almost in a whisper, "I really don't feel like having company right now, T. Thanks anyway. I just need a little more time."

Tanya understood, so she replied, "I understand, girl. Call me if you need me. I'll be here."

Anari hung up the phone. She felt bad about telling Tanya not to come, but she just didn't have the strength to deal with anyone besides Von. She had promised Von that she would try to move on, but how do you attempt to put your life back together after losing your child?

The next day, Anari looked out of her bedroom window and thought about Von. He had been so great to her. He took her in and loved her. He supported her and was really the only solid thing she had in her life. Although he was in the streets a lot, he always found time to make sure she was okay. He had been saving her since the day they met, and she really loved him for that.

Anari called Tanya, but the line was busy. It was then that she realized she hadn't talked to Shawna since the day she sold all her stuff. The last six months seemed like a horrible dream that she couldn't wake up from. She appreciated all the people who had been in her corner. She wanted to thank Shawna for trying to help with the ransom. She reached for her phone and dialed Shawna's cell.

"This line has been disconnected," said the recording. That was strange, thought Anari. She called Shawna's home number.

"This number has been changed. No forwarding number is listed"

Anari hung up the phone and wondered what the hell was up with Shawna. Didn't she know what had happened? Anari thought back and realized she didn't remember seeing Shawna at the funeral.

Anari could not believe that Shawna hadn't even bothered to call. Maybe she didn't know what had happened.

Anari was in the living room when she received a phone call from Von.

"Anari, listen carefully, baby. I only got time to say this shit once. Take the keys to my Benz and get out of the house. Baby, I'm hot. Vice is on they way. I can't come back to the house. I won't make it in time. Pack up some clothes and get the fuck out of there. Grab the stash and meet me at the airport."

Anari ran to their room, grabbing the $200,000 and the ten kilos of dope Von had stashed in the safe. She stuffed the money in his gym bag, put the dope in her Gucci Bag and was out the door.

Anari was almost to Von's car when she remembered that she left the gym bag full of money. She started back for the door when she heard somebody say, "Freeze! Put your hands on top of your head."

Anari dropped her bag and started thinking quick. She needed an excuse to get out of there. She didn't want to get caught with ten kilos of dope. That type of weight carried a life sentence. She gently turned to the officer with her hands raised.

"Oh, sir, I'm just here to sell some cosmetics." She showed him her MAC discount card. "Here, let me show you my card. I work for MAC."

Anari handed the officer her card, hoping he would buy her story and wouldn't ask to see what was in her bag.

The officer read her card, looked at her Gucci bag and lowered his weapon.

"Look, you better get out of here, young lady. Things are about to get real hectic around here."

Anari looked at the officer. "No problem." She grabbed her Gucci bag and walked away as if she really were trying to sell products. She high-tailed it out of there, walking about ten blocks away from the house before she caught a cab to the airport.

When she got there, Von asked what took so long. She explained the situation to him. He hugged her tight.

"Sorry baby, but you did good. You got the stash. Always get the dope first." He told her not to worry about anything because the house and the car were not in his name.

"How did you know about the bust?" Anari asked.

"I got a dirty cop on payroll and he tipped me off." Von explained.

They waited in the airport until one of Von's soldiers came. Von handed him the bag of dope then Anari and Von boarded a plane and flew to Jamaica. It was time for her healing process to begin.

Chapter Nine

Lying on the beach, Anari found herself able to relax for the first time in over a year. She was beginning to accept the fact that her son was gone. Anari knew that she had to let go in order to let him rest in peace. She would always love her son. He was her love and the light of her life, and that would never change. He was with her spiritually, but it was still hard for her to let him go physically.

As Anari sat in the chair enjoying the crashing waves from the ocean, she thought of Maurice. She thought of when she first met him. She had loved him so much.

Everything will be okay, she told herself as she stared out into the ocean.

"Hey, baby" she said as she saw Von walk toward her. She loved Von a lot. She was just going through so much right now. She hoped he could deal with her depression because she really did want to be with him.

"Why don't we go up to our room?" he asked. It

had been so long since Anari had given Von some ass. Anari agreed, knowing what it was that Von was suggesting, and they made their way to the hotel.

Once in their room Von couldn't wait to get shit popping. His dick was harder than a Jawbreaker, and he couldn't wait to feel the inside of Anari's pussy again. Anari was wet too. She wanted to fuck just as badly as he did.

She had so much aggression that she needed to release. She sucked on the tips of his fingers and teased him as he imagined her sucking something else. He bent her over the bed and entered her from behind, making her drip. He pulled her back against him and began to grind into her gently. Anari moaned and played with her clit while he fucked her from behind.

"Maurice," Anari moaned as Von continued to grind into her.

I know this bitch did not just call me Maurice.

Von fucked her harder, getting angry every time he thought about her calling him Maurice. He pumped harder and harder, asking, "Is that the spot, Nari?"

When both of them had an orgasm, he turned her around and held her. He was pissed off at her, but he didn't even think that she knew she had called him by another man's name.

"I love you, Von," said Anari.

Von hesitated when she said this. "I think you love Maurice."

Anari looked at Von. "What are you talking about?" she asked in confusion.

"You know what the fuck I'm talking about. You calling me Maurice and shit while we fucking. I ain't yo' ex. Remember that," Von said, pointing his finger in Anari's face.

Anari sat in silence. She was so embarrassed. It wasn't like she had meant to call him Maurice. She didn't even remember saying it. Anari couldn't believe that she had called Von by Maurice's name.

"I'm sorry."

Von was angry, but he could understand how she would be thinking about the father of her son right now. So he forgave her. The shit just better not happen again.

Anari felt so bad about disrespecting Von the way she did. She didn't try to. She honestly didn't know what she was saying. It was time to let go of all the deceased people in her life, and she knew it. She needed to get a lot of shit off her chest.

The next morning, Anari kissed Von on the cheek and crawled out of bed. She was really sore from Von being so rough with her the night before. She took a long, hot bubble bath and went for a jog. She wanted to run from her past. She wanted to leave everything behind so that she wouldn't mess things up with Von. She didn't feel like she could afford to mess up anything else.

Anari jogged along the beach, saying her goodbyes to her son, her brother, and Maurice. It was time for her to make room for love in her life, and she could not do that with all these burdens that weighed down her heart. As her thoughts grew more intense, she ran faster, sprinting down the Jamaican coast, running from the ghosts of her loved ones. When Anari finally realized that she had run extremely too far, she stopped abruptly.

She slowly walked back to the hotel, feeling a lot better about her life. She got back to the room and saw that Von was still asleep. He looked so peaceful that Anari didn't want to wake him. She just sat and watched him sleep.

Anari got up and went into the bathroom to take a shower. When she got out, Von was sitting on the edge of the bed counting money. She walked over to him, still dripping wet from the shower she had just taken. Von looked at her and licked his lips.

"You better put on some clothes 'fore I do something with you."

Anari laughed. "You better quit licking your lips like that before I give you something else to lick."

Von shook his head. "You hungry, li'l mama?"

Anari said "yes" and they ordered breakfast from room service. When it got there, she fed Von in bed. She apologized again for calling him by another man's name, and he forgave her.

"Don't worry about it. It's over." He kissed her on the head as if she were his little girl then continued to eat his breakfast.

"So, what's up for your birthday?" Von asked.

Anari had been so absorbed in everything else that had been going on that she hadn't even thought about her birthday.

"I just want to spend my birthday with you. Just me and you on this luxurious beach." Anari jumped on top of Von and kissed him all over his body, using her tongue with every kiss.

After they chilled in their room, Anari wanted to go shopping to get her some fly Jamaican shit. She loved collecting souvenirs, and she was not leaving Jamaica until she bought something.

"Baby, let's go shopping."

Von wasn't feeling that shit. Every time he went shopping with Nari, she spent hours in one store.

"Nah, baby. I'm straight. Just grab my wallet and go have fun."

Anari frowned. "But, baby, that ain't gon' be fun. Just come with me, please." Anari gave Von her saddest face, but Von wasn't falling for it.

He laughed. "Nah, you go ahead."

Anari smacked her lips and grabbed Von's wallet, spilling the contents all over the floor. She knelt down to pick up his stuff, noticing a picture. It was Von, standing next to a light-skinned chick. Anari looked through the rest of his pictures and found a photo of two couples. It was Von and some girl, and Mann and Shawna.

"What the fuck is this shit? Who are these people in this picture?" Anari yelled.

Von looked at Anari and went to see what she was screaming about. He looked at the picture.

"Damn, Anari. Why you tripping? That's a picture from high school. That's me and my high school sweetheart, my boy Emanuel, and his girl Tiffany."

Anari stared at the picture to get a better look. "Von, that's Shawna in that picture, and she's standing with Mann," screamed a frightened Anari. "How do you know Mann? What is Mann doing with Shawna?"

Von didn't know what Anari was talking about. He just stood there looking dumbfounded. She grabbed Von's gun from the drawer and pointed it at him.

"What are you doing? Calm down, Anari. That picture is over five years old. We were freshmen in high school. Baby, look at how young I look. I ain't fucking with that bitch no more," Von yelled.

Anari was frustrated. "Fuck the ho you standing with! It's the other people I'm talking about. I don't give a damn how old this picture is. I know Shawna, and this is her, and that's Mann. I know I am not crazy," she screamed.

Von tried to calm Anari. He kept his hands in front of him because she still had the gun pointed at his chest.

"Listen, Anari, I don't know who this Shawna person is. All I know is that you got a friend named Shawna. I've never even met her. The girl that Mann is standing with in that picture is Tiffany, and I ain't seen her since we took that picture. I do know Mann, though. But he died a couple years back. Some bitch shot him."

Anari stared at Von with hateful eyes. "I know. I'm the bitch who killed him."

Von looked at Anari then looked at the picture. *This bitch was crazy,* he thought.

Anari tried to absorb all the information Von was giving her.

"Oh, my God. That bitch! It was Shawna. I killed my only son. I let Shawna into my home. I trusted her. I should have known. I answered her phone that day. I remember at the party he called her Tiff. I trusted Shawna—I mean Tiffany, Shawna . . . no Tiffany."

This was all too confusing and overwhelming for her. She could not live with the fact that she was responsible for her son's death. She saw Von approaching her and she stared blankly at him, not believing that she had let this happen. She slowly took the gun off of Von and turned it on herself.

I killed my son, she thought as she pointed the 9mm to her head and pulled the trigger.

Click!

Von tackled Anari and took his gun from her hands. He embraced her. "You didn't know. There was no way you could've known." He was just glad that he always kept the first barrel of his gun empty. If there had been a bullet in the chamber, Anari would have taken her own life.

Anari cried hysterically. "I told her the code to my alarm system. She knew I had a son. She tried to have me shot at the club that night. Some dude called her on her phone and I answered it. He said that he wouldn't miss next time, thinking that he was talking to Shawna. I killed my child. Von, I killed my baby."

Anari told Von her life story. She told him all about Maurice and everything that he had taken her through. She told him about killing Mann, and he finally understood why she was so troubled.

Anari's body shuddered as she blamed herself over and over again for her child's death. How could she have let this happen? Why had Anari befriended Shawna so quickly? She had told Shawna personal things that she had only shared with Tanya.

Rage bubbled inside of Anari's heart. Anari looked Von in the eyes. "Tomorrow we got to go back to Jersey."

I'm about to kill this bitch, she thought, knowing that she would not stop until she avenged her son's death.

Chapter Ten

From the time they arrived back in Jersey, Anari started making plans. She became a little bit more curious about Von's business. If she wanted to find Shawna or Tiffany or whoever the fuck the bitch was, she knew she needed to have some power.

First, you got to get the money. Once you get the money, you get the power then you get the woman.

She wanted to get this particular woman more than anything in this world, so Anari started plotting. She had to find Shawna and make her pay for what she had done to her son. Anari said fuck the "good girl" look. She didn't give a fuck about what people thought of her anymore. She went and got her son's name tattooed on her neck and cut her hair in a cute but sassy style.

Anari wanted to cut Von's ass off, too. She loved him, but him being in that picture with the enemy made him an enemy too. She needed Von, though.

He could teach her how to hustle. After that, she would drop his ass.

Anari listened in on phone calls and kept track of his transactions. The first thing she needed to do was get a connect. She wanted to get that pure cocaine. She wanted that shit that hadn't ever been stepped on. She wanted that girl. Even though Anari knew almost nothing about the drug game, she knew if she had a good product, then customers were guaranteed.

Anari studied all the gangster movies. She watched *Scarface, Paid in Full, Blow, The Godfather,* and *Goodfellas*. She thought watching these movies would give her a better idea of what she was getting herself into. And the tapes did teach her things that she could use. They helped her develop her persona and taught her some valuable techniques.

Anari knew she couldn't take over by imitating what others had done. She needed her own style. She would soon find it. She knew she had to find a connect, but she didn't have the slightest clue on how to begin searching for one.

Damn, they need to put drug dealers in the phone book, Anari thought. *This shit is harder than it looks.*

She thought back to the days when Maurice used to hustle. Before Maurice died, he had been a well-respected hustler in Jersey, and she knew she needed the same product that made Maurice's business prosper. She needed to find his connect.

Her thoughts were interrupted by Von's footsteps.

"Nari, don't make no plans for Saturday night. I got this business meeting I got to go to. It's very important, so go and buy you something to wear."

Anari took $10,000 from Von then went and bought herself a $3,000 dress. She put the rest in a private account that Von knew nothing about. She was about to start a six-month hustle plan to save money for her own investment in the drug game. She would skim money off the top from Von whenever she could. By the end of the six months, she should have saved $50,000. That would be enough to do something with. Even though Anari didn't know a lot about what dope was going for, she knew that $50,000 would be enough to give her a good start.

Anari went back to the apartment that she and Von had rented when they came back from Jamaica. She saw Von in the living room watching Sports Center.

"Baby?" said Anari in an innocent voice.

Von motioned for her to sit on his lap. "What up, girl?"

"How much a kilo cost?"

"A kilo of what?"

Anari gave Von her baby look. "You know."

Von laughed at his nosy girlfriend. "Eighteen thousand on the street, but with a connect like mine, you can get it for sixteen five."

Anari made mental notes of those figures. "Oh, well how you know if you got that good shit?" she asked.

He stopped what he was doing and looked at her. "You'll know by the amount of customers you attract," he said. "A good hustler only has two or three that always come back for more and more. Stupid niggas have so many customers that they don't know who they dealing with, and if you don't know who you dealing with, you don't know who you selling to. Patience is the key. Good dope sells itself."

Anari absorbed all that information, trying to remember all of the important facts. She paused for a minute then continued her grill session. "What's the number one rule?" asked Anari.

Von laughed, mocking Scarface. "Don't get high off your own supply. And what the hell is up with all the questions?"

Anari looked for a quick explanation. "Oh, I didn't tell you? I'm writing a book. My main character is a drug dealer."

Von hugged Anari. "My entrepreneur. Just don't put my name in the shit." With that statement, the conversation ended.

Anari went back every day with new questions for Von. In a matter of days he taught her everything he knew, without knowing her intentions. Now it was time for her to find a right-hand man. Every hustler had one, and hers would be Tanya. Even though T was acting shitty, Anari knew that she was the only person she could trust with her life, and the drug game is one of life or death.

Anari called Tanya. "Can we meet somewhere?"

Tanya was hesitant because she had not heard from Anari in a while, but she said yes anyway. They met at Starbucks across the way. When they saw each other, they embraced and began to cry. It was at that moment Anari knew Tanya would always be her best friend. No matter what they went through, the genuine love they had for one another would always bring them through.

Anari and Tanya found a table and Anari immediately explained why she had called. "I know who killed my son," said Anari.

Tanya looked confused. "Anari, what are you talking about?"

Anari looked across the table at Tanya. "It was Shawna."

Tanya's eyes bucked when Anari said her name. She never really liked Shawna in the first place. She had tried to warn Anari about befriending her so quickly. Tanya knew that this was no time for "I told you so." Instead, she reached across the table and held Anari's hand. "How do you know?"

Anari took her hand away from Tanya's. "I just know."

Anari explained what she thought had happened. She told her everything from Shawna killing her son to her wanting to enter the drug game.

Tanya looked at Anari with pain in her eyes. "You know I'm down with whatever, but are you sure you want to do this?"

Anari nodded. "Yeah, I'm sure, T. The first thing that we need to do is find a connect, and I think I need to find Maurice's old connect. Do you remember Lance?" Anari asked.

Tanya laughed. How could she forget the nigga that got her pregnant? In fact, she thought about him constantly. He had begged her to have his baby, but Tanya just wasn't ready. She had an abortion at age sixteen, and she regretted it every day of her life.

"Yeah, I remember him. He moved to Detroit about a year ago. I heard that he's the man now."

Anari smiled. "I think it's about time for you to rekindle that relationship. I need to find Maurice's old connect, and I know Lance can help me do that. Set up a trip to the D for next Friday, and we'll go see what's up."

Anari and Tanya agreed on the terms and went their separate ways. Before departing, Tanya said, "By the way, I like the new look."

Anari pulled out a cigar and lit it. "Say good-night to the bad guy." Anari handed Tanya a cell phone and walked out of the restaurant.

Anari looked at her clock in the car. She had to get home so that she could get dressed for Von's meeting. She sped home and kissed Von as she ran through the door.

"Where you been, li'l mama? We gon' be late. I told you about this shit a couple days ago. Hurry up!" he yelled.

Anari ignored Von's fussing. *Shut the fuck up. I'm gon' be ready. Damn, just gimme a minute,* she thought as she hopped into the shower and washed herself as quickly as she could.

She put on the black Versace dress she had picked up and some diamond earrings. She made sure her hair was still intact then she was ready to go.

A limousine picked them up from their house. Anari walked out the door with Von watching her walk to the car. She looked good, but he hated that damn tattoo on her neck. It reminded him of a hood rat. He often wondered if she had gotten it for her son or for her ex. He really couldn't say anything, though, because her other features over-shadowed the blemish.

The limousine pulled up to the Waldorf Astoria

an hour later. Anari looked up and admired the
building. They went into the most beautiful hotel
she had ever seen. A middle-aged white man accompanied by three model-type women—one Asian,
one black, and one white—greeted them. Von
looked at the women and knew that Anari outdid
each one.

Anari tried to observe her surroundings. She
noticed muscular bodyguards standing in each
corner of the room.

*Damn, this nigga got bodyguards and shit. I need to
hire me some of them.*

"Ah, Von, who is this lovely young woman you
are courting?" asked the middle-aged man.

Von looked at me. "This is Alexis, my date for
the night. Alexis, this is Mr. Poindexter."

Anari made sure that she gave Mr. Poindexter
her most gracious smile. He kissed her hand and
murmured, "Exquisite," but he barely looked at
her. He was all about business, leading everyone
into the dining room. The waiter put the women
at one table and sat Mr. Poindexter and Von at another.

Anari wanted to know what they were talking
about. She tried her best to read their lips, but it
was no use. She would just have to get the details
out of Von later.

After thirty minutes of conversation, Von was
ready to go. They rode back to Jersey in the limo,
and on the way, Anari asked, "Why did you intro-
duce me as Alexis?"

Von laughed at his baby girl for being so per-
ceptive. "You never let your left hand know what
your right hand is doing. Keep business and plea-

sure separate. They don't need to know your government name."

Anari was silent for a while, thinking that now would be a good time for her to get some money out of Von.

"Baby, you think you can give me some money to go see my moms in Detroit?"

Without thinking or even questioning his woman, Von said, "Of course. What? You gon' be gone for a couple days?"

Anari looked at him, hoping she was making the right choice. "I think it'll be longer than a couple days. I haven't seen her since I had Maurice. We sort of fell out over my lifestyle. Anyway, she's getting sick now, and I want to be there for her before she dies. I really need to be around family right now. Even though we don't get along much, she's all that I have." Little did he know her momma died when she was fourteen, there was no telling where her daddy was at.

Von looked at Anari with sympathetic eyes and held her close. "Take as much time as you need. Look, I'll just give you fifteen thousand. That should take care of you and your family while you're there." He held onto her hand and added, "She ain't the only person who cares about you, Nari."

Anari kissed Von and slept the rest of the way home.

The next day, Anari called Tanya on the phone she had given her. "Hey, I'll be over there in about an hour."

Tanya knew what it was about, and assured

Anari that she would be home. After Anari got off
the phone she went over her plan in her head. She
wanted to make sure that she would not get herself
in a situation she couldn't get out of. She knew
once she was in, there was no turning back. Anari
headed for Tanya's house.

"What's up, Anari?" said Tanya.

"Did you set up the meeting?" asked Anari in an
eager tone. She didn't mean to be so pushy, but if
she was going to do this, she needed to start the
ball rolling as soon as possible.

Tanya looked at Anari. "I don't know about a
meeting, but he is expecting us. He was excited to
hear from me, and even more excited to see you
after all this time." Tanya had set it up right. They
would be on the first flight to Detroit Friday morning.

"I know Shawna is about to be hard to get to.
She was Mann's main bitch, and it hurts me to say
this, but Mann was just as big as Maurice was—to
some people, bigger. We got to do this right because she got just as many killers working for her
as Mann did. She ain't a dumb chick either. She
orchestrated the kidnapping and killing of Li'l
Maurice right under my nose."

Tears began to well up in her eyes, but Anari
promised herself that she would cry no more.
Emotions were a sign of weakness, and she couldn't
afford to have a weakness. The emotional Anari
died with her son. She wiped the tears from her
eyes.

"Did you get the money from Von?" Tanya asked.

She wasn't sure if Anari was really going to go
through with this, but when Anari placed $60,000
on the table in front of Tanya, she knew there was

no turning back. Tanya looked at the money scattered on the table in disbelief. She had never seen so much money.

"This is a lot of money," Tanya said.

Anari started to stack the money up in thousand-dollar piles. "I've seen Maurice turn a thousand dollars into ten thousand in just a week. Think about what we can do with this much. If we stick to the plan and follow the rules, we can come up quicker than Maurice ever did. Maurice could touch any nigga he wanted, just off of his name. He had love in the streets. That's what we need to get, T, love in the streets. It will be easier to find Shawna that way."

Tanya nodded in agreement. "If you get yo' hands on some dope, how do you know you can sell it? I wouldn't even know where to start."

Anari stopped stacking the money. "It can't be that hard. Von or Maurice never stood on a block as far as I know, and they got rich. The method they used was similar, and I was watching both of them closely. I picked up things from both of them. I think we can do this. I'm scared, but I feel like there's no other way."

Tanya was reluctant to get involved in anything drug-related. She had heard stories of what the game could do to a person. It seemed to her like Anari wasn't thinking this thing through. She didn't even seem like the same person anymore. Tanya didn't know about this shit.

She wanted to help her friend, but she wanted to be sure.

"Anari, people die in this game. We chicks. How you know niggas are gonna even take us seriously? I just want to be sure of the outcome."

Anari looked Tanya dead in the eyes and answered, "T, I got to do this, with you or without you. I would rather have you in my corner like it always been. You the only person I can trust."

Tanya started to help Anari put the money in stacks, and at that moment, Anari knew her friend was in.

Anari spent the rest of the day with Von. He spoiled her, and she hated to admit to herself that she would miss him. But she didn't know whose team he was on, and she couldn't afford any slip-ups. Anari had a lot to think about. She was about to tread new waters. She could only hope that she was ready for it.

Von had noticed that his woman had been distracted lately, so he wanted to spend as much time with her as possible.

"Nari, what time are you leaving Friday morning?"

Anari looked at Von and thought about how good it would feel to be in a position of power like him.

"Six in the morning," replied Anari. She looked at her man, her strong, overprotective man and at that moment, she loved him more than anything.

"I love you, Von. Please remember that. No matter what happens between us, I'll always love you. I appreciate everything that you have done for me. Thank you, baby."

Von had never told a woman that he loved her before. He had never found one who was worthy. He had never even told his own mother that he loved her, and when he fell for Anari, he was surprised. But he did love Anari, almost from the first time he saw her. He knew there was something special about her. He would die for her and he hoped that she knew this.

Anari enjoyed her last days with Von. After she left for Detroit, he wouldn't see her again, so she wanted to cherish every moment she spent with him.

She couldn't trust him, no matter how much she wanted to. When she saw the picture of Von, Shawna, and Mann, all her trust for him went out the door. She couldn't help loving him, though. He was so good to her. He always treated her like a queen, and even if Von was broke, Anari would still love him. She knew that she would always love him, but that didn't mean she had to be with him.

The night before he took her to the airport, he made love to her. He wanted to remind her where home was before she went so far away. He made her feel so good that she almost debated staying, but she knew what she had to do. She wanted Shawna's head, and she could not jeopardize her revenge just because she thought she was in love. *What is love anyway?* She wondered as she fell asleep in Von's arms.

On the way to the airport the following morning, Anari held Von's hand. She held it tight, wanting to hold onto him forever, but when they arrived, she let go. "I love you. Please always know that."

Von kissed her passionately. "I love you, too, baby girl. Be safe, all right?"

She nodded. "You be safe too, and I love you," she replied.

With those words, she kissed her fingers and

placed them gently on his lips then turned and slowly walked into the airport with her suitcase in hand.

I love you, Javon Roberts.

She met Tanya on the plane and together they prepared themselves for what they were about to get into.

Chapter Eleven

They entered the Metro airport at around 10 AM. When they arrived, they saw a tall, lean man holding a sign with their names on it. They approached the man, who escorted them to a stretch Hummer.

They stepped inside, where they were greeted by Lance. Anari looked at the sexy man at the other end of the Hummer. He looked a lot better than he did when he was hanging out with Maurice.

"Sorry to hear about Li'l Maurice. I was in jail during the funeral and I couldn't make it. It's nice to see you, though."

Anari nodded her head and said, "It's nice to see you, too, Lance."

Tanya and Lance exchanged glances but didn't say anything to each other. Instead, Lance concentrated on another subject.

"I know y'all ain't come this far to party and

bullshit," Lance said. "What y'all need, some money? Y'all know I'll take care of y'all."

Anari grinned and paused for a moment. She looked at Tanya and noticed that she was fidgeting in her seat.

"I need to meet Poe," said Anari.

Lance looked at Anari suspiciously and answered, "Poe? What you know about Poe?"

Anari, having total control of the situation, said, "I know that he was Maurice's connect and I need to find him. Can you help me, yes or no?"

Lance was reluctant to make the arrangements for her to meet Poe, but he couldn't tell her no. Maurice was the cause of his success now. If his main girl needed this, then Lance had to give it to her. "We'll discuss that later. Let's catch up on old times."

They went to Lance's condo. He offered them a place to stay while they were visiting Detroit. This was one of his many places. Lance was a smart man. He wasn't too flashy. His condo was nice, but it wasn't out of a working man's reach. They accepted his offer and made plans to meet later on that evening for dinner.

Anari and Tanya settled into the condo. Anari looked at Tanya and could sense there was something wrong with her.

"What's wrong?" she asked, not wanting to pressure Tanya into doing anything.

Tanya shook her head. "I just hope you know what you're doing. I mean, I don't know anything about the game, and I just want to be sure that you know what's going on. I hope you do, Anari. That's all I'm gon' say."

Anari hoped so too. She knew she was getting

herself into some shit, but she was determined to do it anyway. The life of her son was worth it.

She looked at Tanya. "I do," she said resolutely.

Later that evening, they joined Lance at a popular restaurant called Fishbones. Two young men accompanied him. Anari thought they looked barely older than eighteen as she looked at the two young faces in front of her. The boys were identical twins with bald heads and muscular physiques. Their thuggish look appealed to her.

They all sat down, and Lance introduced the two boys to Anari and Tanya. "Biggs and Frank, this is—"

Anari cut Lance off mid-sentence and reached out her hand. "I'm Tony and this is Monica."

They exchanged handshakes and sat down. Lance smiled. He knew that whoever had taught her, had taught her well.

"Tony, these youngsters are very loyal to Maurice. Before he died, he was like their father. They have a lot of respect for him and for you because you're his woman. Between the two of them, they have twenty bodies under their belt. I won't let you do this without them. They some straight soldiers, and they'll be loyal to you. I put my life on it."

Anari looked over at the young boys who sat across from her. She stared both of them straight in the eyes and didn't sense any bitch in either of them as they matched her gaze. She glanced at Tanya, who nodded her head in approval.

"When do I meet Poe?" Anari asked.

They enjoyed their dinner and finished the terms of their agreement. Lance gave Anari the number where Poe could be reached and told her that Poe would be expecting her call. Nothing else was said about the connect. Everyone was catching up on old times and laughing—everyone except the twins. They didn't crack a smile. They just sat there and listened. Periodically, they would glance at the entrance, and every time someone stood up, their attention would go to them. They were seasoned, and aware of their surroundings at all times.

After dinner, Anari invited everyone back to the condo for drinks. They all reminisced about how things were when Maurice was alive.

Anari cleared her throat. "I see you two have Reesey's name tattooed on your arms. Can I trust that you will be that loyal to me?" Anari asked as she sipped her wine.

Biggs was the first to speak. "We know how Maurice felt about you. He would always speak highly of you and talk about how he wanted to protect his home from the streets. Now that he can't do that anymore, it's our time to protect you. We wouldn't have it any other way."

Lance shook his head in agreement. At that moment, Tanya came out of the bathroom. She walked around the couch behind the twins and put a gun to Biggs' head. Anari pulled a gun from her waistline and threw it in Frank's lap.

Tanya looked at Frank. "Kill Tony or kill Lance. Either way it goes, somebody got to die. If you don't pull the trigger, I'll put a hollow point through your brother's head."

Biggs felt the cold steel of the gun against his head but he didn't flinch. Without hesitation, Frank aimed the gun at Lance and pulled the trigger.

Click!

Tanya put her gun away and looked over to

Anari. She smiled as Lance said, "I told you them li'l niggas was loyal." He started to laugh.

That night, Anari left Detroit with two new-found friends. She was confident in the team she had put together, and knew it wouldn't be hard to quickly establish herself as the dominant dealer in Jersey. She sent the twins to set up shop in New Jersey while she and Tanya went to visit Poe.

As they were on their way to North Carolina, Tanya wanted to know something. "Oh, yeah. I forgot to ask you. Why Tony and Monica?"

"It was the first thing that popped into my head," Anari replied. "I guess I watched *Scarface* one too many times."

Tanya laughed. "Oh, Tony and Manolo. Hold on." Tanya lifted one eyebrow. "That ain't no good analogy. You killed me in the end."

Anari laughed and looked at Tanya. "I took a million bullets at the end, too, but that don't mean it's gon' happen. But seriously, those are the names that we go by from here on out. You never let your left hand know what your right hand is doing, T. Besides, they don't need to know your government name." Anari reiterated the lesson that Von had taught her a couple days earlier.

Anari's cell phone rang and the caller ID indicated that it was Von. She wanted to pick up her phone so badly, but she knew that she could never talk to him again. She would have to get her number changed because she didn't need Von distracting her.

The flight from Detroit to North Carolina seemed to take forever. She called Poe on the plane. Anari was instructed that she would be picked up by some of Poe's many bodyguards.

Anari was anxious to get back to Jersey so that she could start stacking money.

Tanya looked at Anari and knew that shit was about to get hectic. She hoped that Anari was all right, that she knew what she was doing. Tanya was helping Anari jump into a dangerous game, and she wasn't trying to lose her life at twenty-four.

"Why is this so important to you?" Tanya asked.

Anari thought about all the shit that she was forced to accept. She needed this money. She had sold her house and everything she owned. She sacrificed everything to get her son back. Now she was living off of Von, and she didn't even know whose side he was on.

Anari knew this was more than a battle between her and Shawna. She needed to be independent. She needed her life back, and after she killed Shawna, that was exactly what she would do. She left Tanya's question unanswered and put her head back and slept.

When they arrived at the Raleigh-Durham airport, two business-type men escorted them to a local hotel. She walked into an all too familiar scene. They were directed into a ballroom with a bodyguard in every corner. She stared into the eyes of the same man she had seen two weeks earlier in the meeting with Von.

Poe stared at her as if he remembered her face. "Hello, Mr. Poindexter." Anari held out her hand, hoping that the man did not recognize her.

"My friends call me Poe," he replied, accepting Anari's hand.

"I'm Tony, and this is Monica." Poe stared at Anari, trying to figure out where he had seen her before.

"Don't I know you from somewhere?" he asked.

Tanya stared at Anari and wondered why he would know her.

"No, I don't believe that we've met," replied Anari in a charming voice.

To Anari's relief, Mr. Poindexter seemed to accept that and motioned for them to take a seat. Anari sat down and Tanya stood behind Anari's chair, keeping watch on who was coming in and out of the room. They wanted no surprises.

"From my understanding, you would like to do business with me," said Poe.

"That's correct," said Anari, standing her ground to Poe. She leaned forward. "Let's cut to the chase." Anari just wanted to get down to business. She had no intention of wasting time.

Poe picked up a cigar and lit it. "Okay, let's talk. I'm going to be straight up with you, Tony. This is not a woman's game you're trying to enter."

Anari had been expecting Poe to feel insecure because of her gender, so she replied, "Nothing is a woman's game because this is a man's world, but I'm trying to be the first woman to change that."

Poe shook his head and took a puff of his cigar then replied. "I like you, Tony, but your beauty will make you seem vulnerable. I don't know if I can invest in someone who will appear to be easily intimidated."

Anari understood everything Poe was telling her. She knew the risk she was asking him to take.

"That's why I will not be seen. No one will know who I am, except my partner Monica and two of my most loyal workers."

Poe continued to smoke his cigar and nodded his head. "Since I like you, nineteen a key."

Tanya turned around and looked at Anari and they began to laugh.

Anari remarked, "You're a funny guy." She reached over the table, grabbed one of Poe's cigars, sat back in her chair and lit it. "I was thinking more sixteen-five a key."

Poe smiled at this feisty woman. "Eighteen a key," he offered.

"Sixteen-five a key," Anari said firmly.

Poe grew tired of trying to bargain with this woman. "Look, I don't need you, you need me. Seventeen a key, and that's my final offer."

Anari flashed her pearly whites. "I accept," she said as she began to rise from the table.

"No, sit, eat. This could be the beginning of a beautiful friendship," Poe said. And just like that, she had her connect.

I thought I was 'bout to die when I puffed that cigar, but besides that, this wasn't too hard, Anari thought as she finished her dinner.

The next morning Anari and Tanya were on their way back to Jersey, expecting Poe to contact them in a couple of weeks.

Chapter Twelve

Anari decided that they would set up shop on Maurice's old blocks, which were now run by Rio, a local hustler who wasn't big-time yet, but wasn't small-time, either. Knocking Rio off would be way easier than knocking off Von, so Rio became Anari's target.

Anari set up a meeting with the twins. "Biggs, Frank, how are you?"

The twins kissed Anari's cheek and Frank said, "Good. What's up?"

Anari instructed the twins to sit down. "We're going to take over the blocks between 106th Street and Boston Ave."

Biggs and Frank had been active in the dope game since they were fourteen, so they knew she was referring to Maurice's old territory. "Right now there's this cat named Rio running things around that way," Anari said. "I need to know how strong his business is, and I need to know how hard it will be to shut it down."

Anari didn't have to say too much. The twins knew what needed to be done, and they also knew they could get it done right. Anari directed them to go step on a couple toes to let niggas know that it was a new sheriff in town.

Biggs and Frank drove down to Maurice's old hustle spot, where they saw two of Rio's goons standing on the corner. They approached the two dudes on the corner and called out, "What up, li'l niggas?" as if they were hungry young hustlers who wanted to be down.

"Shit, what you looking for?" asked one of the street dealers.

"Nah, it ain't even like that," replied Biggs. "We was just wondering who block this was."

One of the thugs angrily said, "This Rio's block, and why you and your man so damn interested?"

At that exact moment, Frank pulled his gun and quickly put a hollow point through the thug's neck. He immediately dropped to the ground, and the twins aimed their attention to the other guy who worked for Rio. He was frozen in fear and knew that if he made a wrong move, he would die next.

"Well see, that's a problem because we heard that this here was Tony's block," Frank said.

The guy looked down at his partner, seeing the life leave his body, and remained silent.

Frank put his hand on the gun in his waistband. "Now, I'm gon' ask you again. Whose block is this?"

The thug was not so thuggish anymore. He was filled with fear, and it showed in his eyes when he replied, "This Tony shit, man. This Tony's block."

Frank and Biggs laughed. "That's what we thought, you bitch-ass nigga."

They took the gun and money off the dead man and hopped in the car. They pulled away, leaving the second thug alive so he could deliver the message to Rio.

Rio got the message all right. It got to almost every hustler in the city. Everybody cracked down on their shit after the twins' unexpected killing. They didn't want two little niggas like them to come bringing the heat around their blocks. People wanted their blocks to be safe, and they quickly found out that if they were on Tony's bad side, then they would not be.

Anari knew it would be hard to get to Rio. She needed a good plan so there wouldn't be any mistakes made. She decided that Tanya would be the one to get on the inside of Rio's camp. If anybody could distract Rio, it was Tanya. Then they could get to Rio from the inside.

Anari's cell phone rang, interrupting her thoughts. She looked at her caller ID. It was Von.

I am not answering this. Damn, why didn't I get my number changed?

Anari ignored Von's call. She had other things to do. She needed to find a new place to live, for one. She had been staying at Tanya's place since she got back in Jersey, but she needed her own spot.

Anari wanted something small, even though she knew she was about to come into a lot of money. She didn't want to flaunt it around town, and she didn't want everybody noticing her, because she didn't want Von to find her, and she didn't want the Feds to pick up on her. They would start to question where she got her money. So, Anari looked at regular one-bedroom apartments in a place where she could stay low-key. She finally found some nice ones that were within her means. A week later she moved into an apartment building right outside of New Jersey. It wasn't the greatest spot, but it would do for now.

Anari called Tanya to inform her about how she planned to get to Rio. Tanya was all for it.

"It's a private party going down at a club in New York this weekend. I can holla at him there," Tanya said.

Anari knew she would not be able to attend the party with Tanya. There was a chance she might run into Von, and she couldn't allow that to happen.

Anari knew she would have to keep a low profile if she didn't want to run into Von. They ran in the same circles and were at competition in the same business. She knew that Jersey was not big enough for both of them.

Anari sent the twins to the party with Tanya for protection. Tanya entered the party like she owned it, wearing a silver knee-length Versace dress with sparkles all over it. Her pretty face and voluptuous body attracted a lot of attention, but she was there for one purpose and one purpose only—to find Rio.

She maneuvered her way through the crowd, finally finding him and his crew in the back. He was already surrounded by a lot of girls, so it would be hard for her to get his attention.

She sat at a table near his, trying to observe what he was doing. She sat and watched him for at least an hour before she finally saw an opportunity to approach. He had gotten up and headed toward the bathroom, so she followed him. She entered the women's bathroom to make sure that she was looking good then walked out of the bathroom and purposefully bumped into Rio as he was walking back to his table.

"Damn," she said as she spilled the contents of her purse onto the floor.

Rio looked at her. "My fault, ma." He knelt down to help her pick up her things.

She looked up at him. "Thank you."

He looked at her, noticed her caramel skin tone, and immediately became interested. "Are you here with somebody?" he asked.

Tanya looked around to make sure the twins were watching her. "No," she said. "I was supposed to meet my friend here, but I guess she changed her mind about coming."

Rio rubbed his hands together, trying to be smooth. "So then you wouldn't have a problem if I asked you to join me in VIP."

"I guess I wouldn't."

Tanya didn't really want to go to the VIP with Rio because the twins wouldn't be able to watch her there, but then decided she could handle herself. She followed Rio into the back of the club and immediately noticed that the vibe was different, more laid back. She sat next to him and noticed the other women who had been trying to get next to Rio. Tanya leaned in close to Rio and he put his arm around her shoulders.

"Everybody, this is . . ." He paused, realizing that he hadn't gotten her name.

His boys yelled and began to playfully talk shit. "Damn, Rio. Nigga, you don't even know her name," someone shouted.

She whispered into his ear, using a seductive voice, "Monica."

He smiled. "This is Monica."

She was feeling Rio. Too bad that she wasn't for real with him. They chilled the entire night, and when the party was over, he asked Tanya to spend the night with him. The twins saw Tanya get into the car with Rio and knew that she could handle the rest.

The connection was made at the party, and for the next three months, Tanya made Rio trust her. She went to Hawaii with him and pretended to love him as if he were her man for real.

As Anari observed their relationship developing, she hoped Tanya remembered whose side she was on. She needed Rio dead so she could take over his spots.

One day, Tanya was sitting in her apartment, thinking about what she ultimately had to do with her newfound lover. Rio wasn't a bad guy. Matter of fact, he treated her like a queen. Maybe . . . maybe . . . fuck it. She needed to get this shit over with. No guts, no glory.

She called Anari on her cell. "Nari, I have to do the shit tonight."

Anari interrupted, instructing her to go outside and call her back on the pay phone near her building. Anari had her own phone burned so that it couldn't be traced or tapped. Tanya's phone wasn't, so Anari took every precaution. She thought about every aspect before she got into her new profession, and she wasn't willing to let her empire fall over some petty shit.

Tanya walked outside and got on the pay phone. She told Anari that she and Rio had plans to fly to Atlanta that night, and she planned on killing him in the hotel room.

"Listen. Go to the beauty salon and get your hair rinsed blonde. Get some tracks added to your hair so that it will be shoulder length. You walk into the hotel a long blond-haired woman wearing dark shades. Wear something outrageous. It doesn't matter what, just make sure that you don't look like yourself.

"After you kill him, rinse the dye out of your hair and remove the weave. Change into something conservative. You walk out of the hotel a well-dressed, business-looking woman with short, brown hair. Don't forget to take all your shit with you. Don't leave anything in his room. The twins will be waiting for you outside the hotel," instructed Anari.

Tanya listened carefully, and that night she was on a plane to the ATL, looking like a different woman. Rio liked the change.

Tanya sat beside him with butterflies in her stomach. Her hands were sweaty and she hated to admit it to herself, but she was scared. She had never killed anyone before. What if something went wrong? What if he knew?

Rio looked at Tanya and noticed how nervous she was. "What's up with you? Why you all silent tonight?"

"Oh, I'm just tired of sitting on this damn plane. Baby, can you order me a margarita?" Rio ordered the drinks and Tanya cuddled against his shoulder.

The plane landed about an hour later. They were supposed to go straight to dinner, but Tanya just wanted get this over with.

"Baby, can we go check into the hotel first? I want to take a shower before we go to dinner."

Rio looked at Tanya. "I want to do something else before we go to dinner."

Tanya smiled and kissed Rio as they walked toward the limo that took them to their hotel. Tanya did exactly what Anari had told her to. She walked into the hotel looking nothing like herself. Rio didn't seem to care, though. He was feeling Tanya.

They went up to their room, and as soon as Tanya opened the door, Rio began to take off her clothes. She let him, too. Just because she was about to kill his ass didn't mean she couldn't have fun first.

She teased Rio, putting her mouth on every part of his body, except the one part that he wanted her to. When he was hard as a rock, she excused herself and went into the bathroom.

"Baby, what the fuck? You leaving a nigga like this?"

Tanya laughed a sexy laugh. "I'm just going to freshen up. You gon' get this. Hold on."

He smiled. *Monica knew how to please a nigga,* he thought. He got up to get a condom from the dresser. He wasn't trying to have no shorty running around up in this bitch. He lay in the bed and waited for Tanya to come out of the bathroom.

Tanya felt as if she were going to be sick. She glanced in the bathroom mirror and noticed how green she looked. She didn't want to do this. Rio didn't deserve this. There had to be another way.

She ran some cold water and splashed it onto her face, trying to build up enough nerve to go through with the plan. She picked up her cell phone and called Anari.

"Hello?" Anari answered.

"Nari, I can't do this," Tanya whispered into the phone.

"You have to do this." Anari's tone was firm. "This is the only way."

Tanya hung up her cell phone and turned it off. She was scared, but she knew Anari was right.

Tanya was taking a long time, Rio thought as he knocked on the bathroom door. The knock startled Tanya. She looked at the door and spoke in a sweet voice.

"I'll be just a minute, baby."

Rio thought, *I'm 'bout to fuck da shit out of her tonight.* He pumped the air with his hands in front of him, imitating how he was going to hit it from the back. He started to walk toward the bed, holding his manhood in his hand, anticipating the sex that was about to occur.

Tanya opened the door and came out of the bathroom wearing nothing. She approached Rio and hugged him from behind. She started massaging his shoulders, and when she felt that he was comfortable, she pulled a knife that she had gently hidden in between her ass cheeks. She sliced Rio from ear to ear and watched him bleed.

He collapsed to the floor, holding his neck with both hands. He never saw it coming.

Tanya stared into the eyes of the dying man as she watched the blood seep from his neck. She couldn't stand the sight of the blood. Instantly, she became nauseated and vomited on the floor. Tanya tried to gain her composure, but the sight of a dead body was overwhelming.

Scattered thoughts raced through her head and her hands shook as she tried to remember exactly what Anari had instructed her to do. Tanya paced back and forth, finally scuffling to the bathroom to wash the color out of hair and remove the weave. Then Tanya went into her suitcase and took out a two-piece suit.

After she was fully dressed, she retrieved the knife from the side of Rio's body. She went into the bathroom to rinse off the knife, and as soon as she turned on the faucet, someone knocked at the door.

In a panic, Tanya dropped the knife and made her way to the window. She opened it and realized that her room was too high off the ground for her to jump out. She heard another knock at the door.

She made her way to the door and yelled, "Who is it?"

"Room service."

Tanya looked through the peephole. "I didn't order room service."

The man looked confused. "I'm very sorry."

Tanya watched the man walk away, and as soon as he was gone, she gathered up her things and took the stacks of hundreds from Rio's suitcase. Tanya left the hotel room and met the twins outside. When she was safely in the back seat of their car, she called Anari on her cell.

"It's done," she said as soon as Anari answered.

"Did you get everything?" Anari asked.

Tanya tried to steady her voice so Anari wouldn't sense that she was shaken up from killing someone. "Yeah, I got everything."

"Everything?" Anari asked

Do she think I'm stupid? Tanya thought.

She shook her head. "Yeah, I'm sure."

Anari hung up the phone. Now that Rio was gone, it was her time.

Chapter Thirteen

It only took a couple months for Anari to take over Rio's spots. It wasn't very hard to take over his spots, because unlike Rio, Anari allowed everybody to eat. Anari was fair in her tactics. She instructed the twins how to handle her business and gave specific instructions to never let her identity be known. All of Rio's old workers were recruited by the twins. Anari ruled her empire with an iron fist, and everyone knew not to overstep their boundaries.

Anari learned the trade through trial and error and with the twins' former experience; it wasn't long before she became a mastermind herself. Anari's bank account started to grow, and things were going very well for her. She realized that if she sold dope cheaper than what the streets were asking, it would sell twice as quick. Even though she didn't get back a big profit at first, she copped almost twice a month. This made Poe love her, and the streets love her even more because she had the best dope and sold it at the lowest price. Everyone had love for this Tony character. Dealers were losing their soldiers because everyone wanted to get down with Tony.

With the devotion of Biggs and Frank, Anari picked up on their street savvy ways. They thought they were learning from Anari, but in actuality, Anari learned from them. She would specifically ask them to cook, chop, and weigh the dope in front of her so she could learn. Once she learned, she taught Tanya, and they cooked all the dope themselves. In the beginning, Anari made many mistakes, but in time she became a pro.

Biggs and Frank recruited a flock of young niggas to set up shop on corners and abandoned buildings. The dope houses almost looked like factories. It felt good to be back on the streets of Jersey. It had been a long time since they had hustled in those parts, and it reminded them of when Maurice was alive. They learned everything about the streets from Maurice. Life was real good for everyone at that time.

Tony had a reputation of allowing people to eat, as long as they got dope from her. Anyone who worked for her always made that paper as long as they were loyal.

Biggs and Frank also grew a name for themselves. People knew that they were natural born killers, and any beef they had usually didn't last long. There were only two things that could happen if someone challenged them. One, they lost their life or two, they lost their respect by being punked in public.

Anari always made sure that she communicated with her crew. She often called the twins and Tanya over for dinner to discuss and touch bases with each other.

Anari had acquired a lawyer, Mr. Wallace, who also acted as her accountant. He took care of investing her money. He instructed her to invest in a business that had non-traceable funds. He suggested opening a salon, explaining that salons usually didn't keep many records of their income.

Anari took heed to everything that her lawyer said, and a couple days after his suggestion, she drove to New York to look for a place to start a hair salon. Mr. Wallace referred her to a real estate agent in New York City. She went into the city and found the small real estate company.

She parked her car, and as soon as she closed the door, a white woman with a navy blue business suit walked out and greeted her.

"Hi. You must be Ms. Simpson. Your lawyer called and told us to be expecting you. Mr. Wallace is a dear friend of mine, and he speaks highly of you. Shall we?"

Anari smiled graciously and followed the woman into the office. The woman led her to a desk where there were pictures of buildings within the Manhattan area.

"Now, these are some of our finest properties. They're square in the middle of Manhattan, and should attract prestigious clientele."

Anari sat up and looked at the pictures that lay sprawled across the woman's desk. "Now, I think this area of the city would be best for your venture because it would only attract big spenders. I'm sure that we could negotiate a reasonable price."

The realtor was trying her hardest to sell the property. Anari wasn't looking to open a salon that would draw attention to herself. She needed something low-key.

It needs to be low-key. It's not really the profit of the salon that interests me. I just need it as a shield. That way if anybody questions where the money's coming from, I'll have the salon. This bitch is trying her hardest to sell me. I ain't having it.

"I was looking for something in one of the other boroughs."

The realtor frowned in confusion. "Oh no, you don't want to start a business in that type of neighborhood. That would be financial suicide for a beginning businesswoman like yourself."

Anari was tired of the bullshit. She knew what she wanted and didn't want to waste time. She stood up. "Thank you anyway, but I think I'll be doing business with the real estate company down the block."

Anari began to walk out, smiling to herself. She knew that the woman was too greedy to let a sale walk out the door.

Five, four, three . . . Before she could even get to two, the realtor stopped her.

"Wait! I do have a building in Brooklyn that is available."

"Let's see it."

Within a month, Anari owned a building in the heart of Brooklyn. She hired a contractor to remodel the building and bought all the supplies she needed to fully stock a beauty salon. She named the shop New Beginnings and promised herself that she would hire the first four girls who inquired about the job.

Mr. Wallace convinced Anari to invest in some other business ventures also, and to become a silent partner with local businesses. He also had an old college buddy who owned a chain of banks throughout New Jersey. Wallace arranged for her money to be rinsed for a small fee. Anari's money was growing by the minute, becoming untouchable. She was achieving the status of a real don.

She was a different breed, though. She didn't want the fame, just the respect and power—all of this without ever revealing her identity. Her main goal was to find Shawna, but in the process, she became legendary and notorious in such a short time. She was building an empire. Tony's name sent chills through people's spine every time it was mentioned.

After seven months, Tanya was collecting from Biggs and Frank weekly, and they were running numerous drug houses throughout Newark. After Newark was on lock, she expanded her drug trade into different parts of Jersey. Anari was building an empire.

No one ever dealt with her directly, so she felt safe and untouchable. The only people who had ever seen her were the twins and Tanya. Anari slowly began to feel happy again. She wasn't happy with her life, but happy that she was powerful and soon she would have her revenge.

Anari and Tanya had several disagreements. The more money they made, the more shit Tanya started to buy. Tanya believed that fast cars and designer clothes were a part of the game. Anari disagreed. Anari told Tanya on several occasions to save money now and enjoy it later. Tanya took it as Anari trying to control her.

One afternoon, Anari and Tanya were having a casual conversation at Anari's house and Tanya asked, "Yo, have you ever thought of dropping Biggs and Frank?"

Anari paused. "Now, why would I want to do that?" Her voice remained calm.

Tanya raised her arms and yelled, "More money for you and me! We can do what they're doing. Only thing they do is check up on the spots and slap around a couple of little niggas to maintain order. I can do that. Don't let the pretty face fool you."

Anari shook her head. Her voice was raspy when she spoke. "That's how beefs get started. You have to let everybody eat. Keep everyone happy. Loyalty is more important than money. Them little niggas is my security. Without them, shit will start to fall apart."

Tanya didn't reply. She just continued to watch the movie on television.

Anari thought, *This bitch is stupid. Biggs and Franks are more valuable than her ass. Only thing she's doing is picking up my money. She better check her damn self.*

Anari knew that Tanya had transformed into Monica. She was a very different person. She missed the crazy, funny Tanya she grew up with. She didn't have a lot of respect for Monica, the money-hungry bitch, and Anari knew she would have to clean up after Monica's mistakes if she kept going at this rate.

Anari's system of divide and conquer continued, and her reputation became more notorious. Anari and Tanya took over half of New Jersey within a year. Jersey had never seen anything like this. Anari had managed to take over the street and rise to the top more rapidly than any drug dealer had ever seen. It was unbelievable. The best dope and the strategic tactics equaled success, and Anari knew this. It also helped to have the twins as her spokesmen. Everybody knew who Tony was, but no one had a clue what she looked like. Everyone just assumed that Tony was a man. Anari didn't care, though. She figured that it would be harder for people to find her if they were always looking for a man. Instead, she concentrated on her business. She started bringing in over $80,000 a month with her shops.

Tony's fame grew. She was notorious for her cutthroat tactics. No one could figure out why all the bosses were getting knocked off. The twins were well taken care of. They had made a name for themselves. No one wanted to fuck with Tony because they knew they would have to deal with the twins. No one ever did direct deals with Tony. She had the twins make all the arrangements. Everything that went down in the city, Tony knew about. Now she had more soldiers than Maurice ever had, and she was ready to go to war.

She hadn't heard anything about Shawna since she had come back to Newark, but she was determined to find her. She was just being patient.

When Anari felt she was ready, she put a contract out in the streets for Tiffany "Shawna" Davis' head. No one seemed to know where to find her, though.

If I can't find her, I'm gon' make her come looking for me. I think it's time for me to take a trip to Mr. and Mrs. Davis' house.

Chapter Fourteen

Tanya was enjoying the fast life. The whole game appealed to her. She had never made as much money as she had in the short time that she and Anari had been hustling. Drug money meant quick money, and just as quickly as she made it, she spent it. There was nothing she couldn't afford, and she made sure that everybody knew it. She stayed in the spotlight and bounced from club to club, flaunting her money.

One of the reasons she was so flashy was because she knew she had to twins to rely on if anybody tried to jump stupid. People started to speculate about what she was doing, but no one knew exactly how Tanya was getting her money. Tanya loved the attention her newfound status was getting her. She knew that wherever she went, people would know her, and if they didn't, they soon would.

After the business began to move more dope than Anari could cook alone, she and Tanya told the twins to hire a few ladies to do it. Anari instructed the twins to never allow the women to wear clothes while they were cooking the drugs. "It will be harder for them to steal from me if they don't have anywhere to hide it. I don't trust anybody, so make sure it gets done right."

Biggs and Frank sat back in one of the dope houses and monitored the workers as they were cooking dope in glass jars, preparing them for distribution. The women were walking around butt naked except for doctor's masks, and the twins were enjoying the sight.

As Biggs watched the money machine count the cash, Frank looked at his watch. "Damn, Monica was supposed to be here by now."

Before Biggs could comment, Tanya walked through the door carrying an empty gym bag. She looked at the ladies' behinds.

"It looks like y'all having a ball in this piece."

Neither of the twins responded. Biggs reached for the gym bag and began to fill it with the money. He said to Tanya, "Tell Tony we're ahead of schedule. We moved a month's worth in eight days. We're going to need to re-cop soon."

Biggs passed the bag to Tanya and she raised the bag up and down. "It's eighty thousand in here?"

Frank and Biggs both nodded.

She winked at them. "Good job, boys. I'll deliver this to Tony in the morning. I'll drop off y'all cut tomorrow evening."

As Tanya entered her apartment, she went straight to her safe and opened it. She took two stacks of money and put them in her safe. She was supposed to drop it off to Anari, but she thought this would be the perfect time to give herself a raise. She put the gym bag with the rest of the money under her bed. She would meet Anari the next day to give it to her.

She thought about everything that had happened. *I can't believe this shit. I'm on top. Me and Anari are running the streets of Jersey. Life is lovely right now.*

Tanya looked around her tiny apartment and immediately felt the urge to spend money. *I'm so tired of living here. With the kind of chips we making I should be able to buy me a house.*

Tanya walked into her bedroom and stood in front of her closet. She pulled out a short, backless, red dress. She laid out her outfit, went into the bathroom and ran a bath. She pulled up her hair and relaxed in the tub, letting the warm water soothe her tense body.

I need to relax. So much shit has been going on. Anari's ass don't even want me to take a break. She need to chill and let me enjoy my money. What's the point of making it if you can't spend it?

Tanya sat in the tub for a half-hour then got out to do her hair. She looked in the mirror and noticed that she had bags under her eyes from running the streets in the daytime and partying at night. She never gave herself any time to rest.

Tanya styled her hair in a ponytail and went back into her room to get dressed for the party. She put on the dress and was out the door by 10 o'clock. She got into her car and drove to the club.

When she walked in, she knew she had everyone's attention. The atmosphere in the club was crunk, and she could smell the sweat coming from the hot bodies on the dance floor. She headed straight for the bar.

She was sipping on a drink and chilling by herself when she overheard a conversation between two young chicks were having next to her. One of the girls was bragging about her boyfriend.

"Yeah, he be buying me everything, girl. He told me that he would move me in with him, but he said it's too dangerous. You know, with him hustling and all."

The other girl shook her head in disbelief. "I can't believe that. How did you end up fucking with Tony? I heard he's the man."

Tanya almost choked on her drink when she heard the girls mention Tony's name. She couldn't believe that shit. They actually had the streets fooled. They even had girls out here lying, talking about they were Tony's woman.

Tanya laughed quietly and picked up her cell to dial Anari's number. She answered the phone on the first ring.

"You'll never guess what I just heard," Tanya said.

Anari heard the loud music in the background. "Where you at?"

"At the club," Tanya replied, "but listen. I just heard the funniest—"

Before Tanya could even tell Anari about the girls, Anari cut her off. "You need to make yourself less visible. You always out. You need to just chill out for a minute. You don't know who got a beef with you. You being too sloppy."

Tanya grew more upset with each word that Anari said. She was tired of Anari telling her what to do. Tanya hung up the phone and continued to sip her drink.

Whenever Anari tried to tell Tanya what to do, it just made her party harder. She bought out the bar and was so drunk that by the end of the night she didn't know where she was. When she was ready to leave the club, she had made two new friends. She was too drunk to drive, and she wasn't trying to get into an accident, so she called Biggs and Frank to pick her up.

As she waited, she treated her friends to more drinks. When she thought the twins might be outside, she motioned for her company to follow her. They tried to make their way through the crowd, holding their drinks above their heads. A man bumped into her and made her spill her drink.

Tanya yelled, "Damn! Watch where you——"

The guy turned around, and her words got caught in her throat.

Von stared down and studied her face. He couldn't remember exactly what Tanya looked like so he wasn't sure if it was her. "My fault."

Tanya didn't stay around to make small talk. She walked out the door and hopped into the twins' car before Von could say anything else.

Von walked outside and saw her get into the car with the twins. *I know that was Tanya. What is she doing fucking with them wild little niggas?*

Tanya woke up next to two model-type females in her king-sized bed. All three of them were completely nude. Tanya smiled, remembering the night she had with the two ladies.

She received a phone call, interrupting her thoughts. "Hello . . . Hello . . . Hello?" She hung up the phone and felt on the dark-skinned girl's breast.

The phone rang again and she picked it up. "Hello . . . Who the fuck is this? State ya name, playful-ass coward." This time, she hung up the phone with force.

She had been receiving phone calls like this for about a week. She didn't have a clue who it was. Only Anari, Biggs, and Frank knew her home number. She made a mental note to call the phone company and get her number changed.

Tanya climbed over the two sleeping girls to get out of the bed, and went to her bathroom. She heard the phone ring and first thought not to pick it up, but she wanted to tell whoever was playing with her how she felt.

"Do you know who I am, motherfucka?"

Anari replied on the other end, "Who the fuck is you talking to?"

Tanya froze. "Sorry. Someone been playing on my damn phone all morning. I thought you were them."

Anari said, "Well, you thought wrong. Get some clothes on and meet me at my house. I know how to get Shawna, Tiffany, whatever you want to call that bitch."

Tanya told Anari she would be there as soon as she could.

"Come now," Anari said.

Thirty minutes later, Tanya was sitting face to face with Anari.

* * *

Anari and Tanya went to Newark where Shawna's parents resided. It was easy to find out where they lived. Some of Anari's customers knew her as Tiffany, so the twins got the information right out of them.

That afternoon, Anari, Tanya, and the twins sat in a rented car in front of the Davis' house. Anari's plan was to wait until nightfall and kill Shawna's parents, but things changed when she saw a school bus pull up and a little girl walked into the Davis house.

"That little girl look just like Shawna," Tanya said.

"It must be her sister," said Anari, then she laughed. "Change of plans. I want her sister."

They drove away from the house and went to one of Anari's shops. Anari explained her new plan to Tanya and the twins.

"I want Shawna, but she's too smart to let me know where she's at, so I'm gon' hit her ass where it hurts. I want y'all to snatch the little girl we saw outside their house today. Do it on her way to school. Close down one of the shops and take her there. I'm gon' give you a note to leave in the girl's book bag, and I want the book bag to be placed on they porch. Do the shit right. The girl can't be no older than ten, so she ain't gon' put up much of a fight."

Anari returned to her apartment. When she stepped inside the door, her cell phone began to ring. It was Von again. Anari began to cry.

I know, baby. I miss you too. I love you, Von, but I'm scared. There are too many things that don't make sense to me. Why did you have to be in that picture with Shawna?

Business had been slow for Von lately. Some new nigga named Tony had moved to Jersey and was taking all his business. In the last year, people suspected Tony in over 100 murders. He had these wild little niggas working for him that no one wanted to fuck with.

In all his years in the drug game, Von had never witnessed anything like what was going on now. Everybody was scared to make a move. It was like the city was in a standstill. Tony was doing everything that was happening.

He was knocking boys out the game, too. No one knew where in Jersey he resided, but his dope reached Newark, and that was Von's main money-making spot. Von needed to regain his territory, and that meant knocking Tony out of the picture. Von knew the only way to get to Tony was to get to the twins, and he knew exactly where to find them.

Von stared at the picture of Anari and put it face down. *I can't be thinking about her ass if I'm 'bout to move on Tony. I don't need any distractions.*

Von began to think about the other woman who had failed him like Anari had done—his mother. Von had grown up in the heart of the ghetto, and he was an only child in a single parent household in Jersey City. As long as he could remember his mother had been addicted to drugs. Her habit was so bad that she would spend all of the money just trying to feed it. He remembered constantly being teased in school because of the raggedy clothes and shoes that he wore. He only had two pairs of jeans and a couple of shirts. He wore the same things over and over, which gave his schoolmates something to tease him about. Often, they would talk about his crack head mother. The comments bothered him, but Von quickly learned not to show emotion. He just ignored them and promised himself that one day he would be on top.

This was what motivated him to have the finer things in life. He never wanted to feel that kind of humiliation again, so he started plotting. His hustling ways came at the tender age of ten. He would shovel snow in the winter and cut grass in the summer to make money. He took that money and bought five-cent candy, selling it to the neighborhood kids for ten cents. He loved making a dollar out of fifteen cents.

At the age of twelve, he was introduced to the streets. The ironic thing about it was that his mother's dealer introduced it to him. One day, he was on his front porch when the dealer came out of his house and glanced over at the young Von.

"What's yo' name, li'l man?"

"Von."

"How old are you?"

Von said in a low voice, "I'm twelve."

"You trying to get paid?"

Von nodded, and the rest was history. He worked as a delivery boy for the next three years, and when he saved up enough money, he decided to dive head-first into the game. He knew he would have clientele since fiends ran in and out of his house daily because of his mother's habit.

A young neighborhood friend, Freddie, became Von's right-hand man. Von realized that his mother was going to smoke, regardless of where she got it, so she became one of his customers too.

Von felt bad every time she bought from him,

but he had to get his. Since his mother didn't care about him enough to stop getting high, he didn't care enough about her to miss a sale.

He soon became a well-dressed young hustler. He always stayed fresh, no matter what. He had a fetish for clothes and shoes, and he cared about his appearance. All the pain he went through as a child about the way he dressed provoked this.

Freddie and Von were making a name for themselves. Von never dealt with a lot of people, and was usually quiet and on the low. He stayed in school and made good grades while hustling. He eventually graduated then gave his undivided attention to the streets. He promised himself if he didn't progress in the dope game in a year, he would go to college. It didn't take a year for him to learn that he was a natural born hustler.

Von's thoughts strayed back to Anari. *Where you at?*

It had been a long time since Von had spoken to or seen his love. He thought about her daily, but did not let it distract him. Von was a very focused person.

Anari was finally starting to get out of his system. He was coming to the reality that his dream woman was not coming back to him. She just disappeared. He wondered every day what he had done wrong.

Von walked through the house he once shared with Anari, and stopped in his back den. He sat at the round table and lit up a freshly rolled blunt from a cigar box at the end of the table. The round table was where he and his company sat and discussed business and, frequently, a spot where Von would go to think.

He felt a vibration on his hip. It startled him, but when he realized that it was just his phone, he answered.

"Hello." Von paused as he listened to his right-hand man Freddie, calling with bad news.

Freddie explained that his operation was decreasing because of the new era—the era of Tony.

Von put down the blunt, balled up his fist and slammed it into the table. "Fuck Tony. This cat is fuckin' with my bread, and I'm not havin' that, son."

Von stood up in frustration and began to pace the spacious room. He screamed into his cell phone, "Who the fuck is this Tony guy? He ain't come to see me yet. Do this cat know who toes he's stepping on? Nothing goes on in this city without me, Bee. I am Jersey. He eating my food, and I don't like it, yo."

Von realized he was yelling at the wrong person and regained his composure. With a calmer voice, he told Freddie, "We have the best dope in town, so his cheap prices will take my costumers temporarily, but they'll come back. Good dope sells itself. It's just a matter of time. This is not the first time this happened, but I fucks with Poe, and that means the best."

Von hung up the phone, picked up the smoking blunt and took a long, hard puff. He made circles with the smoke and leaned back in his chair. After a while, he walked into the living room and sat on the black leather sofa, putting his shoeless feet on the bearskin rug directly in front of the sofa.

He put out the cigar and picked up *The Art of War* by Sun Tzu from the end table. Von loved reading Sun Tzu's work because of the strategic techniques that were given in them. Von was a heavy reader and gained some wisdom as a result.

After an hour of reading, Von closed the book and decided to cruise the city to get some fresh air. He put on some shoes and headed out the door. He started up his Benz and drove on the streets of Jersey. It seemed like every block he rode down, someone yelled out his name. He responded with a simple nod and kept it moving.

He pulled up to a red light and noticed a young lady standing on the stoop, talking to a tall man with loud colors on. He looked closer and thought of Anari.

He noticed a tattoo on the girl's neck and thought it really was her. At the same moment, the man slapped her and roughly grabbed her arms, shaking her vigorously.

Von threw his car into park and jumped out of the car. He drew his pistol and yelled, "Yo, ho-ass nigga, get ya hands off of her, yo!"

The man dressed as a pimp yelled, "This my ho. Mind ya own." The pimp saw Von's gun on his side and quickly changed his facial expression.

Von walked closer and the girl turned toward him. He paused, looking into the girl's eyes and feeling deep disappointment.

"My fault. Handle ya business," he said to the pimp. He turned around and walked back to his car slowly, disgusted with himself for spazzing out like that. He could have sworn on a stack of Bibles that the girl was Anari.

He continued to drive through the city streets. He picked up his phone to call Freddie, but got no response. He decided to stop by a fast food restaurant. He pulled in and turned down his radio then started to order his food.

"Can I have a five-piece chicken and . . ." He looked in his side mirror and noticed a young boy, no older than sixteen, walking behind his car. He figured the fool was walking through the drive through, no car or nothing.

He paid it no mind and continued to order his food, speaking into the intercom. Before Von could react, the young boy jumped into the passenger's side and held a chrome pistol to his neck. Von froze and remained silent.

The boy yelled, "Give me all yo' shine and yo' dough or it's a wrap. I'll blow ya brains out!"

Von put up both of his hands. "All right. Just relax."

The boy began to shake uncontrollably and Von knew the boy was just as scared as he was.

"Do you know what you getting yourself into?" Von asked calmly. The young boy did not respond.

Von said, "You have a choice. You can have my jewelry now and die later, or put down the gun and keep your life." Von knew the boy had no heart, because he couldn't even look him in the eye.

The boy yelled, "Oh, you think it's a game? I'll smoke yo' ass. Give it up!"

Von smiled. "It's your choice. I want you to look behind us and notice that black car sitting with the tint. Who do you think that is? They looking at us right now. I never go anywhere without protection. Please believe it! Life is good. Now, again, you have a choice."

The boy looked back and saw that Von wasn't

lying. There was a black car with tint so dark he couldn't see in it. He lowered his gun, and Von grabbed it with his right hand, punching the boy with his left. The boy instantly grabbed his face. Von emptied the bullets onto his floor, tossed the gun in the boy's lap, reached into his pocket and threw a roll of money at the boy.

He calmly said, "Get money, li'l nigga. Hustle for what you get. Karma will come back to bite you. I never want to see yo' li'l ass again. You trying to stick up a don. You should be dead. Now get the fuck out."

The boy was in fear for his life when he jumped out of the car and ran like hell, trying to get as far away from the black car as possible. Von finished ordering his food, watching three elderly ladies wearing big hats and church clothes step out of the black car, heading into the restaurant. Von looked at one of the ladies and she said, "God bless you."

Von smiled at her. "I know." The lady looked at Von like he was crazy and continued walking.

Von thought, *I thought a nigga was dead. That was close as hell.* He laughed out loud as he drove home.

Chapter Sixteen

Tiffany was reading the *Flint Journal* when she received the call from her mother. "Tiffany, somebody took Jasmine."

Tiffany stared at the phone as her breath caught in her chest. "What do you mean someone took her? Took her where?"

"Just come home. Someone took your sister. Oh, my precious baby. Tiffany, you have to come home. They're demanding two hundred fifty thousand dollars. Oh, my Lord, please protect my child."

Tiffany held her head as she tried to put together all the information her mother was throwing at her.

"Momma, okay, calm down. Call the police. I'll take the first flight back to Jersey," said Tiffany, trying to keep her composure.

"We can't call the police. The note says that if we do, they'll kill her."

Tiffany cried out in frustration. Trying to give her

mother some reassurance that everything would be fine, she said, "Momma, read me the note."

Her mother picked up the note and read it out loud.

> *Shawna,*
> *I want $250,000 cash delivered to 1265 Hemlock Street. You got three days to get the money or the girl dies. Do not try no funny shit, cuz if I think anything is up, she's dead. If you call the police you might as well had killed her yourself. Have the money ready by next Friday at 12:00.*
>
> *Killa*

Her mother dropped the letter. "Oh God, Tiffany, help us. We don't even know who this Shawna person is. Maybe they kidnapped the wrong girl."

Tiffany knew exactly who this letter had come from. Anari had figured her out. Anari knew her real name, and now she had Jasmine. Tiffany's heart pounded in her chest and she fell to her knees.

What am I going to do? She knows I set her up. I can't go back to Jersey. What if she finds me? But what if she hurts Jazzy? How did she find out? I swear if anything happens to Jasmine, I'ma kill that bitch.

Tiffany looked at the picture of her little sister that sat on her table, and she became furious. She decided that she did not have to be afraid of Anari. Tiffany thought about how she could get out of this situation. She knew that she couldn't just go starting any shit. If she made one wrong move, Anari might hurt her little sister, and she didn't want that.

Tiffany hadn't been to Jersey since she set Anari up, but she had heard a lot about some new nigga named Tony. She still talked to a lot of people in Jersey, and for the past year, the only name she was hearing was Tony's. Tiffany had a fetish for drug dealers. She loved the allure of the game, and she knew that if she became Tony's woman, he would want to help her get her sister back. Tony was the only person in Jersey who had enough pull to get her sister back safely.

Tiffany rushed to the phone and booked the first flight to Jersey. She had to find out who Tony was and get him to help her. If he wouldn't, then Jasmine was as good as dead.

"How are you? Do you want something to eat?" Anari stared at the little girl tied up in the chair. She was so small and looked so innocent that Anari almost felt bad about kidnapping her.

"I won't hurt you, sweetie. Here, you have to eat." Anari offered the girl a sandwich.

The little girl stared away with tears in her eyes. She was shaking uncontrollably, and Anari didn't know how to calm the child. Anari turned her head away from the child, feeling pain invade her heart.

What am I doing? I don't wanna hurt her. I just want my son back.

Anari felt the tears well in her eyes and she shook it off. She couldn't get weak now, after all the shit she had to do to get where she was. Anari looked at the girl and saw her tiny body tied to the hard wooden chair.

She's going to be here for a while. I might as well keep her comfortable.

Anari untied her hands and feet. As soon as

Anari was finished with the last rope, the child ran to the door, trying with all her might to pry it open.

"It won't open. It's locked," Anari said.

The little girl stopped struggling with the door and screamed as loud as she could. "Help! Help!"

Anari disregarded the child. She didn't care if the child screamed until she was hoarse. No one could hear her. Anari had made sure that the room was soundproofed.

Anari walked over to the child and knelt down, "How old are you?"

The child shied away from her, afraid to talk.

"My name is Tony. What's yours?"

The little girl looked at Anari. "Jasmine," she replied.

Anari reached out her hand. "I won't hurt you. I promise." Jasmine was reluctant to trust Anari, but she grabbed her hand anyway.

"Eat your sandwich. I know that you're scared, but nothing bad is going to happen to you." Anari gave Jasmine her sandwich and looked around the room. The twins hadn't set up anything in there. They didn't even get a mattress for Jasmine to sleep on.

She picked up her cell phone and dialed Tanya's number.

"Hello," said Tanya.

"Hey, I need you to bring two mattresses, blankets, and a small television to the spot for me," Anari said.

"Fuck that shit. Why you being all nice and shit? I bet Shawna wasn't giving yo' son any shit to keep him entertained," Tanya protested, hoping Anari wasn't getting too attached to this little girl.

Anari became furious. She couldn't believe Tanya had just come at her like that. "Bitch, who the fuck do you think you are? I know what she did to my baby. I live with the shit every day, but Jasmine didn't do it. Shawna did. Don't forget who the fuck you talking to. I'm running shit, not you."

Tanya was silent for a moment. "I'll take care of it," she finally said.

Anari hung up the phone. "Jasmine, my friend is coming by later to give you some things so that you won't be bored. I'm not going to tie you back up. Don't try to get out of here. There's nothing that you can do, okay? The door will be locked, and there are no windows anywhere in this building. Just be good and you'll get home safely." Anari got ready to leave, but Jasmine ran to her and gripped her leg.

"Don't leave, Ms. Tony."

Anari looked at the innocent eyes of the little girl. "I have to, but I'll send someone here to sit with you, okay? I'll make sure there's always someone here with you." Anari called the twins and instructed them that Jasmine was never to be left alone again. She was to have 24-hour surveillance.

Anari left as soon as the twins arrived. She got into her car and drove home.

My life is so fucked up. I just want it all to be over. I'm tired of being Tony. I just want to be Anari again.

She walked into her apartment and thought about all the things she had done, all the lives that she had ordered to be taken. She hated this life.

Anari lay in her bed, looking at the picture of Von on her nightstand. She picked it up and outlined his face with her fingertips. She missed him.

She reached over and picked up her phone.

Though she tried to convince herself she didn't need to call him, she started to dial his number. She dialed the first three digits before she slammed the phone onto the receiver.

It had been over a year and a half since she had talked to Von. There had been so many times she had wanted to call him, but she was so confused. She missed him like crazy, though, and there was no doubt she loved him.

I'll call him, just not today.

he tried any hot shit, Tony's crew would kill him on sight. He needed to be smarter than that.

Von grew tired of thinking about Tony, so he left it alone for the moment. He decided to get out of the house for a while. Just as he was getting ready to leave, his telephone rang.

"Yo."

"Von, I'll have the job done soon."

Von recognized the voice of the hit man he had hired to off Shawna. He had almost forgotten about that shit. He hadn't thought about it since Anari left him.

Von listened as the caller said, "Shawna is supposed to be coming back to Jersey soon, and when she gets here, I'll take care of it."

Von thought about calling the hit off, but Shawna had hurt Anari, and as much as Anari had hurt Von, he still wanted to handle that for her.

"All right," he said then hung up the phone. Von sat there for a minute thinking about the hit he had put on Shawna's head. That's when he decided that was the answer to his problems. He would put a hit on Tony. The shit had to be done right, though, and he knew just who to call.

Von set up a meeting with Boss Sparks for that same night. Sparks was a local hit man who had a notorious reputation. He always got the job done without leaving any trace of who committed the crime. Although Von had never used him, he had heard of jobs Sparks had done. If anybody could get rid of Tony, Sparks could.

He walked into his bedroom and opened his safe, pulling out $50,000. Sparks would get that now, and the rest when he finished the job. Von put the money in a briefcase and got dressed in something casual. He didn't want to look suspicious, carrying a suitcase with some hood clothes on. He strapped on his gun for security purposes and put the suitcase into the car.

He drove to Tammy's Restaurant and found a table where he could wait and observe everyone who entered. He noticed a big Italian walk into the restaurant, surrounded by big men who looked like his bodyguards. Von figured that had to be Sparks. He noticed as everyone stepped out of the way for the man. He shook hands and spoke at most of the tables that he passed. He made his way over to Von's table and held out his hand.

"How are you?" said the Italian.

Von nodded his head as he accepted the man's hand. He expected the man to sit down across from him, but instead, the Italian man moved on and walked straight into the kitchen. Von's eyes followed the man, and when he turned around again, there was a man sitting across from him.

"I'm Boss Sparks."

Von looked at the scrawny man, wearing a tan polo shirt with khakis that were too small. His frame was little, and he appeared to be timid. He looked more like a schoolteacher than a hit man.

Hell nah, fuck this shit. I can't send this punk-ass white boy after Tony.

Von got ready to stand up to leave when Boss Sparks said, "I know what you're thinking, but don't let appearances fool you. I'll get the job done."

Von was reluctant to work with the man, but since he had heard so many good things about his services, he decided to hear him out. He sat down.

"What guarantees do I have that you will take care of the job?"

Boss leaned back. "You haven't even told me what the job is yet, and I have already taken care of a part of it for you. I am very thorough. I knew that you wanted me to take care of Tony for you when you called. I've heard good things about you from small-time hustlers, and I knew that you would be reluctant to work with me, so I have something for you in the trunk of your car. It will prove that I can handle the job."

Von stared across the table and became suspicious. How had this man gained access to his car? What if Sparks was hired to kill him? Maybe it was a bomb or something in the back of Von's car. Von felt the gun that he had secured at his waistline.

Fuck it. I'll see what he talking about. If I die, he dying.

Von stood up from the table. "All right. Let's go." He walked out of the restaurant with Boss Sparks leading the way to Von's car.

"Go ahead, open the trunk," Sparks said.

Von reached for his keys and tossed them to Sparks. "You open it," Von said.

Sparks caught the keys and went over to the trunk. He unlocked the trunk, opened it and motioned for Von to come near. Von walked over to the trunk with his hand on his waistline. He peered inside his trunk.

"Fuck!" he shouted as he turned his head. There was blood all over his trunk. Sparks laughed as he looked at the unrecognizable body he had placed in the back of Von's car.

"Now, can we do business?" asked Mr. Sparks.

Von regained his composure and shouted, "Man, what is this supposed to prove? Anybody can kill a motherfucka. I want to know if you can get to Tony."

Sparks smiled smugly as he replied, "This is not just anybody. It's Frank, one of the twins who works for Tony."

Von couldn't believe what he had just heard. Nobody could touch them little niggas, and this weak-looking man had murdered one of them. Von knew there was no turning back now. He turned to Sparks.

"Yeah, we can do business."

"I'll take care of your car," Sparks told him.

Von handed Mr. Sparks the money-filled suitcase and called a cab to take him home.

Sparks smiled grimly as he replied, "This is not just anybody. It's Vane, one of the guys who works for Tony."

You couldn't believe what he had just heard. Nobody could touch their little nigga, and this well-looking man had murdered one of them. You knew there was no turning back now. He turned to Sparks.

"I want them dead. I don't care what it costs."

Vane handed Mr. Sparks the money-filled suitcase, and called a cab to take him home.

Chapter Eighteen

Boss Sparks was awakened by the beeping alarm. It flashed 6:00 AM, the same time he woke up every morning, no matter what he had to do. He swung his completely naked body to the right side of the bed and placed both feet on the floor. He neatly made up his bed, smoothing out every wrinkle on his crisp, white sheets until his bed was so neat you could bounce a quarter off of it.

He walked slowly to the bathroom and gazed into the mirror as if he were trying to look beyond the image. He continued to stare into his own eyes, never blinking, and in complete stillness. He finally snapped out of his trance and bent down over the faucet, splashing water onto his face then taking a deep breath as he straightened up.

Boss brushed his teeth and walked into the center of his all-white living room. His apartment was completely clean. There was no trace of any kind of dirt. He suffered from an obsessive-compulsive disorder. Even the smallest particle of dirt in his living area drove him nuts. On average, he washed his hands fifty times a day.

He was a perfectionist. His all-white furniture was perfectly lined up, and even though he had purchased it over five years ago, there wasn't one stain on it. All of his furniture was positioned to have an equal distance from the center of the room.

He sat on his bottom and folded his legs to start his daily routine of yoga. By stretching his entire body, he felt that he gained total balance of his body and mind.

After an hour of yoga and meditation, he walked into the back room and focused on his collection of obituaries. It was an inventory of all the lives he had taken. He had newspaper articles taped along his wall, almost completely full.

He began to quote Shakespeare in a near whisper. "Cowards die many times before their deaths; the valiant never taste of death but once. Of all the wonders that I yet have heard, it seems to me most strange that men should fear; seeing that death, a necessary end, will come when it will come."

Boss had an obsession with death. He loved the fact that he could hold someone's life in his hands, and he loved playing the role of God. He felt like the strength of every person that he had killed exited their body and entered his own.

He was raised in an orphanage and had no memory of his parents. By giving him away as an infant, they supplied him with the emotional instability he needed to do the job he had chosen to do—kill. They helped to create this monster.

Boss did not speak his first word until he was ten years old, and that was only because he grew tired of a fellow orphan picking on him. He yelled out,

"Die, fucker, die!" as he delivered a blow to the boy's head with a metal candleholder.

This was the first of many malicious acts he committed. He was in and out of juvenile detention facilities in the state of Alabama during the 1970s. He was often teased for his skinniness and awkward style, but he soon built a reputation as "the crazy white kid" in detention facilities. Anyone who had a problem with Boss and voiced it had a fight on their hands. He grew respect because of his heart and courage. He was only 130 pounds soaking wet, but he could fight like a well-seasoned veteran. This was the transformation from Alexander Sparks to the notorious Boss Sparks.

After being released at the age of eighteen, he decided to move to New York City and begin a new life. With only the clothes on his back, a bus ticket, and fifty-three dollars to his name, he was on his way. He arrived in New York and stepped off the bus, growing uncomfortable with all the different people and the unfamiliar setting. He walked through the city streets for hours, contemplating his next move. Boss was determined to find a job and turn over a new leaf.

The day turned into night as he wandered down the dreary alleyways of the city. Only the moonlight provided light. He stumbled across a big crowd of poorly dressed men, ranting and raving under a bridge. When he stepped closer to see what the fuss was about, he saw two men fighting. People held money in their hands as they urged the two men on. He quickly understood what was happening—they were fighting for money.

One man got knocked out, and the members of the audience dragged him to the side. Some men began celebrating, and some were looking in disgust.

A fat man stood in the middle of the crowd and yelled, "Who's the brave man that wants to get destroyed?"

Everyone grew silent, avoiding eye contact with the fat man. That was when Boss stepped up. "I'll try," he said.

The crowd of men looked at the skinny boy and burst into laughter. They knew there was no way that a skinny kid like him was a match.

Boss stepped forward slowly. Immediately, everyone started to look for bets against him. No one wanted to bet for the underdog, until one older man dressed in an expensive pinstriped suit yelled, "I have a thousand on the kid." The men rushed to get their piece of the action in hopes of collecting from the sure defeat of Boss.

The well-dressed white man walked over to Boss. "I hope your punches are as big as your balls," he said. He patted Boss on the back as he approached the fat man. Boss took off his shirt and tossed it to the side.

The fat man could not stop laughing at the kid, and toyed with him by smacking his own face. "Right here, kiddo."

Boss remained patient, circling around the imaginary line the crowd had formed. The fat man rushed Boss and struck him in his stomach. Boss dropped to his knees and received a kick to the face, which knocked him on his back. The fat man began to laugh and walk away, putting both fists in the air. Boss stood up and showed no pain. His face had no expression, and he acted as if the blows did not affect him.

The crowd grew silent in complete amazement. The fat man turned around and rushed him, but this time Boss stepped to the right and stuck out his foot to trip the man. The fat man fell flat on his face then quickly jumped back to his feet.

"Boy, your ass is mine."

Boss circled the man with no intention of swinging. He just waited for the fat man to attack, and dodged all the punch attempts. The fat man grew tired of swinging, and that was when Boss pounced. He gave the man two punches to the stomach, and when the man bent down in pain, he got a rude awakening. Boss gave him a powerful uppercut that knocked the man unconscious on his back.

Boss approached the unconscious man and kicked him in the face. He stood over the man and mocked him by smacking his own face. "Right here, kiddo."

The place was silent. No one dared to speak a word. Boss picked up his shirt from the side and walked away from the crowd. He took about ten steps before the well-dressed man yelled, "Hey, kid, wait up!"

Boss stopped and turned around to see who was calling him. The only man who bet on him walked over to Boss with a fist full of money he had retrieved from the other men. He counted out five hundred dollars and handed it to Boss.

"Here, you earned it."

Boss took the money and started to walk away again. The man caught up to him.

"I'm Harry," he said. "Are you hungry? Because I know this great place right up the block."

Boss shrugged. "I guess."

Harry began to walk to a black luxury sedan,

and a man stepped out of the car to open the door for him and Boss. They proceeded to the restaurant, where they sat down and placed their orders. Harry ordered a cup of coffee and encouraged Boss to order anything he wanted. Sparks ordered and kept his head down.

Harry asked, "What's your name, son?"

"Boss. My friends call me Boss."

Harry smiled and replied, "Boss, you have balls. I've never seen such a smart fighter at such a young age. You outsmarted that guy with ease. I like that. So, where are you from?"

Boss looked into Harry's eyes. "Alabama. I came here to find work and start my life over."

Harry smiled and sat back in his chair. "Well, maybe I can help you out. I work for an important man who needs security. I've been coming to those street brawls for weeks looking for someone worthy. I think you would be just fine."

This was the start of a beautiful friendship. Boss soon started working for a man named Rolland Vashon, a wealthy man who was well protected. Along with Harry, Boss was Vashon's bodyguard for the next four years. During these four years, Harry shared his knowledge of fighting techniques and mental manipulation methods with the young Boss.

Boss never asked questions about why Vashon needed protection. He just stayed by Harry's side and learned. Harry formed a father-son relationship as Harry taught Boss how to read people and to remain calm in any situation.

As time went by, Boss learned that Vashon was in the drug business and accumulated many enemies over time. He also found out that Harry was Vashon's number one hit man. They called him The Exterminator.

After ten years of working under Harry, Boss was twenty-eight and well dressed, more mature, and very intelligent. He soon began to take more hit jobs, and Harry took less.

Vashon died at age fifty-four of a heart attack. Harry had saved up enough money to hang it up, but Boss wasn't ready to give up the occupation at twenty-eight. Boss had already made a name for himself, and quickly grew an underground buzz as one of the most proficient hit men on the East Coast.

Boss handled business very professionally, and would not work unless he was paid very well. Harry acted as Boss's bookkeeper and handled all the negotiations. Boss Sparks became a legend, and one of the most feared in the underground drug network. Only the elite could hire Boss.

Boss walked out of the room, snapping out of the daze that had him remembering his past. Boss was, at the age of forty, still mourning the death of his mentor Harry. He put on his clothes and walked out his door. He was on his way to New Jersey to find a young hustler by the name of Biggs.

Chapter Nineteen

Biggs was worried about his brother. It had been two days since he'd seen Frank, and the twins had never been away from each other more than two hours their whole lives. Biggs started visiting all the places where he thought his brother might be. He called the hospitals and visited some of Frank's lady friends, trying to see if any of them knew where he was. He began to worry more and more, and it was driving him crazy.

He decided to tell Anari about the problem. He called her and asked if she would meet him at the spot. Anari agreed, and an hour later she was at the shop. She saw Biggs' Cadillac Escalade sitting in front of the shop and knew that he had arrived before her.

I hope I didn't have him waiting long.

Anari made her way into the building. As soon as she stepped in, she saw Biggs pacing the room. The door slammed behind her, and the sound startled Biggs out of his thoughts.

"Frank is nowhere to be found, and this ain't like him. I think something's wrong. If he don't turn up soon, muthafuckas got to die."

Anari sighed and responded, "Look, calm down. He probably just hugged up with one of them hoes he got. If you don't hear from him by nightfall, call me and we'll go from there." Anari could tell by the look in Biggs' eyes that he was itching to kill whoever looked at him wrong.

"You probably right," Biggs said, trying to dismiss his worries.

As Anari walked out the door, she stopped. "Oh yeah, how's the little girl doing?"

Biggs' eyes shot open as he realized he hadn't fed the child in two days. Frank usually took care of that. He didn't want Anari to know the was slipping, so he replied, "She's good."

Anari shook her head. "Remember, she's not the enemy. She's just the bait." With that, she walked out.

As soon as the door shut, Biggs ran upstairs to check on the little girl. He fumbled with the key as he tried to unlock the door. When he finally opened it, he saw her little body curled up in the corner of the room. He dropped to his knees and put his hands to his face, upset that he had starved the child to death.

What am I gonna do with this body? What am I supposed to tell Tony? Biggs asked himself as he picked up the child. When he lifted Jasmine from the ground, her body tensed. Biggs dropped the girl in confusion. He looked at her closely and saw her chest move up and down.

Thank God, this little bitch alive. I didn't need her blood on my hands.

He rushed downstairs to get her a sandwich and some milk. When he returned, she was sitting on the mattresses, clenching her stomach.

"Can I go home now?" she asked between sobs.

"Soon, but for now, eat."

Biggs made sure she finished her food. He turned on the TV and left the room, relieved the girl was still alive.

"I'm tired of Anari. I helped her build this shit," Tanya said as she paced around her bedroom. "I'm doing all the dirty work while she sits on her high horse collecting all the money. I'm only getting a third of what she making, and she be tripping when I try and spend that."

Tanya wiped her runny nose and hit another line of cocaine. "I'm the one who set that meeting up with Lance. I'm the one that killed Rio. What the fuck she been doing besides ordering me around?"

Tanya turned on her radio and started to recite some of 2 Pac's lyrics. She stared into the mirror and noticed that she had dropped a couple pounds, but she didn't care. Despite all the rage she was feeling toward Anari, she could always rely on her newfound friend to lift her spirits. This friend didn't talk, didn't boss her around, and it got her high as a kite.

She leaned over her dresser and hit two more lines. Tanya decided to go over to Anari's to tell her exactly how she felt. She jumped in the same Lamborghini that Anari had instructed her not to buy.

"It's way too flashy," repeated Tanya, imitating Anari's voice.

She sped down the highway, rehearsing what she would say to Anari. As she emptied her new friend on her thumb and put it in her nose, she noticed flashing lights behind her.

Biggs was furious that his brother was gone, and he knew that something bad had happened to him. He had been noticing that his brother was getting sloppy. Frank was too relaxed. Biggs knew that his brother had gotten caught slipping.

Anari was furious, too. She didn't know what to do. Somebody was fucking with her. She knew that Frank's disappearance was not coincidental, and now she didn't know how to console Biggs. He was going crazy. Anybody who even looked at Biggs wrong was reserving himself a spot on the 6 o'clock news.

Tanya wasn't any help at all. As a matter of fact, Tanya was becoming another problem. She was being too flashy, buying cars and clothes. She even had the audacity to inquire about purchasing a $400,000 house.

Anari just wanted to find Shawna so that she could get her revenge. After that, maybe her life would return to normal. Anari was expecting Shawna to come for her sister any day now. All she could do was wait it out.

Anari was stressed out and needed to lie down. She went into her living room and lay on her couch. Feeling the need to talk to someone, she picked up her phone and went through her address book. When she saw Von's name, she felt her heart flutter. She missed him so badly and loved him so much.

She began to dial his number. She finally hit the seventh digit and listened as the phone rang.

"Yo." Von answered.

She was at a loss for words.

"Hello?" Von said with a touch of irritation in his voice.

As tears rushed down Anari's face, she slammed down the receiver. She wanted to run away. She missed Von so much, but she knew she could not go back to him. Von was the enemy, at least for now. Anari struggled with the thought of calling him back for a while before she decided she had to get out of the house.

She grabbed her keys and ran out the door, got into her car and drove to River Rest Cemetery. She parked her car and slowly made her way to her son's grave, kneeling in front of her baby's head-stone.

"Hi, baby boy," she said as she traced the letters on his stone. "I miss you so much. I'm sorry that I haven't been to see you, but I'm here now. I love you so much. You are my pride and joy. I remember how we used to play and you used to laugh and smile at me."

Anari struggled to talk to her son. She just wanted to believe that he was listening. "I miss those times. I'm sorry, baby boy. I tried to protect you. I didn't know. Mommy is going to make them pay. I promise you that. I swear on my life that if she doesn't pay, then you will see me up there with you. I just wish I could do something. I would give my life to save yours."

Anari was heartbroken. She prayed, "Please, God, take care of my son. I know you work in mysterious ways, so I'm not gonna question you. Just please take care of my baby. Let him know that I did love him, and I will always love him. In your name I pray. Amen."

Anari lay on top of her child's grave and gripped the grass as she cried for her son. She sobbed as she felt the anguish conquer her heart. Her insides felt like they were going to explode, and she hated Shawna for taking her son's life. "He was only a child!"

Anari just wanted to be with her son, and although she was lying on the lawn of a cemetery, she slept there, just to feel close to her baby. She slept on her child's grave and dreamed of the good times they had shared. Although it seemed strange, she felt at peace as she rested. She knew that her son felt her presence, and that was enough for her.

The next morning, the cemetery groundskeeper awakened her. "Are you okay?" asked the elderly man who knelt beside her.

Anari was in a daze. She looked at the man. "Yes, I'm sorry," she replied. "This is my son, and I just wanted to be near him." The man shook his head as if he understood, and continued making his rounds.

Anari kissed Li'l Maurice's headstone. "I love you," she said as she stood up and dusted off her clothing. She walked away without looking back.

Anari made her way back to her home. Just as she was pulling into her driveway, her cell phone rang.

"Hello," she said as she got out of the car.

"Anari, you have to help me. I'm in jail."

She stopped dead in her tracks when she heard the frightened voice of her friend. "What are you talking about? In jail? For what?"

I knew that this was going to happen. I told Tanya to stop spending so much money.

"They talking about I killed somebody. I don't know. They're asking so many questions. I'm so scared. I just don't know. You have to help me," screamed Tanya.

A frustrated Anari replied, "All right. Look, don't panic. I'll be there in an hour with our lawyer."

Anari hung up the phone without waiting for Tanya's reply. She called Anderson Wallace, one of the most sought after lawyers on the East Coast. His gift for gab was one of the reasons he never lost a case. He was one of the few people who knew Tony as Anari Simpson. He was aware of what Anari did, but looked the opposite way. They had become good friends.

Wallace met Anari at the police precinct an hour later. He talked to the arresting officers and they informed him that Tanya had been arrested for murder. When Wallace gave Anari this information, she knew exactly what had happened.

They got Tanya for murdering Rio. She must've left something behind or touched something in the room. How the hell am I supposed to get her out of this shit?

Anari paced the room as her lawyer went to find out how much Tanya's bail was. "The judge denied Tanya's bail. She's going to have to stay in there until her trial," Mr. Wallace said.

"What? He denied bail? I can't just leave her in there until her trial. She needs to get out of there. Isn't there something else you can do?" Anari asked, practically screaming at her lawyer.

Mr. Wallace began to gather up his paperwork. "There isn't really anything that anybody can do for her right now. They have your friend's fingerprints on the murder weapon, which was found at the scene of the crime. The two grams of cocaine they found on her doesn't help either. She was also driving a hundred thousand-dollar car with no job or real estate to prove how she purchased it. I'm sorry, but she's going to be in here for a while."

Anari was speechless. She had told Tanya not to leave anything behind in the hotel with Rio, and had warned her about buying all that stuff.

"Well, can I see her?" she asked.

Mr. Wallace directed Anari to a tiny room where Tanya was being held. As soon as she walked in, Anari could tell that Tanya had broken the number one rule. She was getting high. It was written all over her face.

Anari sat across from Tanya and held out her hands. Tanya placed her hands into Anari's and began to cry. She looked bad. Anari could tell that she was terrified.

"Sweetie, don't cry. I'm gonna get you out. It's just gonna take me a little longer."

"I'm never gonna get out of here. They said they have a murder weapon."

Anari's face twisted. "Why would they have a murder weapon? Tanya, I told you not to leave anything behind. I asked you what you did with the knife, and you told me that you took care of it."

Tanya shook her head as tears slipped down her face. "I know, I know. I lied to you. I didn't want you to think that I couldn't handle it. The truth is I panicked. I remember someone knocked at the door and I dropped the knife. I didn't know what to do. I thought I grabbed the knife when I grabbed my bag and stuff, but I must have left it there. I was scared. I slipped up. But it's too late now. The police know I did it. They know about everything. I know they do. They keep asking me where I get my money. I don't know what to tell them."

Anari leaned close and whispered, "You don't tell them shit. You don't say anything. Let them suspect whatever they want, but never back up what they're saying."

Tanya held Anari's hands. "But they said that they would go easy on me if I tell them something."

Anari was enraged. "They're lying, Tanya! You murdered somebody. You killed Rio. They ain't gonna just let that shit ride and forget about it just because you started talking.

"Don't say shit, Tanya. The only person you talk to is me. Do not start naming people, because that would not be good for you. Now, I'm trying to get you out, but I can't do that if you start snitching. I promise I'll get you out of here."

Anari stood up and hugged Tanya, feeling a twinge of guilt. Tanya was a good person. She was only mixed up in the drug game because Anari had asked her to be. Anari knew Tanya would not be able to handle this. She had to get her out of there before she started talking.

Tanya's arrest was reported in the local newspaper the next day, and also was on the 6 o'clock news. The newscaster labeled her a "menace to society." It was also reported that she was charged with money laundering because of a large amount of money found in a safe in her apartment.

She was caught with $1.5 million in her house with no job, no stocks, and no wealthy relatives. Because of the unaccounted money, she became a suspect in local bank robberies, which eventually caught the attention of the Feds. She was now tied to all of Jersey's suspected drug lords. The Feds knew they had something. They just had to make Tanya talk.

Von couldn't believe his eyes and quickly turned up the volume on his television. He saw his Anari's best friend's face on TV and couldn't believe that they were saying about her.

What the fuck? That's Tanya's ass. She was caught with over a million dollars and no source? I hope Anari ain't tied up in that shit. They were always together. She must have been holding cash for a hustler. She had to be. It must have been from an out-of-towner, because ain't nobody getting Jersey like that here except for me . . . and Tony!

Von called Freddie. "Freddie, did you see that shit on the news?"

Freddie exclaimed, "Hell yeah. It's all over the news. Ain't that your girl's people?"

"Yeah, that's her. This shit is crazy. Close down shop, and not even a dime rock gets moved. You hear me? The Feds are gonna be coming to town soon, and I don't want any part of that."

Von closed his phone and sat back on the couch in disbelief. He hoped Anari didn't have anything to do with this. He needed to go see Tanya to find out. Maybe Tanya would know where Anari was. But then he realized he couldn't go see Tanya in jail. He'd be risking too much heat on himself by associating with her now. He tried to convince himself Anari could not have anything to do with this.

Suddenly, he got an idea. He sat up on the couch and reached for his phone, quickly dialing a number.

"Yo, Kareem, this is Von. I was wondering. Are you still a guard at the County?"

Kareem immediately recognized his voice and shivers traveled up his spine. He fumbled over his words when he answered, "Yeah, Von. I'm still in there."

"Well, remember that favor you owe me?"

"How can I forget? I still have my legs," Kareem answered.

"You know that chick that got caught with the money and is being held for the murder wrap?"

Kareem yelled, "Hell yeah! That crazy bitch came in last night. I worked the night shift, and every time I walked past her cell, she was mumbling, having nightmares, screaming and shit. That bitch is crazy. She was talking in her sleep all night. She going down, man."

Von paused for a second. "What exactly was she saying? Did she say a name?"

"I don't know, man. She was talking shit all night." Kareem looked up in the air, trying to remember. "Oh yeah, she was saying Tony this and Tony that. That's all I remember."

"I need you to deliver a note for me," Von said. "I'll drop it off tonight."

Kareem agreed to deliver the note to Tanya,

then before he could make small talk, Von hung
on him.

*I knew it. She was holding that dough for Tony. I
knew it!*

He sat back on his couch and hoped Tanya
could tell him something that would help him find
Anari or Tony. He didn't know who he wanted to
find more. He loved Anari, but he also was in love
with his money, and Tony was interfering with his
cash flow.

Chapter Twenty

Tanya sat in the cold interrogation room, looking at what she was supposed to think was a mirror. She wasn't dumb, though. She knew someone was on the other side, watching her every move. She rocked back and forth in her chair, wondering how she had gotten into this shit.

Tanya was furious at Anari. She needed to hurry up and get Tanya out of there. She was always giving orders, expecting people to follow her, but when the shit hit the fan for Tanya, Anari was nowhere to be found.

Two people entered the room, a man and a woman with guns in their holsters. Both were neatly dressed. The man pulled up a chair next to Tanya and the woman stood by the entrance. He offered her a cigarette, but Tanya declined.

The man gave Tanya a hard stare before he said, "You in a fucked up situation. One and a half million cold cash. That doesn't sit well with the FBI. Is there something that you want to tell me?"

Tanya didn't even look up. She kept her head down and acted as if no one had even said anything to her. The man took a deep breath.

"Okay," he said. "You want to play hard ball?" He got up and walked toward the door.

The woman walked toward Tanya, grabbed her hair, and pulled her head back. She put her lips close to Tanya's ear and began talking in an irritated voice.

"Look, you're facing a twenty-five to life conviction. Your prints are all over the murder weapon. This places you at the scene of the crime. You can tell us who you're holding money for, or you can rot in jail for the rest of your natural life. We have friends in the legal system, and we can make that stay much shorter for you. That is, if you cooperate." The woman gripped Tanya's hair even tighter and stared in her eyes. Tanya stayed silent, and the woman released her grip, throwing Tanya's head forward.

Before they left the room, the woman said, "We'll let you sleep on that. Think about it. Would he go to jail for the rest of his life for you? Guard!" A guard came into the room and escorted Tanya back to her cell.

When they reached the cell, the guard opened the bars and guided Tanya inside. Once she sat on the bench, the guard looked around but didn't leave. When he saw no one was looking, he reached into his shirt pocket and pulled out a small envelope. He threw it at Tanya and whispered, "Von told me to give this to you." He turned around and walked away.

Tanya was shocked to hear Von's name. She waited a few moments before picking up the envelope off the ground. Her hands shook as she unfolded the paper and read.

Tanya,
What's going on? How did you get into this shit? Is
Anari involved? Please tell me where she is so that
I can help. If she is involved, tell her I'm here. And
if you fucking with that new cat Tony, he ain't no
good. Tell me where to find him so that I can help
you out. I can't fix it if I don't have anything to go
on.

She tore up the paper and threw it on the floor. The note enraged her, and she began to think about how things used to be, when she used to fight all Anari's battles for her. She remembered when they were best friends and they were equals.

Images of old times popped in her head. She pictured her and Anari sitting in Maurice's old apartment, eating ice cream and talking about all their problems. She remembered how they were closer than close. Tears streamed down her face and she felt her bottom lip begin to quiver.

Nobody ever thinks about me. It's always Anari, Anari, Anari. Von just wants to find Anari. He can't get me out of here. No one cares about me. No one.

Von and Freddie were riding down the expressway when his phone rang. It was Kareem on the other line, telling him he had a note from Tanya. Von told Freddie what was up then told Kareem to meet him in a vacant parking lot on Third Street.

"Man, I hope I get good news," Von said to Freddie after he hung up the phone. "I don't know what the fuck is going on. I'm trying to kill two birds with one stone. If Tanya tell me where Anari is at and where to find Tony, I'm good."

He got off at the next exit and went to the spot where they were supposed to meet Kareem. Ten minutes later, Kareem pulled up. He extended his hand out the window to give Von the note. Von anxiously grabbed the note and read it.

> *Von,*
> *I don't know you that well, so why would you want to help me? You just want me to tell you where you can find Anari. Anari is not who you think she is. Fuck you and fuck Anari. I will tell you this, though. If you want Anari, find Tony.*

Von was enraged at the thought of Anari being involved with Tony. He yelled, "Tony is dead! He trying to take over my territory and he took my bitch. Fuck Tony!"

Freddie remained silent as he pulled his gun and cocked it.

Chapter Twenty-one

Anari dined with Wallace to discuss Tanya's legal situation. "So, what's it going to take to get Tanya out of jail?" she asked.

Wallace took off his glasses and took a deep breath. "A miracle."

"A miracle? You mean to tell me there are no other options? I want you to defend Tanya to the best of your ability or I will be seeking other legal advice. Defend her as if she were your own flesh and blood. I pay you to make miracles happen."

The waiter interrupted their conversation, asking if they were ready to order. Anari and Wallace looked over the menus quickly and placed their orders.

When the waiter left, Wallace told Anari, "I understand, and I will defend Tanya as if she were my own daughter."

"Thank you, Mr. Wallace. That means a great deal to me."

"Let me make this very clear. It's going to be extremely difficult to exonerate Tanya from these charges. Her prints were on the murder weapon, which places her at the scene of the crime. O.J. couldn't get out of this one with no jail time. Our best bet is to negotiate a reasonable plea bargain. I'm going to shoot for fifteen years in and lifetime probation."

Anari's eyes got wide, and she shook her head, expressing her disapproval.

"That's the best that I can do," Wallace told her, "and that's with a confession from her. If Tanya pleads not guilty and is convicted, the judge will have no mercy when sentencing her. This was a pre-meditated, cold-blooded murder. They're going to try to punish her to the fullest extent of the law if she pleads innocent and is proven guilty."

Wallace closed his eyes and paused, giving Anari time to absorb this information. Anari knew she had to get her friend out of this situation, and she was willing to do anything it took to see Tanya walk. She began to speak, but was interrupted by the ringing of her cell phone.

"Hello?"

It was Biggs on the other line. "Tony, I still haven't heard from—"

"Biggs, I'm in the middle of something," Anari interrupted him.

In the middle of all the chaos, the waiter came to the table. "Would you like more wine with your meal?"

Anari nodded to the waiter then said, "Biggs, I have to go." She closed the phone and redirected her attention to Wallace.

* * *

Biggs looked at his phone and became instantly enraged. "That bitch is out having fucking dinner while my brother is missing."

Biggs dropped to the ground in frustration. Nothing seemed to be right. Tony was out having dinner while his brother was nowhere to be found. They had been so loyal to Tony—too loyal to have her put Frank, her best soldier, on the back burner. If Frank was dead, Tony would be dead. Biggs was pissed that he was there baby-sitting under her orders when he should be out looking for his brother.

Biggs was startled by a knock at the door. He opened the door to Li'l Will, a little hustler who delivered packages for him and Frank. He was no older than sixteen.

"They found Frank," Will said softly.

Biggs' eyes shot open. "Where?"

Li'l Will's head dropped, not wanting to deliver the rest of the news. Biggs grabbed him by the throat and yelled, "Where?"

Will's eyes watered as he struggled to get air. "The river. They found him in the river."

Biggs felt his knees weaken as he dropped to the floor. This could not be happening!

Li'l Will looked at Biggs for a second then ran out of the building as fast as he could. He didn't want to be around when Biggs reacted to this news. Li'l Will knew that something was about to happen, and he wasn't waiting around to see what it would be.

Going over the details of Tanya's case made Anari realize there was a slim to none chance of her friend getting off with no jail time. She wanted to think of a way to get Tanya out of the mess she had gotten herself into, but Anari was running with no direction. She was stuck between a rock and a hard place.

It's my fault that she's in this situation. I need to get her out of this. How can I get her out of this?

Anari wished she had a solution to the problem, but there was no way of getting around it. Tanya was going to jail. Anari was so focused on getting revenge for her son that she forgot she was putting people she cared about at risk. Everything was so fucked up. Tanya was in jail, Frank was missing, and Shawna hadn't even surfaced.

Anari drove through Newark, thinking about everything that had happened to her. She had given up her life with Von trying to find Shawna, and now that the day was approaching, everything she had built was breaking down.

Anari thought about Shawna and how good it was going to feel to watch her die. She decided to call Biggs to make sure he would be there when the drop-off went down. She dialed his cell, but Biggs didn't answer. That was unusual because he always answered her calls.

Anari hung up the phone and redialed, making sure that she had the right number. The line continued to ring without an answer.

Chapter Twenty-two

Tiffany arrived in Jersey on Wednesday morning and spent that entire day trying to find the top man in town, Tony. She wanted to try to get her sister back without giving Anari the money. After hours of searching, she realized her help would not come from the notorious drug dealer. It was literally impossible for her to find Tony. There were only a handful of people who actually knew what Tony looked like, and Tiffany couldn't seem to get in contact with any of those elite people. She went to her parents' house to rest her head and ponder how she would face Anari on Friday.

When she entered the front door, her mother greeted her with worry. The bags under her eyes made it obvious she hadn't gotten any sleep since Jasmine came up missing.

"Oh, baby, what are we going to do?" asked her mother.

"Don't worry about it, Mommy. I'm gonna take care of this."

Tiffany walked into her room, the one she had occupied as a child, and put her things away. She took out the briefcase full of money and counted it to make sure that it was $250,000. Tiffany was shaking uncontrollably, thinking about Jasmine. She didn't know what Anari was capable of doing, and she didn't even know if her sister was still alive.

I should have killed that bitch when I had the chance.

Tiffany paced her bedroom, going over the possible scenarios. She was nervous, having no idea what to expect. In the end, she knew she would either have to kill Anari or trade her own life to save her sister's. Whichever way it happened, she was ready.

She walked into Jasmine's room, imagining her sister's laugh. She sat on the bed, reached in her purse and pulled out a small handgun. She raised the gun and pointed it toward the door.

"Anari, you fucked with the wrong bitch."

At that very moment, her mother opened the door and froze in fear. She started to say something, but before she could get the words out, Tiffany lowered her gun and spoke.

"I gotta go."

Tanya was going crazy in her jail cell. She couldn't take being locked up like she was an animal. The craving for her habit was becoming unbearable. She thought about all the things that had gotten her to this point, and regretted every moment of it.

Tanya worried that she might never get out of there, and it was all because of Anari. It was her friend who had gotten her into the drug game, but now Tanya was the one rotting in a jail cell. Anari was running around playing the part of Tony, but Tanya knew the real Anari. She knew the girl who used to come get Tanya to fight her battles for her. Tanya had been doing things for Anari for so long that she'd forgotten who she really was. Now she'd be spending the rest of her life in a cell, asking "what if?" while Anari was busy living large, worrying about no one but herself.

Another inmate interrupted her thoughts. "Why you ain't in the yard, ma?" Tanya looked at her and remained silent. Her silence enraged the inmate, who yelled, "Oh, you didn't hear me?"

Tanya turned to walk away, but the girl grabbed her arm and swung her around. Out of instinct, Tanya punched her in the nose then continued to hit the girl. The more she hit her, the better it made her feel. All her frustrations were being released. The inmate's face started to look more and more like Anari's in Tanya's mind. Tanya thought about all the shit that Anari put her through, and she took it out on the girl by giving her numerous shots to the face.

After four minutes of head bashing, the other inmates formed a crowd, attracting the guards to the fight. They rushed Tanya, pulling her off of the battered girl. When they finally subdued Tanya, the head guard checked the girl's pulse and reported, "She's dead." She looked at Tanya. "Congratulations. You've just earned a lifetime sentence. Take her to the hole."

Chapter Twenty-three

Biggs paced the abandoned house where the drop-off was going to take place. He was going crazy and had revenge on his mind. The night before, he contemplated suicide to join his brother, but decided to handle unfinished business before their reunion on the other side. He was no longer taking orders from Tony. He didn't give a fuck about what happened to her or to the little girl that he had helped kidnap.

Jasmine had not eaten in days because Biggs no longer felt obligated to feed her. If Tony wanted the girl taken care of, then she should have done it herself.

Biggs had no respect for human life anymore. The one thing that could make Biggs break his loyalty to Tony had happened. She had gotten his brother killed. Biggs felt nothing but hatred toward Tony, and would kill her if it were the last thing he did.

* * *

Anari went to the spot where she was keeping Jasmine. She unlocked the door and saw the little girl sitting in the corner. "Can I go home now? My stomach hurts."

Anari realized the child had not eaten, so she told her to stay put and went to get her whatever Biggs had left there to eat. There were some slices of sandwich meat left, and one slice of bread. She took it and fed it to the young girl. Jasmine was very weak, but she gathered enough strength to eat the much-needed food.

"Can I go home now?" Jasmine repeated.

Anari felt bad about taking Jasmine away from her parents. It wasn't her fault that her sister had crossed Anari. She smiled, thinking of how close she was to getting her revenge.

"Yes, it's time for you to go home now. I'm gonna take you home very soon. We have to play a little game first. You have to put this blindfold on."

The girl let Anari put on the blindfold, then Anari guided the girl to the stairs. Anari grabbed the child's hand and escorted her to the car. She drove to the house where the drop-off was supposed to take place and noticed Biggs' truck sitting outside the house on Hemlock Street. She smiled, feeling reassured that he would never let her down. As soon as this was over, she would help him find Frank.

Anari loaded her gun then pulled the car further up to reach the back door and instructed the girl to get out. They entered through the back, where Anari put the girl in a room and locked it as she exited.

She entered the front room and saw Biggs standing in the corner, waiting. She immediately started giving orders.

"Biggs, this is the day I've been waiting so long for, so I need precision. Don't bring the girl out until I say so. This bitch is dead. This is for my son. By the way, do you know where Frank is at?"

Biggs replied in a whisper, "Yeah, I know were he at. You'll see him very soon, Tony."

"Good, because he had me worried for a minute."

Biggs cocked his gun and began to cry silently. The loss of his brother was tormenting him. He wanted to shoot Tony so bad, but he wanted her to suffer.

Anari paced the room, not noticing Biggs' facial expression and his tears. She was busy thinking about how a chapter in her life would end and a new one would begin with the death of her son's murderer.

A soft knock at the door startled Anari, and she immediately put her back to the same wall the door was on. She pulled out her gun. The door opened slowly, and in came Shawna. Anari's heart jumped when she saw her enemy. She quickly hit her with the back of her gun then shut the door.

Shawna fell to the floor and dropped the black bag she was holding. Anari kicked her in the face.

"Bitch, long time no see." She watched as Shawna struggled to get up, and delivered another blow to her skull. Anari yelled, "Get up, you piece of shit! You pretended to be my friend. I let you stay with me. I trusted you! You killed my baby, and now it's your turn. Biggs, let the girl go and get the fuck out!"

Biggs walked out of the room toward the back.

Anari looked at Shawna's bloody face. "Look at me." Shawna kept her head down, and this made Anari furious. "Look at me!" she screamed. Anari cocked her gun and aimed for Shawna's head.

"I've been waiting for this moment for so long, you grimy-ass bitch." Anari pressed the barrel to Shawna's forehead. She was ready to kill her.

Anari's trigger finger itched, and just as she was about to end it, Shawna shouted, "Wait, wait! He ain't dead."

Anari's heart dropped. "What?" said Anari in complete confusion.

Shawna scrambled to her feet. "Your son isn't dead. He lives in Michigan with me."

Anari smacked Shawna with the butt of her gun, causing her face to swell instantly. "Bitch, don't lie to me. If you fucking lying to me, I will make you wish you was dead."

Shawna held up her hands. "Anari, you don't know the whole story. I know I don't deserve the benefit of the doubt, but I'm telling you the truth. I have your son. He's alive."

Anari kept her gun pointed at Shawna's head and yelled, "Fuck you!"

"I was pregnant with Maurice's baby! That's the real reason why Maurice and Mann were at each other's throats. Mann found out I was pregnant with Maurice's baby," Shawna said hysterically.

Anari's eyes filled with rage and her heart ached as she absorbed what Shawna was telling her. "You lying!" she yelled.

Shawna saw that this was getting to Anari, so she continued, "I was supposed to have Maurice's child. Where do you think he was at all those nights when you couldn't find him? Who do you think he was with? If you believe that, then you're even more stupid than Maurice said you were."

Anari's eyes were welling with tears, and Shawna kept going.

"Anari, he didn't love you! He was only with you because you made him feel guilty every time he tried to leave. You thought that just because you had already killed Mann he wouldn't still get to Maurice? Mann didn't have to physically pull the trigger. He had Maurice killed, and it was all over me.

"He killed Maurice, that other bitch Tasha and their son, and he did it from his grave. Ain't that some shit? But he didn't kill you! You thought you were so special. You walked around Jersey as if you were Maurice's widow, when it was really me. Maurice always had to hide me because of you. 'No one can know,' he used to tell me. So, that's when I decided to take care of you. I took your son because he was supposed to be my son!"

Tears streamed down Anari's face. "Bitch, my son is buried!"

Tiffany laughed cockily. "That's what I made you think. In actuality, I took your son and raised him as my own. That's why you didn't get him back, because he should have been mine. I should have Maurice's son. So see, Anari, your son is still alive, but if you kill me, you'll never find out where he is."

Anari pointed the gun at Shawna. "Where is my baby?"

Before Shawna could reply, Biggs walked into the room, pulling Jasmine by the hair.

"Tiffany!" screamed the frightened little girl.

Anari looked at Biggs and yelled, "Take her to the car like I told you!"

Biggs walked toward Anari and pulled his gun, pointing it at her. "Why should I do that for you? You wouldn't help me find my brother."

Shawna saw that Anari was distracted, so she slowly reached into her waistband and pulled her own gun. She pointed the gun at Anari's head.

"It seems as if you are in quite the predicament, Anari."

Anari didn't know what to do. If she took her gun off Shawna, then Shawna would shoot her, but if she didn't do something about Biggs, then he would put a bullet in her too. She had two guns pointed at her, and only one gun to defend herself with.

"Biggs, what the fuck are you doing?" yelled Anari. "Think about this for a minute. I'll help you find your brother."

An enraged Biggs laughed at Anari. "Shut up, bitch. Frank is dead."

"What?" Anari's eyes opened wide in bewilderment. It was at that moment she knew there was no talking Biggs down. He had come into this situation intending to kill her. She shifted her eyes between Shawna and Biggs, not knowing what to do.

Biggs shoved the little girl at Shawna. "Take this little bitch and get the fuck out of here if you don't wanna die."

Shawna ran toward her sister, picked her up and ran out of the house. Before she left, she looked at Anari. "Nice try, bitch," she said then rushed out of the house, figuring that Biggs would finish off Anari.

Anari heard Shawna's car speed off and she knew that she had failed her son. She became furious at Biggs because he let Shawna go. Anari aimed her gun at him.

"Do you know what you've done? Biggs, she had my son!"

Biggs just laughed. "What I've done? Bitch, do you know what you've done? You had my brother! I've protected my brother since birth, and because of you he's dead now. We were supposed to be untouchable, but you were the only one. You were untouchable because of us, and we couldn't even get no love when we needed it from you. You ain't untouchable now, though."

"Biggs, you and Frank knew the risks of this game, so how is it my fault that Frank got caught slipping?"

Hearing Anari's disregard made Biggs foam at the mouth like a Pit Bull. "Bitch, you didn't even give a fuck when I told you that he went missing! You was out fucking having dinner when you should have been helping me find my fucking brother. Don't worry though, Tony. You'll be seeing him very soon."

He pointed his gun and shot Anari in the leg. The pain raced through her body and she dropped her gun, collapsing to the floor. Biggs watched Anari grip her leg as she felt the blood ooze out of it.

"Yeah, bitch, that's what my brother felt." He picked up her gun and tossed it away from her, then he kicked her in the head. "I want you to beg! Bitch, get on your knees and beg for your life."

Seeing no other alternative, she got on her

knees. "Biggs, please . . ." she began, trying to think of a way to get out of this. She knew that if she begged it would buy her a little time to figure out what to do. "Biggs . . ."

Biggs was harsher than she expected, though. He smacked her across the face with the butt of his gun. She tasted the blood in her mouth and felt the throbbing pain shoot through her right cheek as he hit her again.

"Please, Biggs, stop!" she yelled, looking around for something to fight him off. She grabbed his legs and felt a piece of steel through his pants leg. *Always keep a spare pistol,* she thought as she realized what was secured around his ankle.

She got up on her knees as if she were about to beg some more, but instead of begging, in one swift movement, she grabbed the spare gun and fired two shots into his head.

Biggs dropped the gun and fell to the floor. Anari scrambled to get up on her good leg, but the pain from her gunshot wound was too horrible. She heard Biggs moan as death swept over him. He was struggling to take a breath, but it was a breath that would never come.

She pulled herself over to Biggs' body and held onto his hand as she watched the life slowly leave his body. Biggs choked on his own blood. A single tear traced Anari's face as she sat by the man who had once been her loyal soldier. "I'm sorry," she whispered as she gently closed his eyes and let go of his hand.

Anari looked around the abandoned house, grabbed her gun off the floor then looked for something to help her stand. She saw a board across the room and dragged herself to it to use it as a crutch. She stumbled to her car and the reality swept over her that she had just killed Biggs.

Tears poured from Anari's eyes as she struggled to get into her car. She drove away from Hemlock Street, knowing that she had no one else left, and that her son's murderer was still alive.

Anari knew she had to get to the hospital as she tried her best to drive with her left leg. The pain that vibrated in her right leg was excruciating, and she felt as if she would pass out at any minute. There was blood all over the front seat of her car. She pulled into the first parking space she saw, nearly crashing as she pulled up to the hospital.

She opened her car door with blood all down the left side of her body. Her face felt as if it would explode from the blows that Biggs had delivered. She spit blood out of her mouth as she screamed for someone to help her. Two nurses came rushing out of the hospital. They put her in a wheelchair and immediately rushed her into the emergency ward.

"She's lost a lot of blood!" she heard someone shout. As they wheeled her into an operating room, Anari went into shock.

"We need to get her stabilized," yelled the attending physician. Anari watched helplessly as the doctor filled her with anesthesia. "Miss, can you tell me your name?"

Anari slowly opened her mouth. "Tony . . . I mean Anari . . . Simpson."

The doctor held up his fingers. "Okay, Anari, I want you to count all the fingers that I have in front of me. We have just given you an anesthetic that will put you to sleep." Anari began to count, but before she could get to three, she drifted off into a mind-numbing sleep.

Chapter Twenty-four

After two hours of surgery, Anari woke up in a dark hospital room. She didn't have enough energy to sit up and look around. All she could do was move her eyes. She was groggy and the pain in her leg was better than before, but still painful by any standards.

A nurse entered her room and opened the blinds. The sun felt as if it were burning out Anari's eyes. She shaded her eyes with her hands and weakly said, "While I'm here, could you keep the blinds closed and the lights out?"

The nurse just nodded her head, closed the blinds, and exited the room. A couple minutes later, a doctor came in.

"Miss Simpson, you gave us quite a scare." Anari just smiled, and the doctor continued. "Well, we were able to remove the bullet from your leg, but it chipped pieces of your bone. You probably feel sharp pains running up and down the sides of your leg. This is because the bone needs to heal itself before you will be able to walk again."

Anari couldn't believe what she was hearing. She didn't even know how to respond to what the doctor was telling her.

"Now, it won't take long to heal, but give it a couple weeks. And even then you will have a slight limp because the bone in your right leg will not be as sturdy as the bone in your left leg.

"Your face will be sore for about a week or two. It was bruised pretty badly. We also gave you five tiny stitches above your left eye. We have prescribed some pretty heavy medication that should reduce the amount of pain that you are in. We're going to keep you for a couple days, so if you need anything, just press that red button by the side of your bed."

He looked at her for a minute to let her absorb everything he had just told her. "Do you have any questions?" he finally asked.

Anari shook her head. After the doctor exited the room, she cried, not from physical pain, but from emotional and mental exhaustion.

I can't stay here for a couple days. I have to find Shawna and get my baby back. Thank you, God, for keeping him alive.

Anari tried to sit up, but she was too weak. Her head pounded and she felt nauseated. She realized she might have to stay for a day or two since she really couldn't even move. She tried to make herself as comfortable as possible before she drifted into a fitful sleep.

The next morning, Anari woke up to a dark room. She was glad that the nurse had followed her instructions and not opened the blinds. She reached for the buzzer to ask for help going to the bathroom. When she got no response after about five minutes, she grew irritated, knowing they must have heard the damn buzzer by now. She kept pressing for another few minutes then decided to try to make it to the bathroom by herself, thinking it was only a few steps away.

She struggled to sit up in the bed. After failing, she realized she could just raise the electric bed to sit herself up. She swung her good leg over the side and gently eased up on the leg that had been shot. As soon as her leg hit the floor, she winced in pain.

She took a deep breath and slowly guided herself along the wall. When she reached the bathroom, she searched for the light switch. She couldn't find it and became frustrated, but she had to go. She went into the dark bathroom.

After Anari used the restroom, she sat on the toilet to rest her injured leg for a minute. While she was sitting, she heard the door to her room open. Just as Anari was about to yell for the nurse to help her out of the bathroom, she heard three muffled gunshots.

Anari froze and held her breath, fearing that whoever was in her room would hear her in the bathroom. Anari's eyes widened in horror as she heard footsteps. When they stopped outside the bathroom door, Anari searched for something to defend herself with. To her relief, the intruder left the room and Anari was able to breathe again.

Anari stumbled out of the bathroom, not caring that her leg was injured. The only thing she was thinking about was getting the fuck out of there.

She limped to the stand by her bed and grabbed her car keys. When she glanced at the bed, she noticed the tiny bullet holes where her body would have been. She limped as quickly as possible out of the room.

Anari sneaked down the halls of the hospital, painfully but swiftly. When she got to the parking lot, she realized she didn't know where she had parked her car. She looked around the lot, and when she didn't see it, she pressed the alarm button on her key ring.

She heard her car beep in the back of the lot. She struggled to get to her car, and her leg ached with each step. When she finally made it, she collapsed into the front seat. She was relieved to be off of her leg, but she knew she couldn't sit still for too long. Paranoia swept over her as she put her car in drive and headed to her apartment.

Anari kept her doors and windows locked and made sure that she had her Beretta on her at all times. She was determined to live long enough to get her son back. She didn't know who had tried to kill her in the hospital, but she was determined they would not succeed.

A week passed, and finally she was able to move around, although only very slowly. She went into her living room and noticed that her answering machine was flashing uncontrollably. She walked over to it and pressed play.

"Anari, this is Mr. Wallace. I'm afraid I have some bad news. Tanya has gotten herself into some more trouble. She killed another one of the inmates. She is facing two murder charges, and

the trial begins tomorrow. You should sit right behind us to provide support for Tanya. She needs
it."

The message ended, and the machine announced
the date Mr. Wallace had called. It was a few days
ago. She had missed Tanya's trial!

Chapter Twenty-five

The darkness consumed Tanya as she tried to see through the damp atmosphere of the hole. It had been so long since she had felt daylight. The air smelled like piss, and Tanya felt as if she would suffocate if she breathed in too much at one time. The moss-covered walls were no bigger than a small closet, and they seemed to be closing in tighter and tighter every day. She was mentally, physically, and emotionally exhausted.

Tanya tried to occupy her time by singing to herself, doing sit-ups, counting as high as she could go, but no matter what activities she came up with, they never seemed to take up the time of the day. Tanya was itching for freedom, not just freedom from the hole, but freedom from her life. She felt her sanity slowing leaving her mind, and she knew she was becoming a madwoman.

She sat in the corner of the pitch-black room, hugging her knees, crying, wishing for death.

Tanya? Tanya? Bitch, I know you hear me! Answer me!

Tanya covered her ears, trying to block out the voice. She didn't want to answer her. She hated her. Tanya curled up even tighter and rocked back and forth, humming melodies to herself.

Tanya, why are you ignoring me?

"Go away. Please, just go away!"

Too bad you can't go away, huh, Tanya? You're going to rot in this hole until somebody remembers that you're down here. Look at you, so pathetic! Why are you so upset, sweetie? You killed Rio, so you deserve to die in here. Don't you?

"No, I didn't kill Rio. I didn't. Anari told me to. I was just—"

You were just what, Tanya? You were just following her commands. You were just being her little puppy dog, doing everything she ordered.

"Go away, Monica! Leave me alone!"

Go away? Why couldn't you tell Anari to go away! You need me, Tanya. I am you. You are Monica.

"No! No, I'm Tanya!"

Tanya's dead!

"No, no!"

And what about Anari? Anari should be in here too. If anything, she deserves to rot in the same cell as you. She's the one who started this whole thing. You are weak! If you just tell on Anari, this can all end. You'll be out of here. Do it!

"No!" Tanya yelled, trying to escape the torture going on in her head.

Tanya pulled at her hair, trying to make Monica stop. She hated Anari for introducing her to this life, but she had not been forced. She desperately wanted to get out of jail, but she would not snitch on Anari. If Anari ever did get caught, she wanted it to be because of her own fuck-up, not because Tanya had decided to snitch.

She frantically ran her hands along the walls, looking for the door. She found it and began to beat, scratch, and kick the thing that confined her to this hell. When she had no more energy, she slumped to the floor. There was nothing to do but wait until they wanted to let her out, and she had no idea just how long that would be.

Days passed before she finally heard keys jingle in the locks. Tanya had not seen another human face in weeks, and it felt good to feel human contact, even if it was only a prison guard.

"Let's go," yelled the guard, pulling Tanya to her feet.

She stood on weak legs and managed to walk out of the tiny space that had been her home for two weeks. Tanya's eyes burned as she squinted against the light of the dim corridor. As the guard led Tanya down the hall, she passed her cellblock.

"Where are you taking me?"

The guard didn't respond, but continued to drag Tanya to their unknown destination, a caged conference room where Mr. Wallace was waiting. He looked at Tanya, frowning at her appearance. She was barely recognizable. The confident swagger this woman had once possessed had been devoured by the hunger of the prison. Her once long hair was brittle, short and thin. Her knuckles were bleeding and her eyes were sunken.

He knew the change in her appearance was a direct result of the insanity the hole had induced in her. "Have a seat," he said and looked into her eyes.

"Can we have some privacy?" he asked the guard. When the guard left, he said to Tanya, "You have dug yourself into a hole that you can't get out of. The police have hard evidence that you killed Rio, and on top of that, you've added another second degree murder charge by killing that inmate."

Tanya just stared at the far wall with no facial expression. Wallace snapped his fingers to get her attention and suggested, "We have to plead insanity or they'll push for the death penalty."

Tanya smiled. "Tanya's been dead for a long time, and she has nothing left to live for."

Wallace was shocked, at a loss for words. He gathered his thoughts. "We are going to court tomorrow, so I need you to be on your best behavior in front of the judge. Make eye contact with absolutely no one. We need to sell this insanity plea. I will try to get in contact with Anari so that she can be there."

Tanya stood up violently, throwing Wallace's briefcase against the window. "Fuck Anari!"

Three guards rushed in and pinned Tanya's face to the table as they applied handcuffs.

"Fuck Anari! You tell her Tanya said that!"

As the guards escorted Tanya back to her cell, Wallace removed his glasses and rubbed his temples, regretting ever getting involved in this case which he knew he would not win.

Back in her cell, Tanya lay in her bunk and thought about the trial, which she knew would end in her death sentence. She could not believe that her life had added up to this.

How did I get to this point? How did I let Anari pull me into this?

As Tanya went through the rest of the day, she knew this day would be like every other day for the rest of her life. She would be awakened at the earliest hours and join the rest of society's most dangerous in a dirty dining hall for breakfast. She would live off food that was not suitable to feed animals. Her life would not be one that she lived, but one that she survived. She knew this was her end, and she didn't want to admit it, but she was afraid. She didn't know if she could live like this.

As she retired to her cell that night, she tried to get used to the fact that prison was her new home. In her heart, though, she knew she could never get used to being locked up.

The next day, Tanya woke up and felt remorse for all the wrong she ever did. The murders, the involvement in drugs, the lies and deceit were driving her nuts. She no longer had any desire to live. She wanted to take back what she had done to the other inmate. She had lost total control and beat a person to death with her own hands. The guilt was unbearable. She hated herself for what she had become—Monica.

The guard interrupted her, yelling, "Time to go to court. Assume the position."

Tanya turned her back to the guard and began to walk backwards until she felt the metal bars of her jail cell. She placed both hands through the bars to be handcuffed.

* * *

Tanya scanned the courtroom and noticed that Anari was not there. Her mind wandered as the trial took place.

She didn't even show up to the trial, and I'm here because of her. I have no one.

She searched the crowded room again. Biggs and Frank weren't there either, and it hurt Tanya to realize she didn't mean anything to any of them. She went into this losing game with pure loyalty, and look what it got her. Money couldn't even buy her out of this one.

Tanya looked at her lawyer as he listened to the prosecutor demolish Tanya's character, labeling her a menace to society and a cold-blooded murderer. After an hour of the trial, the judge ordered a recess until the next day, and the guards walked over to retrieve Tanya. Wallace stood up and buttoned his suit jacket. Tanya tugged at his jacket, and Wallace sat back down to talk to her.

Tanya leaned toward Wallace and told him, "Deliver a message for me. Tell Anari I'll see her in hell." Wallace did not understand the meaning of this message, but he would soon find out.

A muscular guard grabbed Tanya by her arm. "Let's go." Tanya saw her opportunity and went for it. She grabbed the gun out of the guard's holster and spun him around. She put the gun to the back of the his head and screamed, "Nobody move."

Immediately, all the guards present in the courtroom had drawn their guns, aiming at Tanya. One guard yelled, "Let him go. Be smart."

Tanya looked the guard straight in the eyes. "I'm not going back. I didn't do nothing. I'm innocent." Countless tears ran down the sides of her face.

"I believe you," the guard replied. "Just drop the gun."

"It's not my fault," Tanya said weakly as she released her grip on the guard. Several shots were fired into Tanya's body, ripping her flesh. Her body dropped to the ground and lay there, lifeless.

The guard who had been held by Tanya kicked the gun out of her hand. The courtroom was silent as the spectators witnessed Tanya experience her death.

As she took her last breath, Tanya whispered, "I'm sorry. I'm . . ."

Tanya was finally free—free from jail, free from Anari's orders, and free from her sins. She was at peace.

Chapter Twenty-six

"**W**e are gathered here today to celebrate the life of LaTanya Morton. She was an artistic child and a pleasure to be around. LaTanya will be missed dearly by family and friends. She was a shining star on Earth, and I'm sure she will shine even brighter in Heaven. We will now allow you to view the body and say your final good-byes." The elderly man stepped off the podium and motioned toward the solid gold casket paid for by Lance.

While the line was forming, Anari limped into the church, dressed in all black, with big black shades that nearly covered her brutalized face. As the mourners gathered, Anari saw Lance standing at the back of the church, his eyes full of tears and his head bowed solemnly. She focused her attention on the front of the church, waiting to give her final farewell to her former partner and best friend.

Anari felt her knees get weak as she approached

the casket. She managed to keep her balance and looked down at her dead friend.

"I'm sorry, T. What am I supposed to do without you? I love you, T. I am so sorry that I brought this on you. I am so sorry."

Tears ran down Anari's face. "Remember when we used to watch comedy shows all night and eat ice cream until we got sick? Remember? That was when we were happy. You have always had my back, and I was on a high horse."

Anari's voice started cracking. "Now it's too late. I'm sorry, T. I love you."

She sat through the rest of the service and paid her final respects to her best friend. It was so hard for her to see Tanya lying there in her casket. It broke her heart.

Anari exited the church and avoided eye contact with everyone. She felt Lance grab her arm.

"Anari, I am so sorry. I know this is hard for you. You and Tanya were like sisters."

Anari kept her head down and responded, "We were sisters."

Lance embraced Anari and rubbed her back. Anari just let him hold her. It was all too unbearable. She had to be strong, though. Tanya would want her to continue to be strong for her son.

Anari looked up at Lance. "I need you to help me. I have no one to turn to. My baby is still alive."

Lance looked at her and wondered if she was going crazy because of the deaths of all her loved ones. He said softly, "He's gone, Anari. He's in a better place."

Anari snatched her body away and gave Lance an evil look. "I don't need your condolence. My son might be alive, and I need your help."

Lance examined Anari's face, trying not to stare too hard. She was really messed up. Her face was swollen twice the usual size. He took her hand and led her to his car where they could talk.

In the car, Anari explained to Lance what had happened at the drop-off and at the hospital. Shocked to hear about the two close encounters with death, he wished he could make Anari stay by his side until he felt she was safe. But he knew she was a stubborn person and would not stop until she got her revenge and found her son.

He wanted to find Shawna just as much as Anari did, but Lance was a more calm and strategic type of person. He explained to Anari that the way to find someone is to catch them unexpectedly. His exact words were, "Rock them to sleep, then attack."

Anari looked out the window and noticed Von walking out of the church. She asked Lance how long he would be in town.

He answered, "As long as I need to be. Get some rest and call me when you need me. I'm here."

Anari hugged Lance and exited the car. She felt a sharp pain shoot through her leg, but did not let the pain affect her. She walked toward Von, who was standing on the steps of the church, looking around as if he was waiting for someone.

He had grown a beard since the last time Anari saw him. He had a whole new look about himself, but her heart still pounded at the sight of him. When she reached the steps to the church, Von's back was toward her.

"Von?" she said softly, barely able to find her voice.

Von turned around, thinking that maybe he

was imagining the voice. When Von faced her, Anari thought her heart would stop beating.

Von looked at Anari and noticed that she was beat up. He noticed her limp as she walked closer to him. Anari's face was swollen and bruised, and Von became instantly enraged. He rushed to her side without thinking twice and asked, "Who did this to you?" He gently touched her face. She looked worn out, as if the past two years had taken their toll on her.

Anari wanted to melt in his arms. It felt so good to be near him again, but she replied, "That's not important. It's good to see you again."

Von felt the sting of her words. He still felt the same urge to love and protect this woman, yet she was talking to him like they were just old acquaintances who had never meant anything to each other. He began to walk away from Anari, not wanting to deal with the pain.

"Von, wait!" Anari yelled, limping after him.

He continued to walk. *Fuck that. I don't have time for this shit. Her ass just disappeared on me more than two years ago and now she wanna act like ain't nothing happen.*

Anari stopped chasing after Von. "I'm sorry!" she yelled. "Von, please wait. I'm sorry."

When Anari saw that Von did not care, she fell to her knees and cried. There was nothing else to do but cry. Her best friend was dead, Biggs and Frank were both dead, Shawna got away, possibly with her son, and Von hated her.

Von turned around and saw Anari looking helpless. No matter how angry he was, he could not just leave her there. He walked back over to the steps, picked her up and carried her to his car.

"I'm sorry," Anari whispered as he placed her in the passenger seat.

Von didn't respond. He just walked around the car, got into the driver's seat and drove her to his house.

When they arrived, he escorted her in and laid her in his bed. "Wait here." He went into his adjoining bathroom and ran a hot bath. He slowly undressed her, thinking that she still had the most perfect body he had ever seen.

He picked up Anari's bare body and placed her into the steaming water. He noticed the wound on her leg and knew instantly it had come from a gunshot. He had been in the game for too long not to know what one looked like. He looked at the bruises on Anari's face and knew that she had been through a lot.

"Why did you leave?" asked Von as he washed Anari's back with a hot sponge.

Her eyes watered because she knew she would have to tell him something; she just didn't know what.

As if Von was reading her mind, he said, "Don't lie to me, Anari."

She quietly replied, "Because I didn't trust you."

Von just sat there in silence, wanting her to continue.

"I didn't trust you, Von. I saw that picture of you and Shawna and I just lost all the trust that I had for you. I thought that you knew her. It was all too coincidental. So, I just decided I had to be by myself for a while."

"It don't look like you've been by yourself to me."

Anari knew he was talking about her battered

body. "Look, Von, it ain't what you think. I haven't been with anyone since I stopped fucking with you. It wasn't even about another nigga. It was about me and you and how I didn't know whose team you were on."

"How do you think I felt when I found out you weren't coming back? You should have known how I felt about you."

Anari got out of the bathtub with his help and wrapped a towel around herself. "Von, I did love you. Remember the last time you saw me? I told you to remember that. I did then and I still do now. It was just hard for me. It still is."

Von looked into Anari's eyes. "It ain't gotta be hard for you. It never had to be. You could've just been with me. I would've kept you safe."

Anari's eyes filled with tears. "It's too late for that. Nobody could've stopped me from doing what I did or what I'm about to do."

Von grabbed her by the shoulders. "What do you mean what you're about to do? You ain't going nowhere, Anari. I'm gon' keep you with me."

She snatched away from Von. "My son is still alive."

Von saw Anari's eyes when she said this and knew that she really believed it. "No, baby girl, your son is dead. You have to move on with—"

"Shut up and listen to me!" she yelled. "I saw Shawna. Well, you know her as Tiffany, but I saw her. I almost had her, but she got away. She told me that my son was alive. Now I have to find her so I can get him back. Von, I have to." Anari was hysterical.

Von grabbed her by the waist and held her. "Shh, baby girl, shh. I promise you if your son is alive, I will find him. I promise. I love you, Anari. I'm here forever, and I won't let anything happen to you. Just promise me that you won't leave again. I need to know that you're here with me."

"I promise."

Von made up the guestroom for Anari, wanting her to be as comfortable as possible, and made his way to the living room. He just assumed that Anari's scars had come from Shawna's hands, and he would kill her for that.

Von sat back on his sofa and realized that he felt good for the first time in a while. Life was good right now. He had Anari back, and his money was picking up because of the absence of Tony and his squad. It seemed like Tony's bitch-ass got scared and dropped off the face of the earth. Von showed his teeth and Tony ran.

It made Von laugh to think that it turned out Tony didn't have any heart. He was probably fat and bald, thought Von, and that was why no one ever saw his ass. Or maybe he got into a freak accident and had some kind of deformity. Whatever the reason, he seemed to be gone, and his little soldiers were coming to Von looking for work now.

Von lit up a blunt, picked up the phone and called Boss Sparks.

"Boss."

"Von, good to hear from you. I'm working on—"

"I know. I want you to handle something else for me right now."

"I really don't like working on two jobs at once. I am a perfectionist, ya know."

"Yeah, but this is urgent. When can we meet?"

"Tomorrow at the Rock Café. Two PM."

"That's good. By the way, why is it taking so long for the other job?"

"Well, I never saw anything like this before. No one seems to know him, and he has no family for bait. But don't worry. I never miss my target. Just give ol' Sparks time."

"His operation is falling apart. Maybe he heard about the hit and decided to run."

"He can run, but he can't hide. I always finish the job."

"I trust your work. I'll see you tomorrow."

Von hung up the phone and continued to puff on his blunt.

Chapter Twenty-seven

Anari woke up confused, not recognizing where she was. It took her a while to remember that she was at Von's house. She got out of bed and walked around the house looking for Von. She was eager to see him, but even more eager to find out if Von had found any information about Shawna. She had a gut feeling about the whole situation.

She found Von in his living room talking on his cell phone. As soon as Anari walked in, Von hung up. She still didn't know what to say to him. It had been so long since she had last seen him that she didn't know how to act around him anymore. She had seen the look in his eyes when she first came back, and she didn't want to make him think that she was using him.

Her first priority was getting her son back. After that, she could focus on making things better between her and Von. She didn't know where to go from here. It was like she was stuck in a rut. All she really wanted to do was find her son. If Shawna had been telling the truth, then she needed to get her son back.

Anari approached Von and asked, "Have you heard anything about Maurice?"

Von looked at Anari. "Anari, he's dead."

She just stared at him, feeling numb. She had already been through the grieving process for her son, and it didn't pain her as much as it made her angry. A single tear slid down Anari's face and she quickly wiped it away. *I'm gon' fucking kill that bitch,* Anari thought as she fumed with rage.

Von walked over to her side and she held onto him. Even though he had told her that her son was dead, this time she wanted to be sure. She gazed up at him.

"Can you take me to the police station?"

Von nodded without questioning her.

When they pulled up to the building, Anari jumped out of the car before it even stopped. Von waited outside for her, because he couldn't risk being seen in the police station.

She approached an officer sitting behind a desk. "My name is Anari Simpson. My son was murdered about a year and a half ago. I want to make sure that the body that was found belonged to my son."

After gathering all the needed details from her, the officer excused himself to search the case files. Anari sat quietly, trying to prepare herself for whatever news he would bring back. Thirty minutes later, he came back with the information Anari had requested.

"I'm sorry, Ms. Simpson, but this report says that the remains that were found at the scene of the crime matched the dental records that you provided."

Without saying a word, Anari arose from her chair and walked out of the police station. She had expected to get those results, but now that she was sure her son was dead, Anari's heart ached.

Now he can rest in peace.

Anari turned to Von in the car. "Will you take me home?" she said softly. Shawna had played with her head and brought back so many painful emotions.

Von pulled Anari close to him and she buried her head in his chest. "It's okay," he said as he kissed her on the cheek and held her.

Von made sure he stayed by Anari's side for the rest of the day. He wanted to make sure that she was taking this news okay. He had seen her almost kill herself in Jamaica, and he wanted to make sure she had the support she needed to make it through this.

She was actually taking the news better than he had expected. It was as if she hadn't gotten any news at all. He noticed that Anari's demeanor was different, totally different. It was something about her that wasn't the same as he remembered.

After Anari fell asleep in the guestroom, Von called Boss Sparks to make sure that their meeting was still scheduled for the next day. When Boss said that it was, Von retired to his room.

The next morning, Von woke up to find Anari sleeping beside him. It was the first time that he had slept comfortably in a very long time, and it felt good to have her near him again. He gently moved Anari's arm off of him, making sure not to wake her.

He went into the bathroom and took a shower then put on a pair of Sean John blue jeans with a light pink-and-blue striped button-down shirt. He threw on a hat and grabbed his car keys.

He walked into the Rock Café, expecting Boss Sparks to be there already. When he saw that he was not, he found a table and waited patiently. When Boss finally arrived, Von motioned for him to sit down.

"So, Javon, what brings us here?" asked Boss Sparks as he sat across from Von.

"I have another job for you," replied Von.

"I told you I usually don't work on two jobs at once. Especially not along with a job like the first one you brought to me." Boss Sparks motioned for the waitress.

"Can you clean this table, please, and bring me a wet nap?"

Von watched as the waitress cleaned the table and pulled a wet nap out of her pocket to give to Boss. "Are you two ready to order or would you like more time to look at the menu?" she asked in a polite voice.

The men placed their orders, and when the waitress left, they resumed their conversation.

"The job that I have for you is simple. I just need you to find someone. I'll take care of the rest," said Von as he put the picture of Tiffany on the table. Boss Sparks just listened as Von continued. "This girl's name is Tiffany Davis. She has also called herself Shawna."

Boss took the picture from Von. "I'll find her as soon as I can. Tony has been lucky, but he will slip. And when he does, I will be there to catch him."

Von nodded his head in approval, admiring Boss Sparks' persistence. "How much will this cost me?" asked Von.

"Ten thousand dollars."

Von threw a wad of money on top of the table. "Get it done."

Boss Sparks nodded, got up from the table and walked out of the restaurant. Von threw a fifty-dollar bill on the table and left also.

When Anari woke up, she noticed that Von was gone. She didn't know where he had gone or when he would be back, but she used this time to contact Lance. She pulled his number out of her Prada bag and dialed.

"Lance, this is Anari."

Lance was glad to hear from her. He was wondering why she hadn't called. "How have you been?" he asked her, genuinely concerned.

"I'm fine. Listen. I need you to find someone for me."

"Anything," Lance replied. "Who is it?"

Anari responded, "Shawna. I need to you to find her."

Lance hesitated. "Anari, you were almost killed the last time you confronted her."

"Lance, do you know how it feels to be stuck in the same spot for a very long time? I've been searching for her for years, and when I finally get her, she gets away on account of the twins that you told me to trust. I'm going to find her Lance, and you are either on my side or you're on hers."

Lance gave in. "Okay, Anari. I'll find her, but in the meanwhile, you need to get back in the streets and manage your money. There are a lot of people getting over on you right now."

Anari didn't care about that money. She had saved over $3 million. She didn't need the money that she had invested out in the streets. As soon as she got the chance, she would go see Poe and tell him that she was done.

When Anari hung up the phone, Von walked in. She walked over to him and gave him a hug.

"Baby, I'm so sorry," she told him. "I'm so sorry for doubting you."

Von put his hands on Anari's face. "Fuck it. We gon' start over. But don't do that shit to me no more. I went crazy without you here."

Anari laughed. "You were crazy before I met you." She kissed him and knew that he was the only person that she had left.

Even though Anari was back with Von, she still had a score to settle, and she still had to cut things off with her connect. Anari decided that she would find Shawna before doing anything.

She was constantly checking on Lance to see if he had heard anything. She was growing impatient, and tried to occupy her days by doing other things. Things with her and Von were going well, but he was out in the streets a lot. She just wanted everything to be over. When it was done and over, they could move somewhere else and just enjoy each other.

Anari started shopping for homes in California. She had always wanted to move to the West Coast, and after she killed Shawna, that was exactly what she would do. She needed peace of mind, and she thought buying her dream home would be the first step in reaching that goal. Anari decided to talk to Von about her plans for their future as soon as he came home that night.

"Baby, we need to talk," said Anari as soon as she heard Von come into the house.

Von gave her a kiss on the cheek. "What up?"

"Baby, I really want to make a fresh start. I want to leave New Jersey. I can't stay here without thinking about everything that's happened."

Von was silent for a moment. "You know I have business here. I just can't pick up and leave."

Anari was afraid she would get that response. It was the response she had gotten from Maurice when she had asked him to stop selling drugs, and now she was getting the same bullshit from Von.

"Baby, I have to leave here. I am leaving here. There's nothing here for us."

Von held her face and spoke through clenched teeth. "How the hell we supposed to eat, Anari? I can't just up and move shop. My money is in Jersey."

Anari snatched away from Von. "Don't give me that shit, Von. You got enough money, and if you don't, then I do."

Von laughed at Anari. "What money? The money that you spend I have to recoup. I'm gonna take care of you. I can't stop. I got a five-year hustle plan. By the end of five years, we'll be sitting on enough money for me to stop permanently."

Anari was outraged. *No, this nigga don't think that he the only one making money. It took me a year to make more than a million. It's something wrong with his plan if it's taking him five years to get where I am now.*

She pulled out a wad of money and started peeling away hundred-dollar bills. "What money?" she yelled. "This money, nigga? It don't take that long to make a mil. Trust me, I know," she said as she continued to throw the bills in his face.

Von's facial expression displayed shock as he watched Anari peel off thousands of dollars. He had no idea how Anari could have gotten that kind of cash, but he immediately assumed that she had gotten the money from Tony or another nigga. Since he didn't want to enrage her any more, he left it alone.

I'll ask her later. That's a lot of money, for her at least. I don't care where she got it from. I just want to start over, here and now. I'll let it go.

"Baby, I can't do this shit no more," she told him when she calmed down a little. "This life that you living has consumed too many of my loved ones. Maurice, my son, my mom, Tanya. This life ain't for me. If I continue to live like this, eventually it's gon' kill me, and if I lose you because of the same dumb shit, I won't be able to handle it. Money isn't everything. Especially this kind of money.

"It's dirty, Von. It's dirty money, and if you stay in this shit long enough, it's gonna make you dirty. Why can't you understand that?"

Von realized what Anari was saying. She wasn't trying to stop him from making money. She just wanted him to be with her, and she was scared of losing him like she'd lost everybody else. He knew

Chapter Twenty-eight

Boss Sparks was getting closer to finishing his job for Von, tracing back some of Tony's footsteps. It turned out that Tony had made a lot of mistakes. It seemed to Boss that he had left some things untended for quite a while now. Boss was able to shake down a few small hustlers to find out minor details about the notorious drug dealer. He found out that Tony's operation was falling apart.

It was only a matter of time before he found Tony, and he was looking forward to the day that he met him. Boss had also made good progress in finding the woman Von had paid him to search for a couple days ago. That job had been easy. He just traced a couple credit cards and wrote down the address. He picked up his phone and called Von with the information.

"Hello?"

"I have good news for you, Javon," said Boss Sparks. "I found Ms. Tiffany Davis. She lives in

Flint, Michigan. I will text you the address after we hang up."

Von was pleased with Boss' work. He hung up the phone and waited for the address. When the text message arrived, he immediately made plans to leave town.

He walked into the kitchen where Anari was fixing dinner. He looked at her and felt pleased that he had found her son's killer. He didn't want to tell her, though. She had been trying to move on with her life and he didn't want to bring up sensitive subjects again.

Anari looked up and saw Von watching her. She walked over to him, still limping slightly. This made him even more upset because he didn't know that Biggs had given it to her. He thought Shawna had hurt Anari.

Anari kissed Von. "Hey, baby."

"Hey, baby girl. Look, I need to leave town for a little while."

"What's a little while?"

"Only for a couple days. I've got to handle some business."

Anari didn't want Von to leave, but this was the perfect time for her to take care of her own unfinished business.

"I'll be fine," she assured him. "It's only for a couple days, and I'm not going anywhere. I'll be right here when you get back."

Anari's words comforted Von. He kissed her. "I got to leave tonight."

"Okay, I'll go pack you some clothes."

Von flew out of the Newark airport that night. As soon as Anari saw his plane take off, she picked up her cell phone and called Lance. He answered on the first ring.

"Hello?"

"Did you find her?"

It must have been Anari's lucky day because Lance replied, "I got her."

"Pick me up from Detroit Metro tomorrow at noon," Anari said.

Anari knew she would not be able to carry her guns on the plane with her, so she arranged with Lance to have a 9mm and her signature .22 waiting when she arrived.

She purchased the tickets at the airport with a big smile on her face, imagining her second murder. This time, she would feel no guilt. She drove home in anticipation, almost tasting the revenge on her tongue.

I am so close.

She went home and enjoyed her night, knowing that the end to all this madness was near. At first this was just about avenging her son, but now Shawna had become an obsession. The murderous thoughts she had about Shawna filled her head 24 hours a day. She just couldn't help it. Anari was determined to kill Shawna even if she also died in the process.

She had waited so long for this. She wanted to make sure it was done right. After this was over, she could start her life again. Shawna's death would also bring about the death of Tony, and Anari could live again.

Anari thought about the events that had taken place in her life. She regretted all the chaos she had helped to cause, and hoped God could forgive her for all the lives she had helped to end. She thought about Tanya and how much she missed her.

It must have been horrible for you, T. I'm sorry I wasn't there for you. I wanted to be. There was just so much other stuff on my mind. I got you caught up in this bull-shit, and I am so sorry. I know how you felt about me when you died, and I just hope that you know that I love you. I love you more than life. You have always been here for me when I needed you, and the one time that I could have been there for you, I wasn't. I'm sorry. I'm so sorry.

Shawna had forced Anari down this road that led to the death of so many people, and she would pay for it with her own life.

I'm coming, bitch.

Boss Sparks picked the lock on the apartment, expecting to find Tony. It had taken him a long time, but he finally found the place where Tony rested his head. Boss knew he was moments away from killing his most elusive target, and it excited him.

He entered the apartment, pointing the 9mm handgun, and was surprised by the appearance of the place. He had expected Tony to live an extravagant life, but it seemed that Tony was smarter than most drug dealers. He lived in a small but comfortable apartment in an ordinary neighborhood.

After Boss checked the entire place, he was certain that Tony had not been there in a while. Everything was clean, and the place had started to collect dust. He searched the apartment for clues about where Tony had taken off to and why he had left everything behind.

Boss looked on the nightstand beside Tony's bed and saw pictures of a young black woman. She was very attractive, with medium-length hair and a beautiful smile.

She's very lovely, Boss thought. He noticed there were no pictures of anyone else in the entire house.

He searched the bathroom and the kitchen, trying to find clues about Tony's appearance and whereabouts. He had to admit that Tony had covered his tracks very well. There was no evidence that a male ever lived in the apartment. There were no men's shoes or clothing in the closet, no male products in the bathroom, and literally no masculine features in the apartment.

Boss grew irritated by the cat and mouse game Tony was playing with him. He had to come out of hiding sometime.

On the kitchen counter, he picked up some mail. Every envelope was addressed to Anari Simpson. He figured she must be the woman in the photograph. Obviously, Tony had good taste.

Before he left, Boss searched the room one more time. This time, he discovered a journal. He put it aside and dug deeper in the closet, finding another picture. He recognized the twins. They were standing with their arms around the woman Boss had seen in the other pictures around the house. He turned the picture over to see what was written on the back. It read: *Tony and the twins.*

A million thoughts raced through his mind as Boss re-read the inscription a thousand times. He went back to the journal and flipped through the pages, trying to find something that supported his new theory. He ripped through the journal until he read an entry that proved him right.

> *I don't even know who I am anymore. This alter ego is not me. I don't know if I'm strong enough to live this double life. I just want to be Anari again. I want my baby back. I will never let him go. He will always be with me. After I finally kill Shawna, I will let the streets go for good. I am so close that I can taste her blood in my mouth. I never . . .*

Boss didn't need to finish reading the entry. He had read enough to know the truth. He picked up the photo again and studied it hard. All this time he had been searching for a man who didn't exist. The person he was after was a woman.

Anari boarded the plane at 8:00 the next morning. She had to hurry up and get this over with so that she could return to Jersey before Von found out she had left. Her hands were sweaty and she was anxious. She had a score to settle and could not wait until she touched down and met with Lance.

She found her seat on the plane and decided she would try to sleep until her arrival in Detroit. She wanted to have enough energy to face Shawna. She knew the fight would not be easy because Shawna was just as strong, respected, and cutthroat as Anari, but Anari was ready for round two. She sat back in her seat and closed her eyes, hoping that she would not be disturbed.

*   *   *

Von woke up feeling refreshed and ready to do the job that he had come to do. He was ready to end this so that he could go back home to Anari.

As he drove down the highway, he thought about Anari. He knew she wanted him to get out of the game, but he was addicted to money, and he only knew one way to make it. He had been hustling for years, and the streets had become his home. He knew he loved Anari, but he didn't know if he was willing to stop his hustle for her.

One thing he was willing to do for her was kill Shawna. He had seen Shawna take Anari through hell and back, and he was more than willing to get rid of her. He knew that by killing Shawna, he would be giving Anari back her sanity.

He pressed the gas harder, trying to get to his destination faster. He drove north on I-75 for about 45 minutes before he saw a sign for Flint. He drove full speed the rest of the way because he wanted to have time to check his surroundings before he made his move.

He found Berkeley Street and parked his car a few houses down from the address Boss Sparks had given him. The house Shawna lived in was a modest-sized red-and-white home, across the street from a high school in what seemed to be a safe area.

I am gon' heat this block up, thought Von as he patiently waited for the sun to go down. It was only noon, but he would sit there and watch Shawna until he was ready to go in for the kill.

Chapter Twenty-nine

Sparks wanted Tony's head so badly he could taste it. He felt so close to ending it, so close to winning.

This job amused him, because Tony was very hard to find. He presented a challenge to Sparks, who had never found it so hard to catch his target. This job was taking a long time to complete, longer than any other he had attempted in his whole career. He was anticipating the day when he could read Tony's obituary.

Boss was skilled with computers and could hack into any database he needed. When he searched Tony's apartment, he found all the information necessary to track her, including her social security number and credit statements. He traced Anari's last credit card purchase and found that she had purchased a one-way flight to Detroit.

He boarded a plane the next morning. It had taken him some time, but the night before, he found out where Tony would be.

He walked toward the front of the plane into first class, and sat next to a snoring woman. This would be a long ride. He sat quietly, growing more and more irritated by the woman's breathing. She had a coat over her head, which made the snores seem even louder than they already were. If there had not been so many people on the flight, Boss might have been tempted to crush the woman's windpipe. Since he was on a crowded flight, he just sat there growing more annoyed by the second.

The flight was long, and when the plane finally landed, he quickly jumped up and exited the plane.

Anari took her jacket off her head and noticed that the plane had just landed. She was drowsy from her uncomfortable sleep, and she just wanted to get to Lance so that he could take her to a hotel. It was 5:00 in the afternoon, so she had about five more hours before she would be paying Shawna a visit.

When she exited the plane, she quickly located Lance in the waiting area. He was pleased to see her, and approached Anari with open arms to give her a big hug.

"How have you been?"

Anari gave Lance a smile, appreciating his genuine concern for her. "I'm fine. How you are?" she asked.

"Oh, you know how shit is. I'm just trying to stay on top of the game."

Anari did understand how it was. She was on top of the game, and it seemed like the more her empire grew, the more haters would come out of the woodwork to tear it down.

He escorted Anari to his car and drove to his
condo. Anari remembered the last time she had
been there. It was the day she met the twins. That
seemed like so long ago. Now here she was, a couple years later, and she was the only one left standing out of her whole team.

Everybody's dead, Anari thought, regretting ever
entering into this game.

She got out of Lance's car and walked into his
condo. Lance offered her a seat then disappeared
into the back room. Anari waited for what seemed
like an eternity before Lance came back. He
brought a black briefcase with him and set it down
on the table in front of Anari.

Anari opened the briefcase to find two shiny
chrome guns, one a 9mm with a silencer, and the
other a small .22.

"Thank you. I really appreciate everything that
you've done for me," she said.

"Don't worry about it. I just want you to be safe.
I don't want you to end up like Tanya did. She de-
served better than that, and so do you. I don't
want to have to plan another funeral, Anari."

Lance was right. Tanya did deserve better, and
Anari was trying to do better for herself. She knew
that if she didn't get out of the game, she would
also join Tanya and the twins in death. She just
had to handle this last thing.

Lance handed her a set of keys, a bus ticket, and
a piece of paper. "This is the directions and the address to where you can find Shawna. It's about an
hour north from here in Flint. Don't worry about
returning the car. Leave it when you're done and
catch the bus back here. Call me, and I'll be there

to pick you up. Are you sure you don't want me to come with you?"

"No, I have to do this myself."

She gave Lance a hug and thanked him again then walked out of his condo and got into the car. On the highway, she drove until she found a hotel just outside the city. She checked into a Holiday Inn, knowing that she would need to rest for a few hours. She needed to be alert when she found Shawna.

Von had been in front of Shawna's house for about seven hours now. When he saw her moving about inside the house, he was tempted to send for Anari, but he didn't want her to have anything to do with this. He would take care of Shawna by himself. It was the only way to help Anari move on.

With Shawna dead, Anari could be more focused on her own life. Von knew how much it bothered her that she had introduced Shawna into the life of her son, and he had to help her rid herself of the guilt that she carried.

Von knew that the time was growing near. By this time tomorrow, the job would be done and Von would be on the first plane back to Jersey. He picked up the phone and called Anari's cell.

As soon as Anari entered her hotel room she heard 50 Cent's popular song, "Many Men." It was her cell phone. She looked on the caller ID and saw that it was Von calling to check on her. She thought about not answering, but knew that if she didn't, he would start to worry. She didn't want him to be concerned and come home early, so she hit the TALK button.

"Hello?"

"What's up, Nari? How you doing?" asked Von.

"I'm cool. What's up?" asked Anari, hoping to get him off the phone quickly. She needed to be focused on one thing only—getting Shawna's head.

"I just wanted to call you and make sure shit was straight. Look, I'll be home tomorrow night. All right?"

Anari planned to fly back to Jersey the next morning, so his schedule agreed with her own. He would never know that she was gone.

"Okay, see you then," she replied. She quickly hung up the phone before he could say anything else.

Boss Sparks scrubbed his body as hard as he could. The hot shower felt good. He hated being in a closed area with a lot of people. There was no telling what type of germs they had. After surviving the flight, he hurried to the nearest hotel and got right in the shower. He wore shower shoes to avoid touching the floor because there was no telling how many people had used that shower before him.

He stepped out of the shower and looked at himself in the mirror. His skin was red from being scrubbed raw. To him, that was good, because rawer meant cleaner. He went into the bedroom and put on his clothes.

After neatly tucking in his shirt, he smiled at

himself in the mirror. This job had been fun for Boss. Tony had actually given him a challenge. But the game was over now. He knew who Tony was, and had already started to assemble the plan that would lead to her demise.

He walked out of the hotel and got into his car, driving toward what would be his greatest kill ever.

Von decided he would move the car to the street behind Shawna's house. He didn't want any of her neighbors to get suspicious of his car. He drove around the corner and parked on the next street. He was growing impatient, but he knew better than to rush into a house that was unfamiliar to him in a strange city. So he sat, he watched, and he waited.

One more hour.

Anari woke up to a dark room. She looked at the clock, which read 10:45. Time to pay Shawna a visit.

Yeah, bitch. I'm coming for your ass.

Anari pulled her hair into a ponytail. She loaded the two guns Lance had given her, putting one pistol in her waistband and strapping the other to her leg. Anari called and requested her car be pulled around to the front of the hotel then exited her hotel room.

A white, middle-aged valet dressed in an all-white uniform brought her car and opened the door for her. As Anari walked over to get her car, she accidentally stepped on the man's shoe. He immediately bent down to wipe off his shoes.

Damn, I only stepped on your shoe, she thought as she watched him vigorously wipe the dirt.

He stood up and looked directly in her eyes. "Have a nice night, miss."

She got into her car and drove toward Flint, Michigan. Her heart pumped with rage, with fear, and with anticipation. She had waited for this moment for so long, and now that it was here, it didn't seem real.

I can't believe that I'm finally here. I have to do this. There are only two ways that this can end—either with Shawna's death or my own. I don't really give a fuck, though. Whichever way it ends doesn't matter to me, as long as it ends today.

Anari was consumed by her thoughts as she sped down I-75. She knew she was about to bring heat to the streets of Flint. She was ready. She had been ready, and this time she would not let Shawna slip through her fingers.

At 11:45, Von stepped out of the car. He concealed his gun in his waistband and went through Shawna's back yard. He entered the house through the unlocked back door then quietly closed it behind him. He kept the lights off, not wanting to attract any unwanted attention from the outside.

He slowly crept around the house, looking for Shawna. After realizing that she wasn't at home, he grew frustrated. *She must've left when I moved my car around the corner,* he thought.

He walked into Shawna's room and sat down on her bed, not knowing whether he should wait for her to come home. He had fucked up and let her leave, and he was not happy with himself. Von lay back onto the bed and put his hands over his face.

He couldn't go back to Jersey without finishing what he started. She would be back, and when she returned, he would be there, waiting.

Anari pulled up in front of Shawna's house at 12:00 on the dot. She turned off the car and took a deep breath. This was it. She exited the car nervously.

Anari was scared. Her heart felt as if it would jump out of her chest, and her stomach was doing somersaults. She had to stay focused. She pulled the 9mm out of her waistline and cocked it.

Bitch, I'm 'bout to send you to your maker.

She walked up the driveway, noticing that all the lights in the house were out. She figured that Shawna was sleeping. Well, she was about to get a rude awakening.

Anari quietly crept through the back door of Shawna's house. She knew that it would be unlocked because when Shawna was staying with her, Anari had to constantly remind her to lock the door behind her.

Anari crept through the house like a cat, making no noise. She made her way through the house, stopping when she saw a figure on the bed in one of the bedrooms.

Anari paused, wondering whether she should shoot Shawna in the dark. She pointed her gun at the silhouette, put her finger on the trigger, and walked into the room. Because she wanted Shawna to see her face before she died, Anari flicked on the light switch. Her heart dropped when she saw who hopped out of Shawna's bed.

"What the fuck are you doing here?" Anari shouted as Von jumped up.

Von looked at Anari in confusion. "Wait. It ain't what you think it is."

Anari's heart throbbed and she put the situation together in her mind. "Shut up! Shut up! I trusted you. You fucking lied to me. Is this the business that you had to handle, huh, Von?" She backed away from him, shaking her head. "I trusted you. How could you do this to me?"

"Listen, you got to listen to me," he insisted. "I came here for you."

Anari wasn't trying to hear what Von was saying. The only person she could trust was herself. All along she had been right about him. She knew her suspicions had been true, but she let her emotions get in the way of her better judgment. She kept the gun pointed at Von.

"You grimey. You fucking with Shawna, the bitch that killed my son? I should kill your sorry ass right now. Where is she, Von? Where the fuck is Shawna?" Anari was going crazy. Tears were flowing down her face, but they were not tears of pain. They were tears of anger. She hated Von. She had loved him and trusted him with everything that she had, but he was a fucking liar.

Anari's heart felt as if it were about explode. She could feel each painful beat from the thought of being betrayed by someone she loved so much. Her breaths became shallow as she tried to cope with the situation.

I have to finish this, she thought.

"Where the fuck is she, Von?"

Von tried to walk toward Anari. "I don't know where she at."

Anari shot at the wall behind Von and yelled, "Where is she?"

Von didn't respond. He had no idea what to say to Anari. She was out of control, and no matter what he said, she wouldn't believe him, so he just remained silent.

"Shawna! Bitch, where the fuck are you?" Anari went storming around the house in search of her. Von chased after her, trying to explain to her what he was doing in Shawna's house. Anari didn't hear any of it, though. The rage, the hatred, and the hurt had taken over.

After she realized that Shawna was not in the house, she pointed the gun back at Von. He put his hands up to show Anari that he was not her enemy.

"Anari, I'm on your side. I'm not the enemy. I love you."

Anari rushed over to Von and smacked him across the face with the butt of her gun. "Fuck you!" Anari spit in his face and aimed her gun at his head. She closed her eyes and pulled the trigger.

Von heard the shot go off in his head, but when he didn't feel the bullet, he opened his eyes. Anari had turned the gun at the last moment. She couldn't bring herself to shoot him.

Anari was shaking uncontrollably. "I trusted you. I loved you," she cried then turned around slowly and began to walk out of the room in a daze.

As Anari walked out of the house, Von's cell phone vibrated on his belt. He picked up his phone and yelled, "What!"

Boss Sparks' crisp voice was on the other line. "I have news for you. You will never believe what I'm about to tell you."

Von wasn't paying attention to Boss. He ran out of the room, trying to catch up to Anari. He saw her get into her car and he ran over to the curb.

"It is really quite funny," said Boss Sparks, continuing to explain to Von.

"Hold on," Von told Boss as bent down and put his head inside Anari's car.

"Wait, you gotta listen to me."

Anari looked at Von and he saw the pained look in her eyes. "Fuck you," she said.

Von heard Boss yelling into the phone.

"What?"

Boss laughed into the phone. "I got Tony. I've got Tony," he announced joyously into the phone.

Von noticed that Anari was about to start her car and leave. He rushed Boss off the phone. "Great. Listen, we'll talk about it later," he said as he reached for Anari's hand and tried to take the keys from her.

Boss couldn't resist himself. "I got Tony. Tony will never expect it, but the next time she starts her car, she'll get a very big surprise."

"She?" Von asked with aggravation. He wanted to get Boss off the phone so he could deal with Anari. If he let her leave, he might never see her again.

Boss continued to talk. "Yes, she. You haven't heard the best part. You'll never guess who Tony is." He paused for dramatic effect. "Tony is a bitch! Tony is a woman named Anari Simpson."

Von looked at Anari and slowly started to put together what he was hearing. He thought about the letter Tanya had written him and Anari's change in behavior.

That's where she got all the money . . . Anari is—

Anari put the key into the ignition and turned it.

Epilogue

Tiffany woke up and rolled over onto a man she barely knew. She had the worst hangover ever, and she barely remembered getting drunk in the club and leaving with this stranger at the end of the night.

He better be glad I was oily, cuz I would have never fucked his ass sober.

She couldn't even remember this dude's name. She crawled out of his bed and went into the bathroom, turned on the shower and washed her body. When she walked back into the bedroom, the guy had awakened and was watching TV. He walked into the bathroom as she walked out, and she sat on his bed and watched the news.

This is Alicia Fields reporting live from Berkley Street on the north side of Flint. Behind me is the car that was blown up late last night. Police have no leads as to who was responsible for this tragedy, but it has been confirmed that there was a bomb planted under the car and that two people were killed due to the blast. Anari Simp-

son, a 25-year-old black woman, and Javon Roberts, a 27-year-old black male, both from New Jersey, were killed.

No one seems to know what the two were doing in the area. Police are still trying to find family members of the victims. If anyone has any information on these two murders, please contact the local police.

Stay tuned for the local weather forecast . . .

Tiffany's mouth dropped as she watched the news play on the TV. She saw her house in the background and a smile spread across her face.

So, Anari, you had the balls to come after me, huh? Too bad I wasn't home. I could have been the one to send you to your maker. It would have been fun. I can't believe this bitch had the nerve to come after me in my own city.

She laughed aloud, happy that this was finally over. She turned off the TV and began to put on her clothes.

The stranger walked out of the bathroom and saw her expression. "You all right?" he asked as she continued to get dressed.

"Yeah, I'm good. Real good."

Tiffany was thinking about all the shit she could do now that Anari was dead. She could not be happier. Everything had worked out perfectly. She had gotten her sister back unharmed, Anari was dead, and since Von had gotten killed and no one had heard from this Tony character, New Jersey was wide open, and Shawna was going in for the kill.

I'll be the first bitch to take over Jersey, she thought, not knowing that she was only following in Anari's footsteps. She thought she would be the first Queen Bee of New Jersey.

Tiffany looked at the guy standing beside her and couldn't stand the sight of him any longer. He wasn't a bad guy or anything. He just wasn't her type.

She stood up. "Look, I have to go, so I'll holla at you later."

She was walking toward the door when she heard him say, "Wait. Here's my cell number." He handed her a piece of paper and she looked down at it.

Lance. So, that's your name.

She put the number in her Coach purse and left. When she got home, she found evidence that they had been in her house. It was turned upside down as if a hurricane had blown through the place with full force.

She stepped over the objects in her bedroom and pulled a shoebox from under the bed. Opening it, she pulled out the obituary of the little boy she had killed. The paper was wrinkled and had started to fade, but she could still see the photo of Anari's son at the top of the page.

Tiffany walked out onto her porch and got the newspaper, cutting out the front-page article about the explosion and Anari's death. Of course, the article mentioned Von too, but it was Anari she was concerned with.

She took the piece of paper to her room and put it into the box with the obituary of Li'l Maurice. She gently closed the box and thought, *she finally has her son back.*

Tiffany walked out of the house, got in her car and headed toward the airport. She was going straight to Jersey.

It's my time now.